FIC
GRE

BIS

T5-BSJ-311

AUG 3 1 2012

AUG 3 1 2012

DATE DUE

		MWS 9.6.13	
SEP 1 8 2012		NOV 13 2013	
	OCT 2 9 2012	OCLC Lexington PL.	
		RI 11189 5137	
DEC 1 0 2012		HWS 1.8.14	
		AUG 0 8 2016	
DEC 2 2012			
	JAN 2 1 2013		
GWS 4/17/13			
OCLC	Alachua County L.D.		
RI	10635 1052		
AUG 2 0 2013			
SEP 0 2 2013			
SEP 0 3 2013			

Demco, Inc. 38-293

BLUE ISLAND
PUBLIC LIBRARY

Copyright © 2010 Nicole Green

All rights reserved.

ISBN: 147768719X
ISBN-13: 978-1477687192

Cover Art by Miss Mae:
http://themissmaesite.blogspot.com

CHAPTER ONE

Melody could have really used a break, but the lemon that insisted on masquerading as a car she drove didn't seem to understand that. Her best friend, Jen, had told her not to try to make it all the way down to Miami by Monday—and taking the back roads to avoid traffic—from Atlanta in the clunker.

"If you have to drive, which I think is ridiculous to start with," Jen had said, "Please, Melody, I'm begging you, rent a car."

But the same stubbornness that had prevented Melody from buying a plane ticket had prevented her from taking her friend's advice. She'd been so sure that old Aretha could make the trip—especially since she'd just gotten a tune-up a few weeks earlier in anticipation of the trip. A year ago when she'd bought the thing, she'd been convinced giving the car her favorite singer's name would bring her good luck. But obviously, she'd been wrong.

Buying a new car was not in her budget at the moment. She didn't make tons of money at New Face Records—a struggling independent label—and she had better uses for money than buying a depreciating, shiny, new piece of metal and fiberglass. That would also mean a higher car insurance premium. Another cost. She'd never save up enough money to go into business for herself as a music manager if she kept increases her expenses.

The new-to-town Used Car Shopping Mall, as it was known on the commercials that flashed across local television stations back home in Midtown, had lured her in with its promises of low prices and CARFAX background checks. When she'd realized the used car industry had crapped on her, The Used Car Shopping Mall had refused to take their jalopy back, and they'd canceled her warranty on a technicality. She'd heard that pursuing Georgia's lemon laws was a useless fight. Besides, a lawyer would be yet another expense. And for a case she probably wouldn't win. She didn't have the energy or money to fight yet another losing battle. She'd had her fill of courtrooms during the divorce.

"Crap, crap, crap," she muttered to herself, glaring at the check engine light. Her nemesis. The thing came on at least three times a week, and usually she ignored it because it didn't necessarily mean anything was wrong with the car. But that day, it meant horrible things. The rattling sounds coming from the engine were a bad sign. Smoke started smoke billow up from the hood. She eased the car over to the side of the road. Just when she got all four tires off the road, the engine spluttered and died.

Making a sound that was somewhere between a moan and a wail, she banged her head against the steering wheel. This was no good. At all. Saeed was going to kill her. With all the cutbacks her company had been making lately, now was not a good time to piss off the new boss. His real name was Saeed Zahedi, but he was known as The Cleaner. He'd been brought in specifically to clean house at New Face Records. He was known for his efficiency. And his ruthlessness.

Saeed had made it clear he thought going to Miami to check out this R&B group was a waste of time. He called them Boyz II Men wannabes who were lacking in freshness and originality even though he'd never heard them sing. He had let her know quite clearly the company wouldn't be covering her traveling expenses.

Driving had not been smart at all. Especially taking the back roads. But Melody had always loved road trips, and she needed time to clear her head. Things had been crazy around the office since Saeed arrived. She needed time to herself to plan her next move. So the road trip to Miami—at her expense, using her own seldom-used vacation time—had seemed like a good idea.

A last-minute plane ticket to Miami would have been exorbitantly expensive, and renting a car would have used up money she could have put in savings toward quitting her going-nowhere job and starting her dream job. She wanted to be a music manager. Finally, she'd be able to foster creativity instead of stifling it in the name of profits and bottom lines. She would still be working in the music industry, but she would be her own boss.

Melody reached into the backseat for her purse. She always kept it there out of a habit she'd formed long ago because most of the time, she had a passenger in her front seat. She pulled it into her lap and groped around inside for her wallet. When her fingers closed over everything but her square brown wallet, her heart dropped. No. She hadn't. Staring down into her purse, she realized she had. There was no wallet in there.

"What is wrong with me lately?" she asked herself, banging a fist against her purse. Sure, she'd been distracted that day, thinking about her last conversation with her boss and about the group in Miami. Things weren't going well at all with her surly, curmudgeonly boss, but that didn't make her any less angry at herself for being so scatterbrained.

She searched the car even though she was almost certain her wallet was back at the little diner where she'd had lunch over an hour ago. She probably looked like a maniac standing out in the sweltering Georgia sun, darting in and out of all of her car doors like a whirling dervish, throwing around maps, reusable shopping bags, her toiletry kit and whatever else she found in the back and under the front seat.

She went to the trunk, poking around and under her yoga mat, the carry-on sized suitcase she'd packed for what should have been no more than a weeklong trip at most, her emergency roadside kit, and other things. Then she sank down behind her car, propped her back against the hot fiberglass, and buried her face in her hands.

She looked up. Her cell phone. She'd stuck it in the center console after talking to Jen before she'd gotten to the diner. She hadn't wanted to talk to anyone else right then. She'd had another fight with Saeed before talking to Jen, and she wanted to eat at least one meal in peace. She'd forgotten to take it out when she got back in the car after leaving the diner. She jumped up and ran to the driver's side door. She could call AAA.

Putting a knee in the driver's seat, she leaned over to the center console and popped the latch on the area where she stored her CDs. There was her smart phone. With a cry of triumph, she grabbed it and held it up. Oh no.

She punched numbers. Held the power switch down until her thumb hurt. Then, she banged it against her thigh. Nothing. It was dead. Maybe the heat had killed off the part of the battery she hadn't used while gabbing to Jen. Her car charger was useless at the moment, and so was her wall charger for obvious reasons.

Walking up to the wheel well, she kicked the front driver's side tire out of frustration. "I used to drive a Range Rover!" she shouted at it like it would care. She'd had to sell her truck—and a lot of other things it'd been very difficult to part with—after the divorce. She'd needed the money to leave California and come back to Georgia to start over.

She was sunk. Out by the side of the road with only a cow pasture to keep her company. Those cows looked kind of wily. She didn't like animals bigger than she was no matter how docile they supposedly were.

She didn't even have a white shirt or anything to stick in the window. Wasn't that what you were supposed to do when your car broke down? She'd seen cars on the side of the road before with a white cloth stuck in the window. She didn't know why it was the standard, but she thought she should have one for her window anyway.

She caught her bottom lip between her teeth, puffed her cheeks up with air, and then blew it out. She was burning up even though she wore only a thin cotton tank top and khaki capri pants, and the sun didn't care one bit. She'd had her hairdresser cut her hair into a bob when she moved to Georgia a year ago, but short hair wasn't helping keep her cool under that hot sun by the side of the road, too close to the baking asphalt.

As car after car passed by without even slowing, she watched, wondering what in the world to do next. She could walk, but in which direction? She hadn't passed so much as a gas station in miles. Did she make the backward trek or take her chances walking forward into the unknown? Maybe there was a closer gas station that way.

The cows started lowing and moving closer to the fence. She glared at them. "Aw, shut up. I don't like me being here any more than you do."

Just as she was about to take her chances walking south into the unknown as opposed to north where she'd come from, a green-and-rust pick-up truck slowed in the road. There being no traffic to be seen on the long, straight stretch of asphalt, the driver must have thought it okay to just back up in the road. The truck eased backwards a few yards until the driver's side door was parallel with Melody.

The driver, a redhead wearing an honest-to-god straw western hat leaned across the seat and smiled at her. She said through the open window, "Car trouble?"

Melody nodded, feeling the uncomfortable stickiness of the sweat pooled at the base of her neck. "The thing just crapped out on me. It's been threatening to all day, and I guess it decided to show me that I wasn't taking its threats seriously enough."

The woman laughed. "I like you. Anybody who can keep a sense of humor on a day like this while stuck on the side of the road's okay with me. If you wanna hop in, I'll give you a ride to town. We can get Austin or one of the other folks down at the shop to tow this thing in for ya."

Melody smiled. Her first lucky break that day. "Thanks. Let me just get some things out of my car and lock it up really quickly." Melody ran back to her car, grabbed her shoulder bag, which constantly held a new batch of demos, and slung it over her shoulder with her purse. After locking her car doors, she went back to the truck. She opened the door and hopped into the cab.

"The name's Regan." The woman held out a calloused hand.

"Melody," she said, shaking the woman's hand.

"So what are you doing way out here, Miz Melody? Passing through I reckon? We don't get many strangers in Sweet Neck. And you're not from 'round here. I know everyone from 'round here."

"Yeah. Passing through. I'm from Atlanta, and I was on my way to Miami." *Was. Back when I had a future. Before my car broke down*, she thought glumly.

"Miami? What in the world are you doing way out here then?"

"I called myself taking the scenic route," Melody said with a sigh. Yet another poor decision on her part. One in a long line of them. "Thought I'd get away from the traffic for a while, and the drive would be prettier."

"Well. That you were. That you definitely were. Miami is far. By car, too?"

"Yeah. I was gonna use back roads to cut over to I-16 down by Metter. Then take that over to I-95. Where am I now anyway?" Her GPS was on her currently useless smart phone. She glared at the dead screen.

"You're about halfway between Sparta and Sandersville. Nowhere near I-95. You still had a good ways to go to get there. I-16's still a good ways off, too. You're a good ways from any interstate a'tall right now."

Yeap. That she knew. And that wasn't the worst of her worries. "You mentioned a tow truck. I don't have any money on me. I left my wallet back up the road at a diner near Covington. I'm convinced of it now," Melody said, looking down at her useless purse. It'd all come back to her. She'd left the wallet right on the red, vinyl booth seat. Picked up her purse and left without it. She'd been looking through her purse for the phone she'd forgotten she'd left in her car earlier. After taking out the money for the server, she laid her wallet on the booth seat next to her while she continued to paw around in her purse.

Distracted by her search, she'd forgotten about her wallet and walked away from the booth without it, still looking through her purse. Out in the parking lot, she'd suddenly remembered where her phone was, and feeling stupid for forgetting she'd left it there, she'd laughed at herself and gotten in the car. After checking the compartment in the center console to make sure it was still there, she'd driven away. This day was possibly the worst of her life.

"You remember the name of the diner where you left it?" Regan asked, pulling Melody out of the memory of what she'd done.

"Yeah. Mindy's." She remembered it because it made her think of that old television show, Mork and Mindy. She sometimes ordered the old episodes on Netflix.

They rolled past a church. They then started passing the occasional house. But mostly, everything was still trees and fields.

"We'll get the number for you when we get back to town and you can call up there to see if anybody's found your wallet. In the meantime, don't worry about it. We're not going to leave your car out there just because you don't have any money. Around here, we help each other out," Regan said. As if to help Regan prove her point, at that moment Melody saw a green welcome sign ahead. The sign was green and blue with white lettering. The state flower, a Cherokee rose, was sketched at the top of it.

She mouthed the words to herself as she read the sign. "Welcome to Sweet Neck, Georgia. We're Happy To Have Ya." How could the residents of a place called Sweet Neck be anything but downright pleasant?

"Okay," Melody said, settling back in the seat. She finally began to feel a little bit relieved. For the first time in hours, she allowed herself to relax a little. They passed a couple more churches. "So what do you do?" Melody asked to make conversation and keep her mind off unpleasant thoughts.

"Own a horse farm a few miles outside of town. And some of the best horses this side of the Mississippi if I say so myself. My goodness. Talk about a girl and her horse. Don't get me started on those magnificent creatures. I'll be talking all day," Regan said.

"I always wanted to learn how to ride," Melody said. One of those "some day" things she'd probably never get around to.

"Well, if you end up sticking around here for a few days, you should come out to the farm," Regan said.

Melody saw some signs of civilization—or something close to it—and guessed they had reached the heart of "town". The buzzing metropolis of Sweet Neck.

Regan guided her truck down what was probably Main Street and turned onto a side road. Pulling up in front of a large square building, she killed the engine.

"Here we are. Holt's Garage."

Melody looked at the dusty building with its faded paint. Both of the tan garage bay doors were closed. There were smatterings of cars parked all around. Some looked like junk cars that would never move again. Those were interspersed with weeds and mostly behind a chain-link fence that ran out from the sides of the building and to the back, probably fencing in the back end of the property. A few cars resembling Regan's in condition—looking worn yet resourceful—were parked near the garage bay doors. There were a couple shiny, newer cars out there as well.

Melody was about to thank Regan for the ride and climb out of the truck when she was distracted by a man coming out of the building, wiping his hands on a rag. His blond hair was cut close, and he filled out his brown coveralls with a broad chest and hulkish shoulders. Even with the brown coveralls doing nothing for him, she could tell there was quite a body underneath.

She tried to push the thought that she hadn't had sex since the divorce to the back of her mind. It wouldn't stay back there, though. She'd been on a few dates, but she hadn't had the energy or desire to take things to the next level. Watching this man take long, confident strides in her direction, she realized that desire was coming back.

He stepped up to the truck and nodded a greeting to Regan. "Hey, Regan," he said in a deep, husky Georgia drawl. His green eyes flitted to Melody, and he smiled. "Who's your friend?"

"Hey, Austin," Regan said, hopping out of the truck. "This here's Melody. She had some car trouble back up the road."

"Did she now?" Austin's eyes raked over her body, staying on her cleavage longer than she should have liked, and she liked it more than she wanted to. She should have been mad at his objectifying move. The fact that she was a little thrilled by it pissed her off.

She looked at his hands. Now that he was closer, she could see that they were blackened, and the rag he'd been wiping them with was even filthier. She moved her eyes to a spot just beyond his head before she responded, not risking a look at that heart-startling face again just yet. "Yeah. She did," Melody said, putting emphasis on "she," making it clear she didn't appreciate being referred to in the third person.

"Hm. Now that's a shame. Where's the car?"

Regan told him.

"Look, I was telling Regan," Melody said. "I don't have any money, I lost my wallet at a diner a few hours' drive away from here. But I'll pay you back, really." Hopefully he'd believe she was a trustworthy person. She really was—she was just also a penniless one at the moment.

"I'm sure you will, Melody," he said, giving her a look that made her want to slap him and jump his bones all at once.

Regan said, "Well, it was nice meeting you, Melody. I have to get to the hardware store and then back to the farm, but I leave you in good hands."

Melody wasn't so sure about that, but she smiled anyway. "Nice meeting you, too. Thanks so much for the ride."

"Don't mention it." Regan straightened her hat and climbed back in the truck. "I'll see y'all."

"Bye, Regan," Austin said and then turned his attention back to Melody. "What, no AAA? I thought you city types covered all your bases at all times." He was mocking her. He wasn't allowed to piss her off and turn her on at the same time, dammit.

"No. AAA. My phone's dead, so I can't call them or anybody else. Now, speaking of phones, can I use yours?"

Austin scratched at the corner of a square jaw, a smile hovering around the edges of his perfectly sculpted lips. Looking like they'd been chiseled there by a Renaissance master of the art. "I dunno, can you?"

"Are you going to help me or what?" Melody snapped. He was starting to get to her. It'd been a long, hot day and all she wanted was to do a little damage control and to have a cold shower and not be sweaty. He made it all the worse by seeming so amused with her. As if she were some wind-up toy, sent there to entertain him instead of a stranded, desperate woman.

"C'mon." He nodded toward the building. "I'll have Donnie tow the car in, and we'll see if we can't find you the number for that diner."

"Okay. Thanks," she said, taking a deep breath to calm herself.

"Of course," he said the words slow and Southern and sexy. Now that she could concentrate on something besides wanting to scream at him, he seemed familiar. She couldn't imagine how in the world she would have ever run into this man from Podunk, USA, but nevertheless she had the feeling she'd seen him before.

CHAPTER TWO

Austin led Melody into the cool interior of his garage. He almost put his hand on her lower back to guide her inside, but he caught himself at the last moment.

"Stay here for a minute," he said to her just outside of the door to his office. She nodded, and he went out to the garage bays where his brother and sister were hard at work.

"Donnie," he said to his brother.

His brother looked up and wiped sweat from his forehead with the back of his arm, which was covered by the sleeve of his dark blue coveralls. "What?" Donnie was about as big around as a piece of barbed wire. His mouth had always been bigger than he was.

"I need you to do something for me," Austin said.

"I'm kind of busy in case you hadn't noticed." Donnie gestured to a car that was suspended in the air by a hydraulic lift. "Get Avery to do it, whatever it is."

Austin's fraternal twin, Avery, slid from beneath a second car. "What did you say about me just now?" Avery had dark hair and blue eyes and was much shorter than her twin brother, but what they lacked in physical similarities, they made up for in personality. Their mother said that was why it was impossible for them to get along. Mom swore she'd never laid eyes on a more stubborn pair of people.

"Austin wants you to do his job for him," Donnie said even though Austin hadn't told him what he wanted yet. He leaned back to look at their sister and pressed the heel of a work boot into the cement floor while lifting the front part from the ground.

"Austin, now you know how Jimbo gets," Avery said. "If this car isn't ready by the time he gets off work this evening—"

"Yes, Avery, I'm well aware of how Jimbo gets," Austin said. "That's why I asked Donnie," he couldn't keep the frustration out of his voice when he said his brother's name, "to do it."

"And what makes you so special you can't go do it?" Donnie smirked.

"The fact that I don't want to," Austin said, leaving out the fact that he'd much rather be in his office with this Melody—who'd caught his eye as soon as she'd pulled those long legs out of Regan's truck—than out bumbling around in the sweltering heat in a tow truck with a chronically broken air conditioner. It quit working so often they'd all but given up on repairing it whenever it conked out. Besides, Donnie deserved to be riled up as often as possible. Maybe he wouldn't deserve it if he didn't look for ways to point out Austin's failures on a daily basis.

"And who's gonna finish this oil change then?" Donnie asked.

"I'll do it. Just go, would ya?" Austin said.

"You haven't even told me where I'm going."

It wasn't like he'd gotten the chance. Pausing for patience, Austin closed his eyes for a moment. Opening them again, he said, "There's a car out on the side of the road near Regan's place. I need you to go get it. Tow it in." He gave Donnie the precise location of the car before heading back over to Melody.

"What's the hold up?" she asked, perfectly arched eyebrows raised. Her flawless skin was the color of chocolate mousse, and he wanted a taste.

He grinned. "I'm sorry. You miss me?"

"About that phone?..."

"Right this way, Miz?..."

"Melody is fine."

He held the door to his office open for her. "Right in here, Miz Melody Is Fine." And she sure was.

"Ha ha," she muttered, stepping past him into the cramped and cluttered space. The office would have been somewhat spacious if it wasn't stacked up with boxes of papers Austin had yet to organize even though he'd taken over the shop four years ago. Also scattered around were old car parts, cases of oil, and other various and sundry items.

"What—you don't find my witty sense of humor charming?" he asked with a chuckle.

"Witty, huh?" She stepped over a red crate that held a couple of old car batteries. "You have a phone book somewhere around here?" she asked. "You think there might be one buried under the rubble in this disaster area you call an office?"

He wondered how long he should let her search around before telling her she wasn't even close to finding the phonebooks. For the moment, he was happy admiring the view.

He watched her calf muscles flex as she reached up to search on top of a file cabinet. Poetry in motion.

"Little help here?" she asked, tottering as she attempted to hold up a stack of papers threatening to fall from its perch on top of the cabinet.

He shook his head to clear it and bring himself back to the moment. "Oh, uh, sorry about that." He rushed over and lifted the papers back onto the top of the cabinet. His arm brushed hers, and he thought he heard her gasp—one sharp little intake of breath. Their eyes met. He wanted so badly to put his arm around her waist and draw her closer. Instead, he backed away and gestured toward the chair behind his desk. "Here, have a seat. I'll get the book."

She sat in his desk chair, and he stood next to her, well aware of how close her shapely body was to his. She crossed those incredible legs, and her arms folded across her breasts. He'd better get to looking for that back before he got himself in trouble.

Opening the left-hand bottom drawer, he dug through his phone books until he found one that included the Covington area. He kept phone books for all the areas within a four-hour radius because of stranded motorists and the need for communicating with other mechanics.

His brother and sister laughed at him and told him to get out of the Stone Age. He didn't like computers, though. Never had, never would. He used them as little as possible. He preferred working with his hands to typing with his fingers. Besides, the internet had helped to destroy his life once, so he didn't see much good in it.

Tossing the phone book onto the desk and pushing the phone toward her, he said, "There ya go." He pushed a few auto part catalogs to the side of the desk and out of her way.

"Okay. Thanks." She sounded wary as if he'd just offered her a piece of candy that might or might not have been poisoned. She said, "You uh, I mean it's long distance. D'ya mind?"

"I think we can handle it and still make the note on this place," Austin said. He stood and stretched. He hid a smile when he noticed her trying not to notice as he did so. "Speaking of which, I better get out there and do some work. Can't leave Avery to do it all. Holler when you're done with the phone."

She nodded and looked up at him. "I really am grateful. For the towing. For this. Sorry if I've been..." She rubbed her fingers over her forehead, and he caught a glimpse of a wedding band on her ring finger. He hadn't noticed that before. Probably because he hadn't wanted to find it. "It's been such a long day," she said with a sigh.

"Understandable. Can't be much fun stranded out in the hot sun all day. Way out here in the sticks," Austin said, realizing he didn't know where she was from. He didn't know very much about her at all other than she had his blood moving faster than it had in years. Faster than the women in town he'd known and been ambivalent about all his life at any rate. "That reminds me, I should have asked you earlier, but do you want anything to drink? I have some bottled water in the fridge in back." He would've remembered to ask earlier if she hadn't distracted him with that body of hers. He let his eyes drift over the soft curve of her neck as she pored over the phonebook. After all, he wasn't handling the married merchandise; he was just browsing around the store.

"No thanks," she said without looking up from the book she had open in front of her.

"Okay, I'm really getting out of your hair this time. I guess you'll want some privacy to call your husband and whomever else you have to call," he said.

She smiled and rubbed the back of her neck again while looking down at her left hand. "I'm not married. Not anymore." She held up her hand. "It keeps away unwanted attention. And there's plenty of it in my line of work."

He nodded. He briefly wondered if his attention would be the unwanted kind. Quickly rejecting the thought, he reminded himself that it shouldn't matter. She was just passing through. "I'll be out in the garage if you need me." He started to move past the desk, headed for the garage bay.

She said, "Hey, hang on a minute."

"Yes?" He turned and looked down at her where she sat in his office chair.

"I feel like I know you from somewhere." She gave a little laugh, exposing perfectly straight teeth. "Crazy, huh?"

Not this again. He hadn't had to deal with this for years. "Yeah." He was careful to keep his face neutral. He wouldn't let his expression give him away. "Crazy." He took another step toward the office door and stumbled over his own two feet. He looked back to see her give a small frown. Crap. Was he caught? Had he been spotted?

"Wait, do I know you from somewhere?" Squinting, she stood and took a step closer.

He backed out of the door, smiling. "I think I'd remember meeting you, Melody." That much was true. "Now if you'll excuse me, that oil's not gonna change itself." He walked toward the bay, grateful to have made his escape for the moment at least.

CHAPTER THREE

"I understand," she said with a disappointed sigh. She did. She hadn't realistically expected anyone to have found her wallet and turned it in, but she'd held a little hope out until that moment. "You'll call me if you hear anything, though?" She tapped Austin's desk calendar with her index finger. Her bracelets jangled around on her wrist.

"Sure, honey," the waitress from Mindy's on the other end of the phone said. "Let me have a number I can reach you at."

Melody fumbled around on the cluttered desk until she somehow, miraculously, came up with a business card. She then gave the woman the number for the shop. After getting off the phone, she walked out to the doorway that opened on the garage bays. Austin stood by a beat-up looking purple sedan, talking to a woman who worked on the next car over, her dark brown hair pulled back into a ponytail.

When he looked up and saw her, a grin spread across his face that almost knocked her off-balance.

"Melody, this is my sister, Avery. Avery, Melody."

Melody said hello to Avery, and she returned the greeting. Then Melody said, "So, this a family operation?"

"Yeap," Austin said. Avery dropped a wrench on her foot, muttered a curse, and bent to pick it up. Austin's eyes flicked to his sister for a moment and then they landed right back on Melody. "Our brother works here, too. He's the one out getting your car."

Melody nodded. Something had seemed to pass between Austin and Avery—an odd vibe of some kind—but whatever it was began and ended so quickly she wasn't sure what it was if anything.

"So, you call everyone you need to call?" Austin asked, walking over to her.

She took a step back almost without realizing it. She didn't like this effect he was having on her. It could be dangerous. She wasn't trying to find out if the town's name applied literally to its residents. "I called the diner. They haven't seen it."

"Did you call your folks?" Austin asked. He sounded concerned. Yet another thing about him to catch her off-guard.

"Um, the numbers are in my phone. Which is dead." She didn't memorize phone numbers anymore—hadn't in years. She didn't even have her mom's number memorized because she'd recently changed cell phone companies and gotten a new number. Melody lifted the useless, dead smart phone from her purse and held it up as proof of her predicament.

When Austin took the phone from her, his fingers brushed hers, sending a tingle racing over her skin. She remembered that tingle. It'd been a long, long time since she'd felt anything like it. Very long. She'd been busy trying to save money so that she could start her new career; she didn't have time to go out looking for men who could produce a tingle like that. Besides, the last one who'd produced that tingle ended up being more trouble than he was worth.

Austin gave a small frown of concentration while staring at the phone then called over his shoulder, "Hey Avery. What kind of phone you got?"

"One of them new ones they just got down at the Radio Shack," she called back.

"Is it like this one?" Austin held up Melody's phone.

Avery walked over, wiping her hands on her dirty coveralls. She scrutinized the phone without taking it from Austin. Moving her dark blue eyes over it, she shook her head. "Naw. Afraid not." She looked up at Melody. "Sorry."

Austin held the phone out to Melody.

She took it from him. "Don't be. It's fine," she said, making a mental note to ask to get her suitcase, which contained her charger, out of the trunk of her car when it got back to the garage. "Does anybody have a computer I can use? I can send some emails if nothing else." The more she anticipated Saeed's reaction to all this, the more anxious she got.

"Austin has that great big old dinosaur in the office," Avery said. "We don't have internet access here at the shop, though. I don't even know if that thing is capable of internet access."

"The library's got a couple, but they're closing any minute now," Austin looked over her shoulder, and she followed his gaze to a clock on the wall behind her. "They close at four on Fridays."

She suppressed a groan. Of course.

"But Mom, she wouldn't mind you using hers. That is, if you'll come on home with us after we close up the garage for the day." He went on to explain though she hadn't asked, "Mom likes having us live there. She says she'd get too lonely if we didn't live in that giant house with her."

Melody really wanted to get things taken care of as soon as possible so she could get somewhere. There was still a possibility—even if a small one—that she could get to Miami on time if she could book a flight and get back to the airport in Atlanta by Monday. She was desperate now. She'd

HIS MELODY

blow as much cash as it took to get to this group in Miami. A lot was riding on them. Like her entire future.

Still, that left only two days to make it back to Atlanta. And she'd be willing to bet there wasn't so much as a bus depot or a car rental place in Sweet Neck. If her jalopy wasn't going to get running again any time soon, and it probably wasn't, she'd need a ride to wherever the nearest car rental office or bus station was. Best to follow the people who had cars.

"Sure," she said. I don't mind waiting." Like she had a choice. "What time do you close on Fridays?"

"'Round six," he said. "We like to give folks an extra hour. So we close down when the banks in town do on Friday.

"There's more than one?" She didn't know if she was teasing or not.

He nodded. "There are two." She didn't know if he thought she was teasing or not, either.

"Okay. I guess I'll wait in your office if you don't mind," she said.

"'Course not." Austin walked back over to the purple car. She didn't realize she'd been staring until he waved to her with that stupid, cocky grin still on his face. His dimples made it even worse. There was no time to be attracted to this man—she had to get back to Atlanta. Flustered, she hurried back to his office.

Melody couldn't find a comfortable position in the desk chair in Austin's office. Not that the chair was the most comfortable thing to begin with. On top of that, her skin was uncomfortable and sticky with salt and sweat. She felt gross and out of place, even in the somewhat dank mechanic's shop. All she wanted was an ice-cold shower. But where in the world was she going to get that?

She didn't even have the money for a hotel. She hoped this town had a Western Union. Maybe once she got to a computer she could email for someone to send her a wire—her mom or Jen. Then she could try to talk the local innkeeper or whoever into letting her have a room until she could get the money to pay him back. She'd have to get some money to pay Austin, too.

She'd been sleepier than she realized. She woke up with a jolt when a door slammed out in the garage. Next, she heard a booming voice. Out of curiosity, she went out to the railing of the walkway that separated the office from the garage bays. She saw a tall, lean man with brownish red hair leaning against the car Austin had been working on earlier. He must have finished with it because the hood was closed.

"Got your car, miss," the man said to Melody.

"Donnie, Melody. Melody, meet the charmer of the South. Also known as Donnie Holt," Austin said. His back was turned to her when he said it, so she couldn't see his expression, but it sounded like Austin was paying his brother only half a compliment.

"Nice to meet ya," Donnie said, walking over and pumping her hand. Then he said to no one in particular, "Yeah, like I said, we're fixin' to get a good one. The sky is darkening up right good out there."

"A storm?" Melody asked. She was pretty sure that was what he meant, but she wanted to be wrong. After all, she still didn't have a roof over her head for the night and didn't know if she would have one.

"Oh yeah. That's putting it mildly," Donnie said.

"Shoot," she said.

"Well, I guess I'll drive this one out." Austin nodded at the purple beater. "Then I'll get your car in here, and we'll have a look at it," Austin said.

"Okay," Melody said, trying not to dread the prognosis too much.

#

Austin walked into the office and sat on the edge of the desk so that he was less than a couple feet from her, and she was very much aware of it. "Bad news," he said.

"That's what I was afraid of," she said. "Give it to me."

"Engine threw a rod." He scratched the corner of his strong, angular jaw. "If we're gonna get a new one in here, it's gonna take a while. It'll be at least a few days, and it's not gonna be cheap." He put a hand behind his neck and screwed his lips to the side. Then he said, "I don't guess you have a warranty on that thing."

She deflated in her chair, shaking her head. "When you say expensive, are you talking hundreds or?..."

"Thousands."

Damn. And there was a good chance she was in the process of losing her job. She couldn't afford this. In more ways than one. Thousands would put a huge dent in her savings account, and she was definitely not in a good place for having that happen. If she forked over thousands, and she lost her job before she was ready to start her own business, she'd be sunk.

"You said a few days. What's the quickest you could get an engine here?"

"I have to make a few calls, but Monday at the earliest. Maybe Tuesday," he said. "Those are your best case scenarios."

"And there's no bus depot close by?"

"Closest one is a few towns over."

"No car rental places?"

"Not here in Sweet Neck."

That was what she'd thought. There couldn't be much at all here in Sweet Neck. "This is not happening," she moaned, burying her face in her hands.

"Sorry," he said. And he sounded like he really was.

She looked up at him, forcing a smile. "Not your fault."

"Look, I can give you a ride to the nearest bus depot tomorrow if you want, but tonight with this storm brewing, it wouldn't be a good idea. Plus, I don't know what the schedule is. They probably don't have any more buses leaving 'til the morning anyway."

"Thanks," she said, her tone dead. "But tonight, I don't know if there's a motel anywhere around here or a Western

Union still open. You see, with no wallet, I don't know where I'll stay." She bit back tears. The pressure of the day's stress was getting to her, but she didn't want to turn into an emotional wreck in front of this complete stranger.

"You'll stay with us. Mom'll love having you over," he said.

She looked up at him. She couldn't remember exactly when it happened—she'd been a little preoccupied after all—but he'd lost the smart aleck routine. It had better not be because of pity. She didn't need any. She was used to looking out for herself. And normally, she was good at it. She'd just come across some bad luck lately. And she'd had a lot on her mind, thanks to the fact that she was almost unemployed amongst other things.

Her ex had been calling lately under the pretense of "business" even though the divorce had been finalized for over a year. She'd heard from friends of hers in California that his new relationship with the practically-a-child R&B singer he'd cheated on her with wasn't going well. Good enough for him. Still, dealing with him always left her mixed up emotionally.

"So...you gonna take me up on it or?..." Austin asked, breaking into her thoughts.

Her smile faltered a little, but she said, "You really don't think she'll mind?"

"Not one bit. In fact, if she heard what happened, and that I hadn't made the offer, she'd've knocked me in the head and asked me why not. When you meet her, you'll understand," he said.

"Okay. Thanks."

"You want me to go ahead with the engine?"

She cringed when she remembered what he'd said about the price.

"We might be able to find a refurbished one in good shape," he said.

"Okay. If you can find one under three thousand, do it," she said, making some mental calculations about her savings and trying to decide if it'd be better to go in for a new car or not. Not having one at all wasn't an option—living in Atlanta without a car was unthinkable. Especially with all the traveling she did for work around the various parts of the city. That would be a sure way to lose her job if she hadn't already.

"All right. Let me make a few calls to see if I can get any leads, and then we'll head out of here," Austin said, hopping off his desk.

She watched while he called various people and had easy conversations with them about car engines. What a smile. And dimples. That laugh. She bet he could seduce with those eyes alone.

He turned to the side to pick up some sort of catalog and suddenly, she had it. For some reason, his profile jogged her memory. She did know him—well, not exactly—but she knew why he seemed so familiar. She sat on the edge of her chair, eager for him to get off the phone so she could share her realization with him and confirm her suspicion.

CHAPTER FOUR

He got off the phone and realized that she was staring at him with a hungry, eager look. He dropped the phone to the desk. He knew that look. When he'd lived in New York, he'd dubbed it the Journalist Look. Or sometimes the Paparazzi Look.

"What," he said flatly, pushing away from the desk. He already knew, but he was drawing this out while debating whether to deny what she was inevitably about to accuse him of being.

"I knew you looked familiar." She sat forward in her chair, and her dark hair fell into her face. "I know who you are. Your hair's different. You used to have more of it, and it was darker and styled and gelled into the heartthrob style at the time. But you're him. From the billboards. The magazines. Weren't you on that reality show for half a season? The one that got canceled? You're Grayson Meadows."

Austin hated that name. It wasn't a part of him any longer. Neither was the life that had gone with it. "My name is Austin Holt." His agent had chosen that phony name to go along with the phony personality she'd tried to pin on him.

"But that was you, right?" A look of doubt flickered through her eyes and for a moment, he thought about reinforcing it.

"Yeah. It was." He sighed and rubbed a hand over his face. He said with his hand over his mouth, "Was is the key word there."

"Grayson Meadows. Male model," she said.

"Austin Holt. Ex-male model," he corrected.

"What happened to you? I mean, why are you here?" she said. "You were so hot. So popular. Everyone wanted you. For a while, I couldn't turn on the television without seeing your face. And then you just…disappeared."

He'd hated it. No, hate wasn't a strong enough word. Neither was loathe, but in any case, he wasn't getting into all that with her. He shrugged. "Career change. Now, that storm is getting closer every minute we sit here. We better get out of this place for the night. Why don't we just go over to Mom's, get you on the internet, and figure the rest out from there? We'll get you settled in for the night, make arrangements for your car, and get you to the bus so that you can get on with your life." It was best for her to get out of there before he got any more ideas that were bound to get him in trouble. And definitely before she could ask any more questions about Grayson.

"Oh. Sure," she said. She seemed to sense he didn't want to talk about it. She had good intuition, he had to give her that. That name alone that she'd mentioned set his teeth on edge.

She walked out of the office. After double-checking the safe and locking up the office, he followed her out into the garage.

When the four of them walked outside, Austin saw immediately that Donnie had been right. The sky was dark purple, almost black. Jagged, ominous, gray storm clouds rolled across it. Wind whipped against them, much cooler than the hot, stagnant air that had settled over them all afternoon. Dust kicked up in the grassless patches of sand near the fence that led around back.

"See you at the house," Austin said to his brother and sister.

"See y'all," they called before heading for a dusty truck parallel parked down the street a bit.

"We'll take my truck," Austin said, putting a hand on her back. She tensed. He hadn't even thought about it. He let his hand drop to his side. "Sorry. Habit."

"It's okay." Her ears and cheeks started to redden. He couldn't stop thinking how adorable that was. She backed away from him a little. "Um, I should have asked you earlier. I almost forgot," she said. "I need to get some things out of my car."

They went back into the garage and retrieved her luggage. He carried her small suitcase and a shoulder bag out to his truck for her.

"This is your truck?" she asked.

He chuckled at the sound of surprise and approval in her voice. "Yeah." He hit a button on his smart key and unlocked the doors to his dark blue custom-built Dodge Ram 3500 complete with a 6.7 liter turbo diesel engine, 350 horsepower, 800 pounds-feet of torque, and 14,000 pounds of towing capacity. Not to mention a mega cab. He had a couple Shelby Mustangs at home—one he'd rebuilt from scratch as a project to get his mind off things when he'd first moved back to Sweet Neck and a newer one. He also had a roadster that he didn't drive much, but the truck was his baby. Cars were his weakness. After all, he'd been born and bred on them.

"Nice," she said, hopping into the seat. He'd wanted so badly to help her into the truck, but she hadn't asked for his help, so it was better for him not to be pushy about it. Besides, he was already having a hard enough time behaving without giving himself extra temptation.

#

When they got to the house, he saw Avery's old pick up truck in the yard, which meant she and Donnie had beat them home. No surprise there considering they'd gotten a head start. Turning to Melody, he said, "Welcome to Bellevue."

"Your house has a name?" she asked.

He shrugged. "Used to be a plantation." Opening his door and grabbing her suitcase from the floor between them, he said, "Let's go inside."

Donnie and Avery were in the living room with the rest of the family. He could tell his mom and Vernon had already been briefed from the eager look on his mom's face.

She jumped up, offering a small, pale hand. "You must be Melody. Welcome to our home. I'm Leigh Anne." She nodded to her the tall, dark-skinned man next to her. "And this is my husband, Vernon. I think you've already met my attractive if unruly brood."

Melody shook hands with them, and everyone exchanged greetings.

"She needs to use your computer, Mom. Her phone died," Austin said before his mom could get sidetracked asking Melody a million questions.

"Oh, sure, sure," she said. "But first, y'all are gonna eat. Poor thing." She put a hand on Melody's shoulder. "After the day you've had, you must want a good meal."

"That'd be wonderful," Melody said.

"Melody, honey, why don't you get settled while I'm putting the finishing touches on dinner?" Mom straightened her back, rising to her full height—all five feet and two inches of it. Despite the fact that Mom was the shortest one in the family, she was clearly the boss of them all. "Austin, you show her to one of the guest rooms on the second floor. Show her the towels and everything," Mom said before bustling off in the direction of the kitchen. Ominous thunder rumbled in the distance.

"A shower sounds so good," Melody said, eyes closed, allowing her head to fall back. She rolled it from shoulder to shoulder. Her slender, long neck was exposed to him. Her throat begged to be kissed. The curve of her neck melted into shoulders that weren't bad at all. He'd always had a particular weakness for a good set of shoulders. He was a leg man, but shoulders were a close second for him.

Tearing his eyes away from her tempting body, he pinched the bridge of his nose. "If you're gonna shower, you better do it quick. This storm is coming on strong and fast." And that wasn't the only thing coming on strong and fast.

"What's the storm got to do with it?" She gave him a curious look.

"You can't shower during a storm."

She snorted. "What's that? Superstition or something? What's gonna happen?"

"Yeah, the kind of superstition that can electrocute you. Besides, Mom won't have it. She'd probably grab you out of there mid-shower, hollering about you trying to get yourself killed," he said. Apparently, he was intent on torturing himself. The thought of Melody in the shower did bad things to him. He was glad he still wore his baggy coveralls so she couldn't see the incriminating evidence of that.

"Okay, show me the way. Hurry. I must shower," Melody said.

Austin led her upstairs.

"This place is huge." Melody looked around as they headed up the stairs. The staircase was made of dark, solid wood. As they ascended, it curved. Melody seemed fascinated by the things he'd seen all his life.

"Yeah. It was the great house for one of the largest plantations in the state right around the time Georgia seceded from the Union in 1861. Then it was an inn after the civil war for a while. It's been in the family since oh…I'd guess about the turn of the century when my great-great grandfather moved to town and made his fortune in bootlegging moonshine," Austin said. "He used the inn as a front for his operation. After he died, my great-great grandmother turned it into a private home."

"How'd he die?"

"Gangsters—rival bootleggers. He wasn't in the safest line of work, you know."

"This place has quite a story behind it, huh?" Melody ran her hand over one of the polished hardwood banisters. She looked up at the family portraits lined the wall above the staircase. Luckily, she didn't ask about those or why Vernon wasn't in them.

"Guess so," he said. He never thought of it as being more than a place to live. In fact, he'd never thought about the house much at all. His mom occasionally had people over from the local historical society, but he didn't have much to do with any of that and had no idea what they did or talked about when they came over for lunch.

He led her to a room at the opposite end of the hall from his. There was an empty room closer to his, but he saw no reason to unnecessarily tempt himself with forbidden fruit.

"Beautiful," she said, walking into the high-ceilinged room and looking around. He guessed if you liked girl stuff, the bright yellow room dripping with lace was a fantasy come true. Like living in a dollhouse or something.

"Well, let me show you the towels so you can shower." A shower didn't sound like a bad idea at all. He might try and sneak in a quick and cold one before dinner. Very, very cold.

She nodded, following him into the hall again. He walked her over to the linen closet just outside the bathroom door across the hall.

"In there," he said, opening the door and gesturing inside the closet.

"Thanks," she said.

"No problem." He started to walk away. She laid a hand on his arm.

"Wait," she said.

"Hum?"

"Thanks. For all of your help today," she said. She lowered her eyes, and her long black eyelashes brushed her cheeks.

"Happy I could help," he said.

She smiled and released his arm. He struggled against the feeling of disappointment he felt and walked down the hall to his room.

CHAPTER FIVE

Melody heard a knock at the door as she headed for the door on her way downstairs for dinner. She opened it and had to hold onto it to keep from stumbling backward. There was no doubt in her mind as to why he'd gotten discovered as a model. He filled out a simple T-shirt and jeans better than she'd imagined anyone could. He'd bulked up some since his modeling days. He was huge, and it was all muscle.

He passed a hand over his buzzed blond hair and settled blazing green eyes on her face after making his own appraisal. It'd been quick and subtler than the one he'd made earlier that day, yet she caught it. She tried to tell herself she hadn't chosen to wear her low-cut yellow sundress to dinner because of him. The one she'd bought specifically because the top was cut just low enough to make her breasts look phenomenal.

"You ready for dinner?" he asked.

"Yeah," she said. He offered his elbow. Laughing, she linked her arm with his. "I can pretend I'm on the red carpet, huh?" A thrill of warmth flooded her when their skin touched. She found it difficult not to tremble.

#

"Sure," he said. "How was your shower?" The last thing he wanted to talk about was red carpets.

"Perfect. Just what I needed," she said. She frowned at a loud crack of thunder. Rain pounded the roof. In the large, cavernous house, the sound was like that of the world crashing down on top of them. "That storm's getting really bad, huh?" she asked as if she were trying to fill the silence. She turned to him, her heart-shaped face framed by her short black hair.

"I guess." He studied the slight pout on her full lips. The soft fabric of her dress felt like silk where it touched his arm. That thin bit of fabric was the only thing between him and her smooth, warm body. A body that was soft in all the right places, and firm in all the right ones, too. At least from what he could tell so far. Investigating any further into the matter would likely earn him a slap to the face.

"I bet your mom's as bad about electrical devices during storms as she is about showers," Melody said, bringing him out of his thoughts.

"Worse," he said. At that moment, as if on cue, the lights went out.

"Great," she muttered. "That definitely means no internet. Or charging my phone."

"You're right about that, but on the bright side, our first dinner together will be by candlelight," he said. He wasn't sure what'd made him say it, but he was relieved when he heard her laughter.

"I can't see a thing," she said.

"I got ya. I know every inch of this house even with my eyes closed."

"A useful skill to have right now," she said.

"I guess it is." He slipped an arm around her. Gripping her waist firmly, he guided her the rest of the way down the stairs. He knew he was holding closer than was necessary, but he couldn't stop himself. He felt the heat of her skin through the flimsy material of her dress. She smelled like vanilla. He let his hand slip down to the top of her hip as they headed for the dining room. Either she didn't notice, or she didn't mind.

They did indeed have dinner by candlelight. He and Vernon set out the candles, and the others, Melody included, brought in the dishes and the water and sweet tea pitchers. Then they all sat down to a feast. Every meal his mom cooked was a feast, no matter how many or few people would be sitting down to eat it.

He hadn't thought it possible, but Melody was even more radiant by candlelight. He wanted to brush her soft, black hair away from her the sides of her face and tease her skin with his tongue so badly that he could barely focus on the dinner table conversation.

"I hope Regan's all right out there in all this," Mom said. "I worry about her when it storms or anything, but she insists on living all alone out at that big farm," she continued while fussing with a casserole dish.

"She's fine, Mom. You know she is," Austin said. Regan was one of the toughest and most self-reliant people he knew. Funniest and smartest, too. He'd always admired that woman.

Once they started eating, the conversation turned to Melody. He found out she was an A&R exec back in Atlanta where she was from and that she'd been on a business trip to Miami. A&R, huh? Life must have thought it was funny, always cracking little jokes at his expense.

"A&R. That must be so glamorous," Avery said. "You probably meet so many stars. Do you know?..." and she rattled off the names of several musical acts. His sister had always been smitten with celebrities. She still was after all that'd happened. She was always picking up some gossip rag at Zip's, the local grocery store. He couldn't stand those tabloids. They ruined lives. They'd definitely helped ruin his.

After Melody got done answering Avery's stream of questions, Melody said, "But you all have your very own star right here. Grayson Meadows."

Everybody got real quiet. The only sounds were the scrape of fork against plate, the background patter of rain, and occasional booms of thunder that were starting to fade farther away. There was no way for her to know what a sore subject it was for his family, but he was still angry with her for bringing it up. He knew his anger was irrational, but if there was such thing as a family wound, Grayson Meadows was it for the Holts.

"Well," his mom said, forcing a smile. "We are right proud of Austin." She folded her hands on the table in front of her plate. "Melody, tell us more about Atlanta. Life there must never be dull." That was his mom all right. Always putting out fires. Hiding her own pain. Protecting him. He felt especially guilty about that last part.

Donnie snorted in his direction before sending him a look. Austin couldn't see him well in the dim, flickering candlelight, but he knew the look Donnie was shooting him had to be an ugly one.

Melody must have sensed the awkwardness she caused because she stumbled over her words when she first started telling Mom about life in Atlanta as requested.

Thankfully, the rest of dinner conversation centered around Melody, her job, and Atlanta. That didn't stop Donnie from jumping in with his little snide remarks about Grayson Meadows. Donnie never had known when to shut his mouth up. That was probably why he had been busted in it so many times. Not by Austin—well most of the times Donnie had been busted in the mouth, Austin hadn't been the culprit.

#

That night, after Melody changed into the sweatpants cut off at the knees and dark blue tank top that were her favorite sleeping apparel, she climbed into bed and quickly realized it was going to be impossible to fall asleep. It was too hot for sleep. The electricity, and so the air conditioning, was still out. Georgia in the summer was not a place anyone wanted to be without air conditioning. Even at night. Rather than cooling things off, the storm was making the air even muggier. Fans and cracked windows didn't stand much of a chance against the humidity and the day's heat that was still trapped in the house. This was especially true in a house the size of Bellevue. The rooms were huge and thus hard to cool. Especially the rooms with floor-to-ceiling windows that soaked up plenty of sun during the day—like the bedroom Melody was staying in.

After tossing and turning for a while, she pushed her sticky sheets aside and got out of bed. She decided to wander around for a bit, check out the rest of the house. If the house had been around since before the Civil War, maybe there was a ghost or something lurking around. And maybe she watched too much T.V.

Glancing down the hall, she saw light coming from under one of the doors. It was the one she'd seen Austin enter earlier that night after they'd finished with dinner and washed dishes the best they could considering the power was still out. Good. Maybe they could keep each other company since neither one could sleep. Plus, looking at him would be more fun and probably a better idea than wandering around in the dark in a place she hadn't been invited to explore on her own. Besides, there was always the possibility that the ghost theory could pan out, and she was certainly no ghost hunter and had no desire to become one.

She padded down the hall and knocked lightly on the door, hoping he hadn't simply fallen asleep with the light on.

"Come in," came a muffled voice from the other side of the door.

She walked in and her breath caught in her throat. A candle burned on his desk, and he sat in the chair in front of it. He leaned back in the chair as she entered the room. He was shirtless. Shadow and light played over the well-defined muscles of his biceps, pecks, and abs. She swallowed hard and pressed her sweaty palms to the sides of her cut-off sweatpants without really thinking about it.

"See something that interests you?" he asked. She heard the amusement in his voice, and it brought her back to reality. She remembered how irritating she'd found him earlier that day. That cocky guy was surfacing again. Not that she hadn't encouraged him to come out of there.

She ignored the connotation behind his words and thought up an excuse to cover her real thoughts. "I was just looking at your tattoo." Luckily, he had one. A tribal band around his left bicep.

He looked down at it as if to confirm it was still there and then looked back at her. "Yeah, my agent thought it'd give me an edge or something." The way he said "agent" sounded even more bitter than the rest of the words he'd just spoken. But he grinned when he said, "My image consultant hated it." He gestured toward his bed. "Have a seat."

She walked over and sank down onto the soft bed. A feather top mattress. It was the kind of bed that made you want to melt into it and fall asleep as soon as you hit it. The king-sized bed was in one corner of the sparsely furnished room, near a window. The lack of furniture made the already large room seem even bigger. His bedroom was almost the same size as her two-bedroom apartment.

"I'm sorry if I made things strange earlier," she said. "At dinner. I didn't know your modeling career was such a touchy subject for your family." She settled back on the bed.

"There wasn't any way for you to." His expression didn't seem to change, but it was hard to tell in the semi-dark.

"You wanna talk about it?"

He hesitated for a moment, but he eventually shook his head. "Nothing to talk about. I was a model. Now I'm running the family business."

"Funny how things work out, huh?" she asked.

He shrugged. "Not so funny. I grew up with cars. Should've known I'd never escape 'em. You can run, but you can't hide." His laugh was forced. He hunched his shoulders a bit and stared at a point to the left of her head.

"I guess I was thinking of me more than you when I said that," she said, partly to make their conversation less awkward by taking the pressure off him and partly because it was true.

"Oh?"

She nodded. Her mother had always drilled being practical into Melody. Mom was terrified of Melody turning out like her dad—a washed up, deteriorating, starving artist. Melody had idolized her dad. When he died, she'd been so devastated that she cut music out of her life altogether for a couple years. Her mom encouraged it. Music was the center of her world, though.

When she realized what a dark place her world was without it, she'd enrolled in some music theory classes at her college. Later, she decided to minor in musicology. That was how she'd met the fool she married who tried to kill her love of music again.

"Yeah. I love music, but A&R exec was never my first choice for a career," she said. "I love my job, but I used to want to be a songwriter. I knew singing wasn't for me, but there was a time when I would've given anything to hear people who had real talent belt out my songs." She chuckled. "I used to dream about writing a song for Jill Scott." She shook her head. "Crazy, right?"

"What's crazy about that?"

She shrugged. Her practical mom could've given him a laundry list of answers to that question if she were in the room.

"You still write? The songs, I mean?" He sounded interested in what she'd said. Excited by it even.

She shook her head. "I realized it wasn't gonna happen, and I gave up on the whole thing."

"Shame."

She snorted. "How do you know? You've never even heard one of my songs. Could be for the best for everybody."

"Sing me one."

"I can't do that."

"Why not? You got any of 'em with you? Or memorized?"

"Maybe." She had lots of them memorized. She wanted to sing, but she was afraid. She'd never sung solo in front of another person before. When she and Jen did karaoke songs together, she sang so low people could barely hear her. Karaoke nights and shower tunes made up the full extent of her singing resume. She was happy with that. Her dad had been the performer in the family.

"Sing to me." He said the words in a low soft voice that made her stomach muscles quiver. He came over and sat next to her on the bed. The world seemed to tilt a little as the bed sagged under his weight. His scent—spice and soap—washed over her.

Lost in his green eyes, she said a stupid thing, "Okay.

"Good." He smiled and leaned back on his elbows.

Watching his muscle flex as he shifted positions made her go blank for a moment, forgetting the song she wanted to sing. There wasn't an inch of flab on him anywhere. Not even half of one. She'd never laid hands on a body that perfect in her life.

And you won't now, she told herself. Behave yourself.

"I hope you're not backing out on me," he said. He was so close, his bicep near her knee. Thunder boomed through the sky, and she jumped. He grinned and put a hand on her knee. "Don't worry. I won't let it get you."

"Ha ha," she said dryly even though her heart was skittering around in her chest; his hand on her skin felt so good. Too good.

"You gonna sing for me or what?"

"Okay." She took a deep, shaky breath and let it out slowly, watching their shadows dance with the candlelight on the wall on the other side of the bed. "I think this one fits right now. It's called, 'Rain on my Window Pane'."

She sang her song for him, and she was afraid to look at him until she finished. Still, she could feel his stare. When she looked down at the end of her song, she was frozen to his gaze. She'd never been looked at in such a tender way. There was something almost adoring in his eyes. Neither of them said a word. The only sound was that of soft rain hitting the roof and the windows.

"That was beautiful. Sad, but beautiful," he murmured. "What were you talking about earlier? You have a great voice."

She looked down at her hands, grateful for the fact that it was probably too dark for him to see her blush because she could certainly feel her cheeks roasting. "Thanks." That was all she could think of to say.

"I didn't expect country, but it suits you. It really fits."

She nodded. Most people didn't. That reminded her of something she hadn't expected earlier. She'd been trying to think of a way to bring it up, and now was the best opportunity she'd had so far.

"That guy, Vernon, is he your dad?" She took in Austin's blond hair and green eyes and the border between pale and golden skin on his arms that came from his farmer's tan.

"Step-dad," he said.

She leaned in and murmured, like it was a secret or something, "He's black."

He leaned up and murmured back, "I know."

"Isn't that a problem? In a town like this?" A small Southern town? Even in Atlanta, she'd sometimes seen interracial couples get strange looks.

He shook his head. "Nah. People mostly mind their business in Sweet Neck. We all know too much about each other to start throwing stones at each other's glass houses. Well, most everybody. There are a few—aren't there always a few—like Miz Hardy who lives on the farm next door. Mom calls her Miz Busybody." He grinned. "Let's just say this much. It is never a good thing to attract the attention, scorn, and hateful eye of a busybody." He added, "But generally, things are copasetic. Most everyone in town loves Vernon and Mom anyhow."

She nodded. "What happened to your dad?"

"Dead. Stroke." He said the words with no emotion in his tone at all.

"I'm sorry."

"It was a long time ago," he said, watching the candle on his desk as he spoke. "Back to you." He trained his gaze on her again. "You're into country music then?"

"Yeah. I listen to everything. The label I work for is mainly R&B. A few hip-hop artists. We're getting into some neo-soul and jazz now, which I love. But I have a special place in my heart for country. My grandpa babysat me a lot when I was a kid, and it's all he listens to," Melody said. She thought about all the time she'd spent with her grandparents before they moved to California, and the time she'd spent with them while she was in college out there. After her dad died, they couldn't bear to stay in Georgia any longer. He'd been close them, and he was an only child. They'd moved back to California thinking the change of scenery would help them deal with their grief and because both of them were born there.

"She has Nashville in her heart, but she lives in Atlanta." Austin hummed a little.

"Ha. So you write country, too?"

They laughed. He scooted closer to her on the bed. His arm brushed against her leg, and his skin was hot. Almost feverish. Part of her wished he'd pull her down to lay on the bed next to him. Another part was glad he didn't.

Still leaning back on his elbows, he looked up at her. "I'm sorry you got stuck here and all, but I'm enjoying this. Talking, laughing, singing with you," he said. The way he dropped the "g's" off the ends of his words and drew them out with his drawl was delicious to her ears.

"Me, too." For a moment, she almost leaned in for a kiss. Putting more distance between them, she turned the conversation in a safer direction. "Tell me more about this Mustang you rebuilt."

He did. Then he gave her a crash course about the auto mechanic business and told her about his life in Sweet Neck. After that, she told him about Atlanta until they'd talked most of the night away.

CHAPTER SIX

Melody woke up groggy after just a few hours' sleep. She and Austin had been up until four in the morning talking. Still, no matter how late she stayed up, she could never sleep much past nine. Thankfully, the power was back on that morning. She plugged her charger and phone in before stumbling to the shower. The power being on meant there was running—and more importantly hot—water. After her shower, she trudged back to her room to get dressed.

She went into the kitchen and gratefully accepted a cup of coffee from Leigh Anne. She looked around the sunlit, airy kitchen as she took a sip. The light fixtures were ornate and probably as old as the house itself though well-polished and cared for. The up-to-date stainless steel appliances seemed out of place.

"You want any breakfast?" Leigh Anne asked. She wore a faded pair of jeans and an old flannel shirt over a white tank top.

Melody shook her head no. "Just the coffee is perfect, thanks."

"If you change your mind, there's some leftover bacon and eggs in the oven." She nodded at the stove across from the highly polished, oak kitchen table. "Or I can whip you up something real quick. We have cereal, too, if you'd rather have that."

"I don't want to you to go through all that trouble."

"Oh, pshaw. No trouble at all." Leigh Anne waved off her concern.

"Thanks, I'll keep that in mind." She was too tired to be hungry. Besides, at home, her breakfast rarely consisted of more than grabbing a travel mug full of coffee on her way out of the door in the morning. "Where is everybody?" she asked.

Leigh Anne said, "Vernon went over to check on Regan and see if she needed any help after last night's storm. The kids are down at the shop. It's what, ten now? They'll be back in a couple hours or so. The shop's open 'til noon on Saturdays." Leigh Anne sipped her coffee. "Austin said he'll drive you to the bus station that's a couple towns away from here when he gets home. Y'all can make arrangements about your car, too, when he gets here."

Melody nodded. "Yeah. About the car. And you letting me stay here. I'm going to pay you all as soon as I get home and get everything straightened out. I swear. I'll even sign something if you want me to."

Leigh Anne laughed and put one hand over her heart, the other on Melody's shoulder. "Oh goodness, Melody. I won't take your money. I'm glad to have your company, and I won't hear of it. And I insist on paying for your bus ticket. After all you've been through, it's the least I can do. I'm sure you and Austin can work something out for the car. He's a good boy, but you let me know if he needs a good bopping over the head about this."

Melody was used to paying her own way. "No, really I—"

"Shush now. It's settled," Leigh Anne said, shaking her head and giving Melody a motherly smile.

Melody sipped her coffee. "Well thank you. Very much."

"You're welcome, hon." Leigh Anne said, walking over to the island in the center of the kitchen, which was laden with produce, freezer bags, and packages of meat that seemed to have come from the refrigerator and freezer.

"What are you up to?" Melody asked.

"Just going through this food, seeing what can be saved and what got ruined on account of the storm." Tossing one of the freezer bags aside, she said, "After that, I'm headed out back to do a little gardening."

"Let me help you with that," Melody said.

"Well, come on over here, then." Leigh Anne waved her over to the table.

Melody set down her coffee cup, grabbed a couple of empty plastic shopping bags, and walked over to the island to help Leigh Anne.

#

Once they were done cleaning out the fridge and deep freezer, Melody asked if she could use Leigh Anne's computer.

"Sure," Leigh Anne led her to a room set up as an office just off the living room. She informed Melody it used to be a drawing room back when the house was first built. "You use the phone and give our number as a contact if you need to. I know you're going to say something about it, so let me say it now. I don't care about the long distance. You getting in touch with your folks is what's important right now."

"Thanks, Mrs..." Melody suddenly realized she didn't know what to call the woman. Her last name might not have been the same as Austin's considering they were a blended family.

"Leigh Anne. Please."

"I appreciate it so much," Melody said. Her cell phone should have been nearly charged by then, but it was sweet of Leigh Anne to offer.

"Of course. I'll be out back in my garden if you need me," Leigh Anne said.

"Okay."

Melody sat down at the desk and turned on the computer. She would send Mom and Jen emails and then run upstairs later after she finished checking her email to get her phone. By that time, it would definitely be done charging. She'd use it to call Mom and Jen first. She didn't even want to think about the other phone call she had to make.

She signed into her email account and skimmed her messages. She sent emails to her mom and Jen, telling them she'd call them soon and hopefully before they got her emails. She then explained about her phone being dead and everything else that'd happened yesterday. Then she canceled all of her credit cards and check cards and had new ones sent out. She took care of the rest of her online errands before going upstairs to get her phone.

She had two difficult phone calls to make. One to the R&B' group's manager to tell him there was a chance she wouldn't make it to the club to hear the group sing. And the other to Saeed.

CHAPTER SEVEN

She found the manager's phone number in one of their email exchanges and made that call first. He took it pretty well, and he seemed more optimistic than she was about the situation. He still believed she might actually make it to Miami in time to see the group perform.

"Believe me," she said to the manager, who was also the father of two of the group members. "I really want to be there. Seeing the group perform is my number one priority right now."

"I know," he said smoothly into the phone. "I'm not worried. You've been on top of things so far."

She winced. Yeah. He hadn't seen her yesterday. "Okay. Good. Hope to see you all Tuesday night," she said.

"You will," he said.

When the call was finished, Melody held the phone to her temple and closed her eyes. This group was her big chance. They were really good, and they were definitely going to go places, whether New Face signed them or not.

Their manager had expressed an interest in stepping down and letting someone else run the group because he had two businesses to run that he'd started and that he loved running. He'd only gotten involved with managing the group to look out for his sons and their friends. He didn't have a real passion for music, and he'd told Melody that several times. He kept hinting that as soon as he found someone professional and capable to replace him, he planned on stepping down as manager. And he'd made it clear that he thought Melody would make a perfect replacement for him.

This group was her ticket out of New Face in more ways than one. Even if Saeed wouldn't let her offer them a contract, they could be her first clients. No, they would be. As long as she found a way to get to Miami by Monday night. She didn't care if she had to get off the plane and get a cab straight to the club. No matter what it took, she was going to make this work.

After talking with the group's manager, she had to make the most dreaded phone call.

Taking a deep breath, she speed dialed the main line for the record company. She followed the prompts and entered Saeed's extension at the appropriate time. Her stomach churned while she listened to his voicemail greeting. She then left him a message asking him to call her back as soon as possible. She flagged the voicemail message as urgent and hung up the phone. She cradled her head in her hands, trying to will away the beginnings of the dull ache she felt creeping into the base of her skull.

Saeed hadn't been crazy about the idea of her going to Miami, and he didn't think there was anything special about the group she was going there to see. However, she really believed in the guys and had decided that she would pay out of pocket—both with gas money and vacation time—to go see them. Despite his initial lack of support, maybe there was some chance Saeed would fly her to Miami. If he would just listen to the demo CD she'd given him, he would understand.

If they didn't snatch the group up soon, someone else would. And whenever they got picked up by a record company—probably by a major label—they would be big. Huge. She wanted it to be a New Face contract they signed when they signed one. And if Saeed had any common sense, that was what he'd want, too.

Saeed had told her the company wouldn't pay for a ticket earlier, and it was bad enough they would lose much of her productivity for nearly a week, but maybe he would have a heart just this once. She had to believe that because the only hope she had left was getting on Saeed's good side. Otherwise, she could probably kiss her job goodbye.

She needed to talk to her mom and Jen. She tried her mom first and got her voice mail. After leaving a voice mail and sending her mom a text to let her know she was okay, she called Jen.

"Melody James!" Jen cried. "I read your email. What kind of mess have you gotten yourself into this time?"

Melody laughed, tears of relief trickling from the corners of her eyes at the sound of Jen's voice. "Jen. I can't even begin to tell you how insane this has all been."

"I told you about that clunker of yours," Jen said.

Melody sighed. It was true. She had. "I know."

"So what are you gonna do now? You want me to come get you?"

"Thanks, Jen, but I think I got it figured out," Melody said before sharing her plan with her best friend.

"Yeah, sounds like you got it all figured out all right. Have you called Saeed yet?"

"Left him a message."

"Good luck. 'Cause you're gonna need it."

"I know." She smiled, thinking of her little friend. Small but tough. And loyal. Jen would have crawled across hot coals to Sweet Neck to get Melody if she had needed her to.

"Sweet Neck, huh? Wow. What's it like there? You run into Andy or Gomer Pyle yet? Maybe Goober?"

Melody laughed. "Not quite Gomer," she said, thinking of Austin. "I haven't had a chance to check out the town yet really. There's a local celebrity, though."

"What, really?"

"Yeah. You remember Grayson Meadows? From the Diet Max commercials a few years back?"

"Uhm...he was on that reality show about the male models, too, right? And then he just kind of disappeared—wait. Don't tell me. Grayson is in Sweet Neck?" Jen's voice became a shriek by the time she finished speaking.

"He is. He's from here." They talked about Grayson and one tangent led to another. Melody had been on the phone for almost an hour when she heard the call waiting beep. Noticing her mom's number, she told Jen that she had to go, her mom was on the phone.

"Melody James!" her mom cried as soon as she said hello into the phone.

"Mom, I—"

"I've been worried sick. I must have left a hundred voice mails on that phone of yours."

"The phone—"

"Don't you know that anything could have happened to you? And where in the world is Sweet Neck?"

The conversation went much like that, but eventually Melody was able to get enough words in to let her mom know that she was safe and that she'd contacted her as soon as she was able to. After reassuring her mother that everything was okay, they talked business. Her mom agreed to pick her up at the bus station and take her to the Hartsfield-Jackson airport in Atlanta when she managed to find her way to a bus depot and make her way back up there. Melody stayed on the phone with her mom until a number beeped in that made her heart sink.

"Mom. I have to go. It's Saeed calling."

"Hmph. That little weasel."

"Yes, but he's still my boss and I need to talk to him about work," Melody said.

"Okay, but you have your charger now. Don't you dare let that phone die again. Call me before you leave for the bus station. If you don't, I'll call you."

"Sure thing, Mom."

"I don't like the idea of you being stranded there."

"I'm fine," Melody said, anxious. Saeed had hung up and called back. She could almost see him getting more and more agitated as he waited for her to answer the phone. Saeed didn't like being told no, even if that no was as seemingly innocuous as an unanswered phone call. "I have to go now."

"Bye, baby."

"Bye, Mom." Melody clicked over and tried to swallow against a dry throat. "This is Melody."

"Melody. Where are you? What is this message you left me?" Saeed's voice was flat. He always sounded like that right before an explosion.

"My car broke down. I can catch a bus back to Atlanta, but I'll need to book a flight to Miami right away."

"Why?" The way he said it made her heart sink.

Already knowing what his answer would be, she still went through the motions, hoping she was wrong. "The R&B group I told you about is performing in Miami on Monday night."

Saeed ignored her. "You mentioned losing your wallet. Were your company cards in there?"

"Yes," Melody almost whispered.

He blew a harsh breath into the phone. "And they haven't been canceled yet?" His voice was tight. Strained.

"Not until today." She didn't carry the phone numbers for the credit card companies around with her. She'd needed to get to a computer before she could cancel the cards. "There was a storm last night, and I just—"

"You lost two company cards twenty-four hours ago. I'm just finding out." Each word was staccato and sounded as if a period was behind it.

"I'm sorry, Saeed, I—"

"You're done is what you are. Done making excuses for yourself. Because I'm done listening to them."

"But if you'd just listen to these guys, Saeed. They're unbelievable. I have to get to Miami. If you could just front me the money for the ticket, I'll pay it back. You'll see. If we don't sign them, somebody else will—a major label will find out about them soon. Probably at the club Monday night. Listen to the demo. Please."

"I've already told you the company's not going to pay for you to go chasing dreams all over the country. I'm up to my neck in troubles, ASCAP and BMI are breathing down my neck, we're looking at potential legal problems here—huge copyright issues—because of an artist your subordinate brought to me, and you do what? You do nothing but go out and find more troubles to bring to my doorstep."

Melody knew the artist he was talking about, and she'd tried to warn him about the potential copyright issues, but he hadn't listened to her when it would have made a difference. Just like he wouldn't listen to her now. He preferred to bulldoze on ahead and blame someone else whenever he got into trouble. "But it's not—"

"No, Melody. I don't wanna hear it. I am done with your hair-brained Lucy and Ethel schemes. I'm not wasting another single resource on this long shot group of wannabes. You've already wasted all kinds of time on them that you could have spent on groups that are actually making money."

She had to bite her tongue to keep from reminding him about all the flop acts he'd insisted they sign to the label. Instead, she said, "Send June. She knows—"

"Nobody's getting sent to Miami on this company's dime, including you. And take your time getting back to Atlanta. You are putting us right into bankruptcy court."

"Well, how is that my fault?" Hold on. He wasn't about to blame all the company's financial problems on her. Especially when he'd been responsible for most if not all of them.

"Excuse me?" Saeed's voice gave away the fact that he was not used to being talked to this way. Too bad. He'd crossed a line. After the last twenty-four hours, and after the way she worked her fingers to the bone for his ungrateful little tail every day, he was not going to talk to her this way and get away with it.

"Nobody likes you," she said. "Not your employees, not the artists, not their managers. Nobody. You're alienating the acts we already have faster than I can bring new ones in. None of the acts you've insisted we bring in have made us any money. The board brought you in to save us? Well, it seems to me that all you're doing is running us into the ground quicker."

The line went dead silent for so long, she thought at first that he'd hung up. Finally, he said, "Enjoy your vacation in the middle of nowhere wherever you are."

"What is that supposed to mean?"

"Consider yourself fired."

"Fired?" In that moment, she could barely comprehend what the word meant. "Wait, no, no. I'm sorr—"

"Yes, fired. Done. That's it. I'll have someone pack your things. You can pick up the boxes when you get back or have someone pick them up for you."

Melody crushed the phone to her ear, wanting to say so many things to him, but not able to get the words out. The word "fired" had paralyzed her tongue.

"We can discuss wrapping up loose ends, paperwork, and all the minor details when you get back to Atlanta."

Still no words would come.

"Have a good vacation, Melody. I wish you well." It didn't sound like he wished her well. And then there was silence on the other end. She was holding the phone in her hand, staring at it, when Austin walked into the room.

CHAPTER EIGHT

Austin was filthy, but he'd seen Melody in the office and he wanted to say hi to her before going upstairs to wash up. As soon as he entered the doorway, he could tell something was off.

"Melody, what's wrong?" he asked, walking into the center of the room. He'd left his work boots near the back door so he now wore only socks on his feet.

Melody jumped a little at the sound of his voice. Setting her phone on the desk next to her, she looked up at him with large brown eyes. She looked stunned. That was the best way to describe it. Like somebody had clubbed her over the head with something and she was trying to pull herself together after the blow.

"Huh? Oh. Hi, Austin," she said.

"Hi," he said. He moved closer and rephrased his earlier question. "Is everything okay?"

She shook her head and burst into tears. He wasn't entirely sure what he should do. Probably hug her, but he was covered in gunk and grease. He walked over to the desk chair and squatted down next to her. "Melody?"

"I won't need you to take me to the bus station." It took her a while to get the words out. She spoke a few words at a time around her sobs. "The group. I have to call...manager...gone!"

He didn't understand what she was talking about, but her certainly understood that she was upset.

"I would hug you, but I don't want to get you all dirty," he admitted. She slid off the chair and into his arms. Taken off guard, he almost fell backward. He caught himself just in time, got back on balance and held her to him. She then sobbed out enough of her story into his shoulder for him to know she'd gotten fired and she hated her boss—well, former boss.

"And now I have no job, no car—nothing." She said, pulling back a little and swiping at her tears. Her hair was a little mussed and fell over one of her cheeks. Even tear streaked and with a black smudge of dirt from his coveralls on it, her face was beautiful. The face of an angel. He reached up to wipe the smudge from her cheek. He always scrubbed his hands clean before leaving the shop.

She sniffled and put her hand over his as he started to pull it away from her cheek. She gave him a watery smile. "Thanks for letting me cry on you."

"Any time," he said, his voice husky with desire. He was very much aware of how close her body was to his. He shouldn't have been tempting himself so much, but he didn't want her to move from where she knelt between his legs either. Her leg brushed against his inner thigh as she shifted positions. It took all his strength for him to not start tearing at her clothes right that moment.

She moved her hand from his, and he let it fall away from her cheek. "I guess it's time to figure out the next move," she said.

"That reminds me. I found an engine if you want it for under two thousand. I'll have to let the guy know something soon. He said he can only hold it a few days. No labor charge of course. I insist." The engine was closer to four thousand, but she didn't need to know he was cutting the cost in half for her. He had a feeling she wouldn't have it if she knew.

"You don't have to do that," she said. "I can pay for the labor."

"Do you want my mom to kill me? Besides, I want to." And he really did. He had a strong urge to do anything he could to take away any of her sadness or frustrations that he could. He knew she'd had a lot of them in the twenty-four hours since they'd met. And after staying up all night talking to her, he knew she was something special. He'd been pretty tired at work all morning, but it'd been worth it.

She smiled. "Thanks. Let me think about it, okay? I'll let you know on Monday. I might just take the bus home and buy a new car. Let you have that one for scrap metal or something. I have no idea what my next move will be right now."

"Okay. But it really is a pretty decent car excepting your engine. I think with this new one, you could get some decent mileage out of it before you have to get another one." He didn't want her to leave town so soon. And if she did leave, he'd prefer it if she had a reason to come back. So he really wanted to fix that car for her.

She nodded. "I need to make a call." She rubbed a hand over her face and seemed stressed at the thought of that call. "After that, would you mind just taking me to get a few things? Is the Radio Shack open?"

"Radio Shack closed at noon, but I'll take you Monday."

"Okay." She sighed. "That's right. I don't have any money yet anyway. I'd still like to get out of here for a while. Maybe I'll go for a walk."

"I have to go to the grocery store for Mom. If you give me a minute to get cleaned up, you can come with me if you want."

"Sounds great. Thanks." She stood and stretched. Her shirt rode up, exposing a flat, smooth inch of brown stomach. She walked to the doorway and looked over her shoulder. "Coming?"

"Um yeah. In a little bit." He needed a minute. And to think some very boring thoughts.

She nodded. "I'm going to go see what all your mom needs from the store. I'll be out back in the garden with her."

"Okay," he said, watching her walk away. It only made his, uh, problem worse, but he couldn't keep his eyes off her.

#

Her call to the group's manager had been exhausting. It'd taken all her effort to hold it together as she told the man it was all over. That she wasn't going to be able to make it to Miami. All hope wasn't lost for the group, not by any means. But it was all lost for her.

After that horrible conversation, Austin drove them into town. When he stopped at the red light on Main Street at the one and only major intersection in town, she looked over at him.

"Is this the only traffic light in Sweet Neck?" she asked in a teasing tone.

"The only real one." He gave an easy grin. "There's one farther out. One of those blinking yellow ones."

"I can't decide if that's funny or not."

He laughed softly. The light turned green, and he drove forward.

"What does Vernon do for a living? And Leigh Anne?" she asked as they drove past the store fronts that lined either side of Main Street.

"Vernon's a truck driver. Long distance. He's leaving in a few days for a trip as a matter of fact. Sometimes, he helps Regan out with her horses. Mom works part-time as a bank teller."

"Oh." She continued to stare through the windshield after that, and their conversation died away. She caught him glancing her way more than once from the corner of her eye, but she was lost in her thoughts and didn't turn his way.

#

HIS MELODY

At the far end of Main Street, Austin turned onto a side street. After passing an empty lot, Zip's was on their left.

He pulled into a small parking lot, which was in front of an unimpressive squat brick building with glass double doors. The wooden white sign on the roof had faded red letters on it reading, "Zip's Supermarket".

She looked at him and then back at the store.

"What?" he said.

"It sure ain't New York, huh?"

"Nope. Not New York." Thank goodness. He'd left New York behind in a coke haze with only bad memories and shattered dreams to show for it. Nothing great about that place. If Leigh Anne, Vernon, and Regan hadn't helped put him back together again, he probably wouldn't have made it.

They climbed out of his truck and headed for the store. He held the glass door open for her, appreciating the way her polo shirt hugged her curves as she brushed past him. Apparently, he was never going to learn when it came to her. Un-tucking his own shirt in what he hoped was a subtle move, he followed her into the store. He greeted almost everyone they passed.

"You really know every single person in this town, don't you?" she asked as they walked up and down the aisles. The aisles were packed in a little too close together, and the beige tiles were scuffed and cracked with age. These were things he'd never noticed as a little kid when he, Avery, and Donnie had raced up and down the aisles, chasing each other around the store and giving Mom a headache.

He grinned. "In case you hadn't noticed? Sweet Neck ain't all that big of a place."

She laughed, and he tried to think of something to say that would allow him to hear that beautiful sound again.

She said, "I was thinking. About what we were talking about last night."

He nodded and concentrated on putting things into the basket. He'd told her about life in Sweet Neck, carefully evading her every time she asked about New York. Grayson

Meadows was dead, and he didn't want to talk about anything connected to that life. He hoped she wasn't going to try to turn the conversation in that direction again.

They wandered up and down the narrow aisles for a while, tossing the things Mom had requested into the basket as they did.

"So it seems like we've run into every person in this town except your girlfriend," she said, picking up a can of peas and shifting them from hand to hand. Her diamond ring flashed under the store's lights as she did so. He reminded himself that she wasn't really married before reminding himself that it wouldn't change a thing for him if she were. He couldn't allow anything to happen with her. Nope. He wasn't even going to think about it.

"Ah. There's a simple explanation for that." He shifted the basket from one hand to the other. "I don't have one."

"Really?"

"Not right now. Not for a while actually. There's Kristen," he jerked his thumb at a brunette cashier. "She was my high school sweetheart. Married with four kids now. Remember the Miz Hardy I mentioned? The busybody? Well, that's her daughter."

The brunette looked up at them briefly and then ducked her head back toward her cash register. He suppressed a sigh. He truly did ruin everything and everyone he touched.

Austin pointed across the store at the deli. "And Lil. We sort of dated the summer before I moved away. Regan and I spent a little time together when I first came home," he said, leaving out the fact that she'd held him together for a while, and he'd leaned on her too much and taken more than he should have from her. He felt guilty about it, but he didn't want to get into all that. Getting into it would mean talking about New York. "All past. No current."

"Regan? Really?" She put the peas back on the shelf and turned her full attention to him.

"Yeah. Why'd you say it like that?"

"I guess I didn't expect it is all. Isn't she a lot older than you?"

"If you call fifteen years a lot," he said with a shrug. "But things like that don't matter to me."

"So you two don't have anything going on at all anymore?"

"Nope. Just good friends. She's one of the best friends I've ever had," Austin said. She'd saved him.

"I still can't believe the women in this town would let you stay single," she said with a shake of her head.

He gave a little laugh. "Around here? People don't get dazzled by things like Grayson Meadows."

"But I'm sure they still appreciate a good looking man." Her eyes flitted over his chest.

"I'm good looking am I?" He avoided telling her that he was tainted. No respectable woman in Sweet Neck would be caught near him. But he spent some time with the less respectable ones. He hadn't even done that in a good while, though.

"Please. Don't pull that. Ex male model? What do you see when you look in the mirror? Gollum?" She snorted.

"Let's just say I don't look in mirrors all that often anymore," he said. Vanity hadn't gotten him anywhere he wanted to be.

She moved closer to him. "What happened to you, Austin Holt?"

He almost wanted to tell her. She was so close and beautiful and soft. But he couldn't allow himself to do it. He was done with opening himself up to people other than Leigh Anne, Vernon, and Regan. Plus, she would be gone in a few days.

He pointed behind her, brushing his arm against hers as he did so. "Mom needs new batteries for the flashlights. Over there. By the cash registers." He murmured the words much closer to the soft curve of her ear than was necessary.

She stumbled backward a little, bumping into a display rack of some sort of kitchen gadgets. He steadied the display as she nodded and turned toward the cash registers. She was adorable. Those shorts were torture for him, though. Very long legs, very short shorts. She couldn't have possibly gotten them any shorter without showing off her panties to the world. If she was wearing any. Why was he thinking about her panties? Why torture himself like that? Time to get his thoughts away from that very dangerous place.

That evening, before dinner, Melody and Austin sat in the family room, which used to be called a parlor back in the house's original, high-society days. Melody sat on the davenport—which as far as Austin could tell was a fancy name for a big, old couch. The high-ceilinged, vast room was mostly filled with furniture his great-great-grandmother had placed in it years before his parents were even twinkles in their parents' eyes. He guessed it was all antique stuff by now. His mom would know. She loved that Antiques Roadshow.

They made small talk. He could tell she wanted to ask him more about his past, but he wasn't encouraging her to bring it up. All that was better off left where it was—behind him.

All was fine and good until Donnie bounded into the room.

"Hey, y'all!" the tall hayseed said in his booming voice. By normal people's standards, it would have been a shout. That was just the way Donnie talked, though. Full volume. He walked over to Melody and sat on the opposite end of the davenport from her. Austin stayed where he'd been sitting all along on a chair across from them. "What are y'all talking about in here?" Donnie asked.

"Not much," Melody said, giving Austin a look he couldn't read.

"Pshaw. Austin has a lot of good stories. You haven't been telling her any of your real good stories, Austin?" Donnie gave him a challenging look.

"I don't have any worth telling," he said, giving his brother a warning look.

HIS MELODY

"Aw, he's just puttin' on," Donnie said. "There's lots he could tell you." Donnie put his elbows on his knees, leaned forward, and smirked before saying, "Don't let him fool you."

"I reckon you'd be best off keeping your mouth shut when it comes to things that don't concern you," Austin said.

Donnie chuckled. "That's my brother for you." He paused and put on an exaggerated show of tapping his chin with his finger and trying to look like he was thinking about something. Must have been hard since thinking wasn't something Donnie had a lot of experience with. Finally, he said, "Yeah, Austin. I guess you're right. Your life in New York couldn't have been all that great. I guess you screwed that life up and then had to come down here looking for someone else's life to steal."

Melody looked back and forth between the two of them. He could tell from the tilt of her head and the confusion in her eyes that she didn't know whether she should say anything or not.

"Ignore him," Austin said. "He's bitter about the fact that he's never really been good at anything his whole life."

"You know." Donnie shot to his feet. "You, Grayson Meadows, can go fuck yourself." He turned to Melody. "Sorry you had to hear that." He walked out of the room.

Austin turned to Melody and cut off the question forming on her lips by speaking first. "I think I'll go see if Mom needs any help in the kitchen."

"I'll come with you." She stood.

As they walked out of the room, the scent of vanilla trailed her. He wanted to push her soft black hair away from the sides of her face and find the source of that smell with his mouth. His charming brother had just reminded him of why he had to stay away, though. One thing Donnie had right—Austin screwed up lives. He'd done it to his own and to the people he cared about too many times to count. He wasn't going to drag Melody into that mess as well.

He'd made his decision about this long ago after he and Regan broke up. It was best for everybody if he didn't get involved with anybody.

CHAPTER NINE

That evening, after dinner, Austin said, "There's something I want to show you."

Melody raised her eyebrows. "Oh yeah?"

"In the basement. C'mon." He waved her toward the basement, and she followed him down there. As they descended the stairs, he said, "I used to be a D.J." He flipped on a light.

"Looks like it. You have an impressive collection here," she said as she looked at the crates full of records stacked all around her. In a corner were several sets of speakers, a turntable, and other D.J. equipment. Out of all the rooms in this huge house she could probably get lost in if she went wandering around by herself, this small room in the basement was easily her favorite. Music was a big part of her life, and down here, it surrounded her.

He reached into a bin, grabbed an album, and handed it to her.

She looked down at the sleeve and grinned. "Miles Davis."

He handed her another.

"John Coltrane."

And another.

"Peabo Bryson." She nodded. "Very eclectic."

He shrugged. "I like what I like." The once over he gave her as he said that made her shiver.

"I see," was all she could think of to say in response.

"I thought this might cheer you up, but we can go back upstairs if all this is a painful reminder." His green eyes were filled with concern.

She warmed all over. "What? Oh. No." He must've taken her silence as a sign that she was upset. "No. I like it down here." She liked that it was just the two of them and that he wanted to share this with her. She fanned herself with an album sleeve.

He shifted a few crates to the floor from an old tattered loveseat. He sat down and patted the space next to him. She walked over and sat next to him.

"Hand me that," she said, pointing at one of the crates that rested on the floor.

He picked up the crate and set it in her lap.

She began thumbing through the album sleeves. "M.C. Lyte," she said, pausing to look at one of the covers.

He fingered the brightly colored album cover, his hand brushing against hers in the process. "That's one of my favorites."

"Really?" She turned to look at him. A mistake because his eyes had a hypnotic effect on her.

He nodded.

She moved her gaze from the bristles of blond hair on his head to his strong jaw line and then down to appreciate the way his T-shirt fit over his biceps and pecks. She couldn't help herself. It'd been so, so long. Since the divorce. And her ex-husband was the only man she'd been with since her junior year in college when they started dating. She bet—hoped? No, hoping was not the right thing—Austin could do things to her that her ex had never even heard of. Well, whether it was the right thing or not, she definitely hoped he could. More than that, she wanted him to.

Trying to turn her attention to something else, she asked, "How many records do you have?"

He grinned. "Lost count a while ago." He sat back on the loveseat and rested his arm over the top of the seat cushions. "I didn't use all of this for D.J.'ing, but it's all music I love."

"I see." It was clear he loved music as much as she did if not more.

Once again, she was fascinated by what she learned about Austin. That didn't help her deal with her constant desire to touch him one bit. She was very much aware of how close the arm he'd slung over the top of the sofa was to the back of her neck.

"You know what I'd love to do?" Besides you, she added that last part silently. She wanted to share a little of herself with him because he'd shared so much with her that night.

"What?"

"I want to be a music manager. Nobody to tell me what to do or when to do it. I could help artists pursue their dreams instead of being the one to curb those dreams because I have to keep some record company's bottom line in mind. I already have a few people in mind who could be huge with the right management." Her heart sank a little as this made her think about the hard call she'd had to make to the manager of the R&B group in Miami. When she'd had to tell him she wouldn't be at the club Monday night, she'd felt like the walls were caving in around her. The group would be taking the stage in less than forty-eight hours and some lucky person would discover them. Her dream would become someone else's reality in less than two days.

"Why haven't you done it yet?" Austin asked, breaking into her thoughts. "You probably have lots of contacts at the record labels and all the other right places. You've worked in the industry since you got out of college, right?"

"Yeah," she said, distracted by the fact that he'd been paying so much attention last night when they'd talked for hours. She'd told him that right after college and getting her C.P.A. license, she'd started out in the accounting department at a division of a major record label in California. She'd barely mentioned her ex who'd been a vice president there. The same ex who'd been the reason she moved clear across the country and back home to Georgia so she could start over free and clear of his shadow.

"So you could let them know you've jumped to the other side, decided to be a manager," Austin said. "You could let those artists you mentioned having in mind know that you could help them with their careers. Instead of looking for a job, you can create your own. Why not go for it?"

"I don't have enough money saved." She said it more defensively than she meant to, but he'd touched on a question she asked herself constantly. A question Jen also kept putting to her. "After this little fiasco, I don't know when I'll have enough. It seems like every time I get close to having enough saved, something bad happens."

"Something bad is always happening." He said with a shrug of his broad shoulders. "You can't control that. What you can control is whether you hand out updated resumes to jaded record execs or brand new business cards to hopeful artists when you get back to…Atlanta." He looked away from her when he said the last word.

"Guess it's something to think about."

He laughed.

"What?"

"Oh. Nothing. It's just that I say that same thing when I'm not fixin' to take the advice someone has given me."

She grinned. He had her there. She looked up at him and was lost in his gaze. What was she doing? She was only here for a few days. She shouldn't—couldn't—be getting wrapped up in this person she would never see again.

Grayson Meadows, Austin Holt, whatever name he wanted to use didn't matter. What mattered was that he was getting under her skin in a very disconcerting way. Warning bells should have been going off. Instead, all she could think of was how good it felt to be close to him, talk to him, hear his voice.

And the only thing she wanted, sitting in that basement with him, was for him to wrap those big strong arms around her. Even if her car got fixed within a week, she had the feeling she wouldn't make it out of Sweet Neck without falling for Austin. The scariest part of that was the thought of falling—and leaving—alone.

CHAPTER TEN

The next day, Melody went for a walk to try and get her head on straight. She needed to figure out what to do about the car. Should she stay until it was fixed? Should she get it fixed at all? Austin had said it would be in pretty good shape with a new engine. And why should she be in a hurry to get back to Atlanta? It wasn't like she had a job waiting for her there. She needed to start looking for one, though. She didn't have enough money saved to strike out on her own yet.

She really didn't Especially now with a huge car repair bill hanging over her head. It wasn't just some lame excuse to avoid taking the scary step of striking out on her own. She didn't care what anyone said.

Shuffling along on the shoulder of the road, she looked around her at the cypress, beach, and oak trees and acres of farmland that expanded on both sides of her. It was so quiet and peaceful out there. So many acres of nothing noisy or impatient. Just green and brown and blue everywhere.

There was another reason besides looking for work that she needed to go home. Austin. She was becoming attached to this man who would never be in her life again after she left Sweet Neck. Not only was he attractive, but there was so much else about him she adored. He was funny. Smart. Sexy.

There was just enough of an air of mystery about him to draw her in and make her want to know more—want to know about the few things he wouldn't mention. Like Grayson. The smart thing to do would be to go back to Atlanta the next day whether or not she had him fix the car. Now, about having him fix the car...

Melody was so lost in her thoughts that she didn't even notice the old woman with a white scarf wrapped around her head and tied under her chin until she'd almost run into her.

"Oh. Excuse me. I'm sorry," Melody said.

The woman smiled and held out a papery, gnarled, pale hand. "Such a pretty girl." The woman touched her hand to Melody's cheek. The hand was oddly cool on the sweltering summer day. "Hot out here," the woman said with a thick accent. "Would you like a nice cool glass of lemonade? You come with me." The woman pointed down a dirt path that branched off from the main road. Tall pines grew on either side of the lane. The old woman looked harmless—after all, nobody she'd seen in Sweet Neck looked harmful—but why in the world was she inviting a stranger in for lemonade?

"I'm sorry, you are?..." Melody said.

"I am called Blanche Leroux," she said. "You're new here. I seen you with that Holt boy. Ha, I can tell you things about that brood." Blanche threw a sharp look over her shoulder. "Plenty o' things."

"Leroux? Is that Cajun?" Melody asked. They were quite a ways from Louisiana, but upon listening closer, she realized the woman had a Cajun lilt to her voice.

"Yes, chère." The woman wrapped her shawl closer around her shoulders. Melody briefly wondered how she could stand wearing one when it had to be at least eighty degrees out. Then she remembered how cold the woman's hand had felt and gave an involuntary shiver. "You coming or not?" Blanche asked.

"Why do you want to tell me about Austin?" Melody asked. She was wary even though curiosity was killing her.

The woman just smiled and started walking down the dirt path she'd pointed to earlier, the long skirt of her emerald dress dragging on the ground as she moved. She waved over her shoulder, gesturing that Melody should start moving, but she never stopped walking or turned around. She seemed certain Melody would follow her.

Curiosity won out over caution, especially after what the woman had said about "that Holt boy," and Melody followed. After all, she should be able to outrun this old woman if anything crazy happened.

At the end of the path, they came upon a wood cabin with kudzu creeping over it. The warped gray planks making up the siding could have used a good layer of primer and some paint. Maybe they needed replacing instead. Really, someone should have torn the whole thing down and started over.

The woman walked up onto the sagging porch and opened the door. She beckoned to Melody with a crooked finger but didn't wait for Melody to enter before she walked into the house.

Melody wandered inside, but stood just inside the door. Inside, it was cool and dark. Zydeco music played on low volume from another room.

"In here," a voice called from Melody's left.

She inched into the house and peeped around the corner into the room from which the voice had come. Thick pieces of velvet—not curtains, just long rectangles of velvet fabric—covered the windows. A few chairs were scattered around the room. In the center of the room sat a small metal table. It reminded Melody of a card table. On one side of it was an armchair, and on the other side was a stool. In fact, the few pieces of furniture in the room were all mismatched.

HIS MELODY

The Zydeco music she'd heard upon entering the house came from this room. A phonograph sat in one corner of the room, and a record was rotating around on it.

Melody caught sight of a one-eyed alligator and muffled a scream.

The woman laughed. "Relax, chère. It's stuffed. Ain't gonna hurt you." Blanche had pulled the scarf back from her face. Melody walked into the room, and as her eyes adjusted to the low light, she could see that the woman's watery eyes were pale blue. Her gray-blonde hair hung in unkempt tangles around her neck.

"So..." Melody started, but she was unsure of what to say after that.

"Have a seat." The woman pointed to the armchair on one side of the card table.

"I could take the stool—"

"Sit."

Surprised by the woman's commanding tone, Melody went to the armchair and sat.

Blanche scuttled over to the stool and had a seat. She clasped her gnarled, arthritic-looking hands together and closed her eyes. Taking a deep breath, she sat rigid on the stool. There was complete silence except for the Zydeco music for a moment. Then she opened her eyes and smiled. "Just reading your aura, making sure I was right about you. Yeah, you the right one. I'll be right back with that lemonade, chère. The woman bustled off to the kitchen, which was room two out of three rooms in the cabin. Melody could see a small bedroom off the opposite end of the living room.

At least Melody could watch what this strange little woman was doing as there was no wall between the kitchen and the living room. If the woman didn't pour two glasses of lemonade from that same pitcher and take a sip before Melody drank hers, Melody would leave her glass on the table untouched.

The woman laughed and set a glass in front of Melody. "You think I'm crazy, chère. I see that in your eyes." Blanche took a sip of lemonade from the glass she'd poured for herself. "You're not the only one. Talk to anybody in Sweet Neck, and they'll be right in league with you. But I've been on this earth a very long time. I see things other people don't see because they can't see past their own noses. I take in more than they do."

"Oh." Melody took a sip from her own glass.

"I think something special brought you into that boy's life." Blanche shrugged. "The universe? Fate? Whatever it is, it's 'bout time. He needs you. I can tell you be good for him."

Did the universe have to screw me over so severely in the process? she asked herself. "How can you know that?" she addressed those words to Blanche.

"I tell you things, and you don't listen," Blanche said with a reproving shake of her head. "But I like you chère, so I'm gon' try to help you see." She tapped the side of her head. "I know things."

Know things? What things? Melody thought. Maybe Blanche was just a busybody. Regardless, she seemed harmless. "Were you born here?" she asked, trying to gauge how well the woman might know the Holts.

"Louisiana, chère, but you already knew that." Blanche winked at her. "Cajun country."

"How'd you end up in Sweet Neck?"

"I got to travel, chère. I got to see this world. But you don't want to know about old Blanche Leroux. You want to know about that Holt boy." Blanche seemed sure of this fact.

"I do?"

Blanche nodded, continuing to treat their conversation like a perfectly normal and logical one. "Oh yes. Of course you do. That's why you followed me on down that lane even though you half-thought I was half-crazy. You shouldn't be asking me how I ended up in Sweet Neck. You should be asking yourself how you ended up here."

"My car—"

"Hush now, chère. Do you want me to tell you 'bout this here or not?"

Melody nodded. "Please do."

Blanche settled back onto the stool across from Melody.

"Them two brothers, they don't act like brothers now. I'm sure you seen that."

Melody nodded. She had. The two of them seemed to avoid each other whenever possible. And her first night at the house, when the electricity had gone out, Donnie kept making smart remarks about Grayson after Melody had unwittingly brought him up.

"There's a lot of pain and anger between those boys. Because of it, they both hurt that dear sweet mother they both love. Them boys don't mean her no harm, they love her. They just so angry they don't know how to do any better than they do." Blanche looked up at her solemnly. "That's where you come in."

"Me? I—"

"Hush now, chère, hush now. I ain't tell you it was time for you to do the talkin' yet, now did I?"

Melody shook her head.

Blanche shifted on her stool and folded her hands together. "Now then. Like I was saying. That sister, Avery, she angry at Austin, too, but she do her best to keep the peace between those two. But getting Donnie and Austin back to acting like brothers, that's the key to the healing that family needs." Blanche closed her eyes and began humming.

Melody sat up in her chair. "That's nice, but I should probably be going now."

Blanche's eyes popped open. "That boy come from a cold place. A cold and dark place, and I ain't just talking about winter in New York City. He don't think nobody understand, but I think you just might do."

Melody nodded and stood. "I don't know about all that, but thank you for the lemonade. It was very good."

"He needs you, Melody James," Blanche said, using her name for the first time and giving her a stare that made her think the woman could see clear through to her soul. Melody tried to remember whether she'd given the woman her name. She couldn't remember giving it to her, but maybe she had. Blanche couldn't have known it otherwise. Right? "He needs you," Blanche said again.

Melody nodded and stumbled backward in the direction of the door.

"You afraid of me, I know it, but I'm afraid of you failing those brothers. Such a nice good family. I hate to see it fall apart and them good folk lose each other. You could stop it from happening." Blanche stood and folded her arms into the wide sleeves of her dress. "You got a good heart. You'll see your purpose and fulfill it." Blanche looked satisfied with herself as she said these last lines. Confident even.

"Okay, well, bye now." Melody wrapped her hand around the doorknob.

Blanche waved her off, but was singing along with the music coming from the phonograph and seemed to have forgotten Melody was there. Anybody just walking in the door would've had no clue about the creepy and intense nature of the conversation they'd just had. Melody stepped out of the door and into the heat. The warmth was welcome against her skin after the chill that pervaded Blanche's house. She hurried up the dirt path and back to the main road.

CHAPTER ELEVEN

For some nagging reason, Melody couldn't dismiss the woman's words no matter how much she wanted to. After she left Blanche's, she went back to the Holts' and called her mother to tell her she wasn't coming home right away.

Melody told herself she needed a break from Atlanta anyway and she wasn't giving any credence to the old lady's ramblings. Still, she couldn't shake the feeling that maybe the woman wasn't crazy. Blanche had somehow seemed more wise than crazy.

She hadn't looked forward to the battle with her mom, but she was able to eventually convince Mom that everything was fine and not to worry. That Melody would be home soon. In a couple weeks at the most. Her mom would express mail Melody's cards to her when they arrived from the credit card companies and the bank.

The replacement cards Melody had ordered online for her personal accounts were supposed to arrive some time that week. Mom had insisted on wiring some money to Melody that Monday, but Melody had convinced her that she'd be fine without it. She didn't want Mom straining her budget like that. Melody had just lost her job, but she at least had her savings to rely on for a while. And a severance package once she worked out the details with Saeed.

And she could always sell off more jewelry. Oh, what a painful thought, but she usually sacrificed a piece or two when things got really rough money-wise. In addition to the Range Rover and condo in the Poconos she'd already sold to get her new life set up in Atlanta and start saving up money for breaking out on her own, she'd taken the small things with her in the divorce like her jewelry and clothes. She didn't want alimony or any of that. Luckily, though, her ex had paid off her student loans when they got married as a wedding present to her. After the divorce, she left with the bare minimum—the things her lawyer had convinced her to take basically. She didn't want to admit she needed that fool for anything.

One thing about her ex. He hadn't been a cheap man. He liked for his woman to look good because she was an extension of him. At least that was the way he saw it. Melody had sold most of the things he'd given her right after the divorce, but she tried to save back her favorite pieces. That meant she had thousands of dollars worth of platinum and diamond jewelry as well as her remaining designer clothes and shoes stashed away at her place in Midtown and at her mom's house in Marietta. Occasionally, she'd sell things on eBay—or sometimes take the jewelry to a local pawn shop—to add to the fund when she had no other choice. Maybe this was one of those times she had no other choice.

The money could come in handy. It would've been nice to get a room at the one motel in Sweet Neck so she didn't feel like she was imposing on Leigh Anne and the rest of the Holts. But she knew enough about Leigh Anne already to know the woman would have taken her leaving as a personal insult, so she let it go.

After the long, somewhat painful conversation with her mom, Melody hadn't been able to stand the thought of telling another person about her decision to stay in Sweet

Neck. She decided to call Jen the next day. For the moment, what she really needed was a bath.

She sank gratefully into the tub and pressed a damp washcloth to her face, letting thoughts of the past few days' craziness flit around in her head.

Austin needed her. For what? He seemed perfectly happy and normal and well-adjusted to her. Blanched seemed so sure of it, though. So he wouldn't talk about his past. Maybe he didn't feel like telling his whole life story to someone he barely knew. And even if he never wanted to talk about it, he still didn't seem to need saving. Her life was more of a mess than his was.

Why was she even worrying about anything Blanche had said? She would get Austin to fix her car, she would go back to Atlanta, and she would deal with Saeed and then find a new job. Those were the things to worry about—not some enigmatic bayou woman's ramblings.

Still. Family was important. She thought about how difficult it was to lose someone you loved. She'd lost a father, too, even though the circumstances had been different. Her dad died of cirrhosis of the liver when she was a senior in high school. He'd only lasted a few years after the divorce; he drank himself to death. Austin didn't have to lose a brother as well as a father. Donnie was right there. It didn't seem like either of them was interested in reaching out to the other, though.

She dozed for a while and realized with a start someone was pounding at the door. She sat up, shivering as her wet body made contact with the air. "Yeah?"

She heard Donnie's voice through the door. "Just wondering if you were still alive in there," Donnie said, laughter in his voice. "We're going out to Regan's farm in a little bit. Gonna invite her to Sunday dinner. I was checking to see if you wanted to come along."

"Okay. I'll be out in a minute." She sighed and reached down to drain the tub. She stood and stretched, arching her back. What was she? A narcoleptic? She kept falling asleep.

Then again, it probably had something to do with the fact that she hadn't been sleeping so well at night.

After she got dressed, she went to Austin's door and knocked softly.

"Come in," he called out in that soft Southern accent. The combination of deep voice and soft accent made her knees weak every time she heard it. She'd avoided speaking with an accent all her life, but it sounded good on him. And that threadbare white T-shirt looked good over his broad chest and shoulders.

"Donnie said y'all—everyone—is going down to Regan's," she said.

He chuckled.

"What?"

"It's just funny to me the lengths you go to not to sound like you're from the South."

"Ha," she said. "I've come to a decision about my car."

"Oh?" He fixed those deep green eyes on her.

She stuck her hands in the back pockets of her jeans. "Yeah. I want you to put in the engine, and I want to stick around here while you do it. If it's okay, I'd like to stay here with you a—fine, y'all, happy? But only if you let me work off the cost. At least part of it."

"And how do you plan on doing that? You know your way around a carburetor?" The corners of his mouth twitched with a smile as he said it.

"Um...not hardly. But I do know math. I could help with bookkeeping. I'm a C.P.A." She'd been a music and accounting double-major in college because her mother had insisted she do something "practical" in addition to studying music. It was ironic that a mother who named her Melody wasn't more supportive of her dreams of making a career out of music. Then again, Melody's name had been mostly her father's idea.

"Yeah, I remember you mentioning that," Austin said.

"I still have my license. I could also help you clean up that office. It needs it desperately. I don't even know how you can get through the door with all that junk lying around."

Austin's smile faded. "Yeah I guess nothing's really been done with it since Dad died."

She thought back to their talk in his room on the night of his storm. He obviously didn't like to talk about his father. "Oh. Austin, I'm sorry." She started to walk toward him.

He stood and grabbed his keys from his desk. "You ready to head out to Regan's? If we don't get going, Donnie's gonna come up here after us."

"Sure." She backed off and let him walk past her. As she followed him downstairs, she thought about what Blanche had said again. About Austin needing to be saved from himself.

CHAPTER TWELVE

Sunday night, Austin sat in his room staring at a blank page of his notebook. Regan had just left after eating Sunday dinner with them. He didn't know if he'd ever be able to look at Regan without having bittersweet feelings, but he definitely couldn't do it yet. They both agreed that they weren't right for each other. They cared about each other and were still friends. Still, he felt guilty about what had happened between them.

He'd been needy and angry and immature when they were together, and she had been so patient with him. He'd never be able to thank or repay her. He really hoped she'd find someone who would make her happy one day. She swore out she'd never get married. Whenever he threatened to marry her if she didn't hurry up and find somebody, she'd just laugh.

They'd never had much of a real relationship. It'd been more like a quick affair; it'd been good except for the times when he'd been an idiot. He hoped she remembered it the same way—mostly good. She said she did.

He flipped through pages of lyrics and poems in his notebook as he thought about Melody. He hadn't been able to keep his eyes off her at dinner, and Regan had noticed. He didn't know if anyone else had. After dinner, Regan had asked him about it. He'd simply stated the part of the truth that he was sure about—Melody wasn't going to be around long.

Melody. What to think about her? She was the reason he'd gotten out his notebook for the first time in months. He'd been blocked for a while, but suddenly he felt inspired.

He used to go to poetry slams at a place up in Glennville every week, but he hadn't been in a while. He simply didn't have anything to say. His material had been really angry right after he left New York. Then it mellowed out. Next it was sad. Then empty. Just words with no emotion behind them. No feeling.

He snorted when he thought about the way his agent had tried to turn him into a white rapper gimmick. She'd tried to make him into something he wasn't. He didn't want to be anybody's stereotype or wildly skewed expectation. He wanted to share his views—his feelings—with the world or nothing at all. At least that was the way he'd once felt. Now he wrote for himself. Nobody else needed to know, see, or hear what he was writing about.

He didn't want to be a part of that world anymore. He'd found out the hard way that the fast-paced life of the entertainment world wasn't for him. Life in Sweet Neck suited him just fine. The only people he cared about, and the only people who cared about him, were here. Forgetting that had led to the destruction of not only him, but those he loved. From Isadora, his girlfriend who'd died of an overdose, to his friends and family, he'd let them all down and he couldn't stop blaming himself for the deaths of two of them, no matter what anybody said—Isadora and his father. Well, any of them besides Donnie. Donnie agreed with him completely about at least that one thing.

Austin hadn't spoken to his father for five years before his death. He'd last spoken to his dad when he was nineteen. He was twenty-nine now. Still, his father had left the shop to him. In the letter that Austin wasn't to open until after his father's death according to the will, Dad had said that he hoped the shop could do for Austin what his father hadn't been able to. After everything that'd happened, his father still held out hope for him. That night, after the lawyer gave him Dad's letter, he'd gone to his mother and asked for help. The next day, Regan and his mother took him to rehab.

He wondered what Melody would think of him if she knew all that. Probably not a whole lot. In any case, she'd be gone soon. He had no business wondering what she would think about anything.

After smoothing his hand over a blank sheet of paper, he wrote her name at the top of it in big, block letters. He stared at the letters—black ink on a white sheet of paper. Then, the words started to flow, faster than he could write them. He spent the next couple of hours scribbling furiously onto the pages.

CHAPTER THIRTEEN

Monday morning, Austin stood in the kitchen, sipping coffee as he waited for Melody to finish breakfast. He'd sent Donnie and Avery ahead to the shop, telling them he'd be a little late that morning.

"You not eating anything?" she asked. She shook her short black hair out of her face and sipped from a glass of orange juice.

"Not hungry." He never ate breakfast no matter how much his mom fussed with him about it. His compromise with Mom was a protein shake after his morning run. Sometimes he'd throw an egg or two in the shake. Mom wouldn't let him out of Sunday breakfast before church, though. Sunday breakfast and dinner were mandatory for everybody who wanted to live in that house in peace.

"It's delicious," she said in a sing-song voice. So was she in a low-cut sundress that clung to every soft curve she possessed. And those shoulders. Soft and definitely feminine, but still well-defined. He was going to have to buy a burlap sack for her to put on if she was going to continue living in his house and wearing dresses like that, or he'd never be able to think of anything other than her body. Then again, with that body, she'd probably make a burlap sack sexy, too.

"I know," he replied, using the same sing-song tone.

Melody brought a forkful of eggs to her luscious lips. His eyes moved to her slender neck when she swallowed.

"Your mom can really throw down in the kitchen," she said. "Can I take her home with me?"

"Not a chance."

She grinned. "I don't blame you." Her fork scraped the plate as she scooped up more eggs. "I told her I'd help with dinner tonight."

"I hope you can cook then."

After polishing off a piece of toast, she stood. "I like to think so."

"Good," he said, tugging a baseball cap with the shop's logo on it on his head backwards. "What?" She was staring at him.

"I usually don't like the backward hat thing, but it's kinda sexy on you," she said. "That's all."

"Melody James. Are you flirting with me?" he asked as they walked out of the kitchen.

"Austin Holt. I just might be."

He chuckled. "Well, let's get you over to Radio Shack, and then we'll head to the shop." Donnie and Avery had opened up that morning since he wanted to wait around until Radio Shack opened and take Melody over there like he'd promised to. Donnie would've thrown a fit, he knew, except for the fact that he liked Melody. Donnie made it clear that he didn't want any extra responsibility if he didn't get to be in charge. He showed up, worked on cars, chatted up customers—most everybody in town loved Donnie—and that was it. "You ready?" he asked as he opened the kitchen's side door that led out to the wraparound porch.

"Let's do it," she said, walking through the door that he held open for her. He followed her at a slight distance, admiring her the sway of her hips as she walked followed the porch toward the front of the house and to his truck.

HIS MELODY

At Radio Shack, Austin let Melody borrow some money that he didn't plan on letting her pay back, but she didn't know that yet. She picked up a pack of batteries for her CD player, headphones for it and her mp3 player, and a few other things. When they were done in the store, they headed to his shop. In his office, she made a point of stepping over a pile of boxes in the middle of the floor. He admired her calf muscles as she did so. She had to be a runner, or maybe she was naturally blessed, or both.

"Okay, so, obviously I need to get to work," she said as she looked around the cluttered office. "Where should I set up?"

"Anywhere you can find a spot."

"Do I get a desk?"

He lifted his cap and scratched the back of his head. "I don't think there's really room for two, do you? But we can share."

She grinned, sitting on the corner of his desk. "This is my side." She reached over, putting her palm in the center of the desk to mark her territory. He couldn't stop his eyes from drifting downward. He just couldn't help it. She couldn't be wearing a bra with that dress, but could her breasts really be that perky without one? They were kind of on the big side for that to be so. So perfect and round. The idea of reaching out and touching them almost seemed worth the slap he would surely get if he did so.

Melody cleared her throat, and he was jarred out of his mental calculations. He tore his eyes away, his face feeling like it was on fire. "Uh, sorry. What was that?"

"I asked if you were enjoying the free show," she said. She now sat up straight, and her arms were crossed over her chest.

"I'm sorry. I just—I well…" What could he say? The answer was yes, but he couldn't say that for obvious reasons. He rearranged some pencils and order slips lying on his desk in lieu of an answer to her question.

She got up from the desk. "That was harsh. You're a good guy, Austin. I can tell that about you." She walked over to him. Twisting her wedding ring around on her finger, she said, "It's just that I'm often surrounded by guys who think I'm part of their signing bonus or who think networking involves sex. I'm used to being defensive about these things."

"It's okay," he said.

She put a hand on his arm. "You're so easygoing."

He put his hand over his, running his thumb over her knuckles. "I try to be. No use in getting worked up over the small stuff. Won't change anything anyhow." At least that was how he felt about it now. He hadn't always been a laidback kind of guy.

She leaned her forehead against his shoulder. "That's a good philosophy."

"Hm." It'd sure taken him long enough to cultivate it. Standing there with her so close had his blood running hot. She often did that to him. All he wanted was to get her undressed. He couldn't think that way.

Remember Isadora? You're poison to every beautiful thing you touch.

He realized his hand had found its way to her lower back. What was he doing? "I need to get to work," he said. He pulled away. He had to get out of that room because the thing he wanted most in the world was to back her against a wall and pull that sundress up over her hips. Then find out if he was right about her not wearing a bra or not.

"Yeah, me, too," she said. Was it just his lust-filled overactive imagination, or did she sound disappointed?

"I'll be out in the garage if you need me," he said.

"Yep. You got a shredder? Some boxes? Garbage bags?" She swiveled her neck, doing a visual search of the office as she spoke.

"Sure." He showed her where to find everything she'd asked for and then escaped to the place where he was always able to find peace—his garage, surrounded by cars.

HIS MELODY

Out there with the cars, he could feel close to his dad again. Cars were the thing that had always brought them together. They still did, even after his dad's death. Out in his garage, he felt peace. As long as Donnie kept his mouth shut, that was.

CHAPTER FOURTEEN

Donnie burst into the office a little after noon. He was tall and skinny—the definition of lanky—with brownish red hair. Nothing about him reminded Melody of Austin except for the long, straight nose—they definitely shared a nose. Except Austin's was a little crooked, as if it'd gotten broken somewhere along the way in his twenty-nine years.

"Lunch!" Donnie hollered into the room. "Whoo, girl, I'm starving. C'mon. Let me treat you."

Melody put the papers she'd been sorting through back into the box from which they'd come. "I don't want to impose."

"You'll hurt my feelings if you don't let me buy you lunch. The prettiest thing in Sweet Neck? Psht, impose? You'd be doing me a favor, not to mention wonders for my reputation," he said before giving her a crooked smile. "I'd be the one doing the imposing."

"Okay, let me just tell Austin—" Melody started toward the door, but Donnie shook his head.

"Aw, girl, don't worry 'bout him. He's under some lady's car right now, and he's doing a lot of cussing. I think we'd best leave him be."

She laughed at the mock serious expression on Donnie's face. She'd already learned you couldn't be around Donnie too long without catching his infectious smile. The only time he seemed to lose his jovial nature was when he was talking to his brother one-on-one.

"Okay, let's go," she said. She grabbed her purse—habit. After all, nothing was in it—and followed Donnie outside.

They got into his black Impala SS low-rider. Everyone in the family had a thing for rebuilt classics apparently. She slid onto the leather front seat and Donnie removed the sun blocker from the windshield and tossed it into the backseat.

Raking a hand through his dark hair, he said, "Okay. Get ready for the best meal you've ever had in a restaurant. Outside of Mom's cooking, Rose's is the only cooking I trust."

"Okay," she said. "I'm ready."

Donnie had shed his coveralls and left them back at the shop. He wore a white, ribbed, sleeveless undershirt and baggy jeans, emphasizing his skinniness. He drove them a short distance they could have walked out to main street and down a bit, parallel parking in front of a storefront with the words "Rose's Diner" etched onto the frosted glass. A giant pink rose was painted beneath the words.

They walked inside, and Melody closed her eyes for a minute, relishing the rush of cold air as they did. The smell of deep fried food greeted them at the door as well. Suddenly, her mouth watered for fried potatoes. A buxom woman with brown, rosy cheeks and a huge smile along with a nametag reading "Rose" greeted them. She wore a peach short-sleeved dress that had a row of buttons down the front. It reminded Melody of what a waitress in a diner in the fifties would've worn.

"Hey, Donnie!" Rose exclaimed. "And you must be Melody," the woman stuck her hand out to Melody.

"Yes," Melody said, a little stunned the woman knew her name.

"Nice to meet you," Rose said.

Melody returned the greeting, and Donnie leaned in, supplying the answer to her unasked question. "Word travels fast in Sweet Neck. We don't have much to talk about down here." He then formally introduced the two women before nodding at Rose and saying, "She gets all my money."

Rose laughed. "Y'all find yourselves a couple seats, and I'll bring you some sweet tea. Donnie, your usual?"

Donnie grinned. "You know it."

"Make yourself useful, boy, and find that young lady a menu," Rose said. In a bustle of words and movement, she was gone.

Donnie guided Melody over to a red vinyl booth and handed her a menu. Customers were laughing and talking all around them. Most of them wore work uniforms of various sorts. Had to be the lunch crowd. Donnie waved to a few people around them, and they waved back. A Patsy Cline song played over the restaurant's sound system.

She looked at the options of meat and accompanying grease. Between Leigh Anne and now Rose, her clothes wouldn't fit much longer if she kept this up. She hadn't worked out at all since getting stuck in Sweet Neck. However, she had to say, everything she'd eaten so far was worth the calories. Telling herself that she'd have to get back to running in the mornings, she skipped over the salads and started pondering the meats.

"You should try the lunch special," Donnie said, rubbing his nearly concave stomach. "Rose's meatloaf. Lord have mercy." He had a look of complete rapture on his face as he spoke.

"Okay, I'll give it a try. So she's owner, cook, and server? Rose?"

"Rose does a little bit of everything. Two things I know for sure. She always makes the meatloaf, and she always makes the tea."

After Rose brought them tea and took their orders, Donnie turned a serious look on Melody. She was surprised by the abrupt change in his face.

"I want to talk to you. About my brother," he said while toying with the salt shaker. He rotated it through his long fingers.

"What about him?"

"Don't let him fool you." Donnie sat back in the booth, keeping his brown eyes on her. That was the same thing he'd said Saturday evening before dinner.

"Fool me?" She thought back to the conversation she'd had with Blanche and wondered if she was about to learn more.

"He's not that nice of a guy. He takes what he wants from people and leaves the rest to blow around like corn husks in the wind."

"Huh?"

"I've seen the way you look at him."

She felt blood rush to her face, and the tips of her ears were on fire. Is it that obvious?

"Just be aware of the fact that he's like poison. A pretty poison."

He sat back in the booth without saying anything else as if he wanted to let that sink in. She turned her glass of tea around in circles on the table. Dishes clanged and people shouted orders back in the kitchen. There was the buzz of conversation at the tables surrounding them, but their table was silent.

"I'm only going to be here a few days," she said. "I'm not getting attached or anything. But he doesn't seem so bad to me." She toyed with her fork "I mean, after all, he doesn't have to fix my car labor cost-free or let me get away with only paying half price for that engine." He probably didn't think she knew about the steep discount on the engine, but she did. She'd figured it out while trying to get his books in order earlier that day.

Donnie shook his head. "You have no idea how good he is at fooling people."

"Oh?"

"Do you know he stole the shop from me? When he came back from the 'big city?'" Donnie said.

She looked up at him, shocked. He nodded. Just then, Rose brought their food, and they chatted with her for a moment. When she went away, Melody still hadn't composed herself enough to have a reply to what Donnie had said.

"I was running the shop before he came home. Dad had put me in charge of everything after his first stroke. Then he comes home like a ghost come back to life. We hadn't seen hide nor hair of him since he left home at eighteen. Six years and not a day of it did he spend in Sweet Neck. He came back soon as Dad kicked the bucket and pushed Avery and me aside." A sour look clouded Donnie's face. "Took charge of everything. Told us we could learn to like it or get out. Everything we built up and had tried to do? Gone." He slapped the table. "Like a fart in the wind."

Melody put her napkin in her lap and smoothed it over her thighs several times. "He must have had a good reason." The words sounded hollow to Melody even as she spoke them.

Donnie snorted. "Yeah? Well, maybe he'll share it with us one day."

Melody pictured Austin as she looked down at her plate. He seemed so easygoing and generous. Could he be the person Donnie said he was also? He and Donnie didn't get along too well from what she'd seen. What incentive would Donnie have to lie to her, though? And there were a lot of things Austin wouldn't even mention.

"I don't want you to think I'm telling you all this because I want to make a move on you or something," Donnie said. "I have a girl. She's coming over for dinner tonight. I don't prey on out-of-towners anyway. Unlike my brother, I'm not always looking around for a quick fling."

When he said the words "quick fling," Melody thought of Regan and the admittedly little she knew about Austin's relationship with the woman. Was Austin that type? A user?

Someone who'd betray his family, cast his brother aside, use people and then throw them away? Could he be someone like her ex? Austin didn't seem like her lying, cheating ex-husband at all, but she had no way to know for sure. She'd only known him a few days. Donnie had known him for years.

"Look, Melody. You seem like a really good person. I don't want you getting mixed up in a bad situation. There's a reason he doesn't have any friends around here except Regan." He shook his head. "Who knows what her problem is? Guess maybe she's still in love with him, poor thing. She can do much better."

"People seem to like him okay." She thought of Austin saying hi to everybody they met on the street or in a store, seeming to know them all.

"Sweet Neck folks are like that. They don't act mulish or ornery outright. But you watch and see how many people he really spends time with. If you'll notice, it'll only be Mom, Vernon, and Regan. He's burned a lot of people in this town, Melody. I don't wanna see him burn you, too." Donnie fiddled with his knife and fork.

"Well, like I said, I won't be around long. Just until my car is up and running again. While I'm here, I just want to show my thanks and work off my debt for the car," she said.

"I hope that's true." Donnie took a large bite of meatloaf.

She did, too.

#

That afternoon, Melody was sweating with the effort she was putting into her cleaning despite the window air conditioning unit in Austin's office blowing out cool air on full blast. She'd pulled her hair away from her face and put it up in as much of a ponytail as the short length of her bob would allow with a rubber band she'd found on Austin's desk. The fabric of her gauzy sundress stuck to her in places she didn't want it to. It was made of thin material, but at the moment she felt like she was wearing a canvas tarp.

After carrying several bags of trash to the dump and shredding some extremely old records she'd made sure weren't needed anymore, she flopped down in Austin's desk chair and looked down at a box of papers she'd brought over to the chair with her so she could sit while she sorted them.

With a groan, she swiveled the chair away from them. She was tired of looking through papers for the moment. Turning to the bookshelf behind the desk, she looked at the spines of the books hiding behind the clutter. On the few inches of shelf space in front of the books, and stacked on top of some of the shorter books, sat various knick knacks and even a few car parts. Most of the spines indicated that the books were about cars. She was about to reach for one that didn't seem to belong—a biography of some sort—when she noticed a spiral notebook tucked into the end of one of the rows, barely visible. The haphazard way it was stuck in there made it seem as if someone had tucked it in there a while ago and forgotten about it.

With a curious frown, she pulled out the notebook and looked at the cover. Doodles covered the black cover. They seemed to have been drawn with a White-Out pen. She opened the notebook and was surprised to see what looked like poetry. Upon closer inspection, after flipping a few pages, she noticed that it was poetry mixed in with lyrics, thoughts about various political topics, and sometimes drawings lined the tops and the margins of the pages.

Some of it was angry, some sad, a lot of it introspective. Mouthing the words to herself as she read them, she realized just how talented the writer was. In all her days at the record company, she'd never come across such talent. Normally, their label went for gimmick over talent thanks to the "vision" of people like Saeed and those higher up than him. That was part of the reason they could barely keep afloat in her opinion. They were always looking for the next flash in the pan as opposed to sustainable artists who could produce quality music long-term. Of course, there was no explaining this to the big guys at the top. After all, she was only a woman—what did she know?

She was so engrossed in the notebook, she hadn't even heard Austin come into the office, so when she heard his voice, she jumped.

"Hey," he said. "It already looks better in here."

She held up the notebook. "Is this yours? Did you write these words?"

He gave her a blank look, impossible to read. Walking over, he took the notebook from her and shrugged. "I've never seen this before. Where'd you find it?" He flipped through it.

"Tucked into the bookshelf," she said, staring up at him. He wouldn't have a reason to lie about something like that, would he?

"Oh. I don't know whose it is. Donnie or Avery must like writing poetry or something. I guess one of them stuck it in there." He tossed the notebook in a drawer and closed it. "You about ready to knock off? Gotta get home to help with dinner, right?"

"Uh yeah. I do," she said as if in a daze.

"I have a few things to finish up here, but I'll run you home first if you want. Mom usually starts dinner around now." He studied her with eyes that remained unreadable.

She glanced at the clock on the wall. It was a little after five.

"Sure," she said.

"All right. Let me go wash my hands. I'll meet you by the truck," he said.

She nodded, grabbing her purse and her shopping bag from Radio Shack. She was anxious to talk to Jen tonight. She felt like she hadn't talked to her friend in forever. Usually, they talked every day, but Melody had been distracted by several surprises—some pleasant and some not—since arriving in Sweet Neck.

Not only did she miss Jen, but she wanted to find out what Jen thought about the notebook. What if there was a musician in the family? Her mind was working overtime, and she didn't pay any real attention to Austin's almost complete silence on the ride home.

A musician in the family could mean a saved job for Melody. Or maybe something more. Something she was afraid to dream could be hers. A musician as talented as the one who'd written the words in that notebook could mean a whole new career for her as a music manager.

CHAPTER FIFTEEN

When Austin returned home for the second time that evening, it was to the irresistible smell of chicken smothered in gravy. He could almost taste the mushrooms.

"Great gawd, something smells too good!" Donnie shouted. Between that booming voice and the fact that he was over six and a half feet tall, Donnie always seemed to take up too much space. That and he was an irksome creature in general.

"Thank Melody. She barely let me do a thing." Their mother's voice breezed to them from the kitchen.

"Not true. I could never be half the cook you are." That was Melody's voice.

Austin ran a hand over his face in an attempt to wipe the stupid grin from it. He definitely didn't want Donnie seeing that. Lord only knew what kind of a big deal he'd try to make out of it.

"Well, I'm going to get cleaned up. I'm starving," Austin said to no one in particular.

"I'll bet you are," Donnie said.

"What's that supposed to mean?" Austin didn't like his tone.

"Nothing. I have to call my girl," Donnie said. "Move." He pushed past Austin. Donnie, the overgrown child.

Austin took a deep breath and walked toward the downstairs half bath. He knew when Donnie was trying to provoke him. It wasn't going to work this time. Knowing Donnie, for whatever reason, he wanted Austin to make an ass out of himself in front of Melody.

Once Nina, Donnie's girlfriend, arrived, they all sat down to dinner. Austin sat across from Melody. He wanted to sit next to her, be closer to her, but he didn't trust himself to do that. Remembering how close he'd come to grabbing her in his office earlier that day, he took the seat across from her, as close as he dared get, and piled his plate full of smothered chicken, greens, and potatoes. He then asked Avery to pass the cornbread. It would have been simpler to ask Donnie because his brother was closer to it, but knowing his childish ass, the cornbread would have "accidentally" ended up in Austin's lap. When Donnie got it in his head to be a pain, he went all out with it.

"So, Melody. How was your first day at the shop?" Vernon asked.

Before Melody could respond, Donnie said, "Probably would have been better if she didn't work for such a tyrant. Had that poor thing doing back breaking labor."

Austin glared across the table. "I believe it might cause you physical pain to keep your mouth shut for five whole seconds in a row."

"Aw, don't be so tetchy." Donnie rubbed Nina's shoulder. "You see how he is? How he treats his only brother in the world?"

He'd be better off not having any brothers at all then.

Melody smiled and said, "It was good exercise. And with all this good eating I'm doing here, I need all the exercise I can get. I need to get back to running."

Before he realized he was saying it, the words came out of Austin's mouth. "I go running every morning at six. If you want to get up that early, you're welcome to come along."

"I don't know if I could keep up with you."

"Only one way to find out," Austin said. He hadn't realized how brazenly flirtatious their tones were until he realized that all conversation at the table—and even all eating—had stopped. Both were nearly unheard of at the Holt dinner table.

Melody's cheeks reddened and he wanted to kiss them right where they did. "Okay," she said. "Tomorrow. Six o'clock."

Mom held up the breadbasket. "More cornbread, anyone?"

"Over here," Donnie said, waving toward himself. Of course.

Vernon said, "I would help y'all put in Melody's engine, Austin, but I'll be gone before it even gets here. I head out for California early tomorrow morning as soon as I load my truck."

"I know you would, but not to worry. The three of us can handle it," Austin said even though he would have preferred to leave Donnie out altogether. Of everything. If it weren't for their mother and the way the shop had been willed to Austin, Donnie would have been fired long ago. And Donnie knew it. That was why he did everything he possibly could to tick off Austin. He liked pushing buttons, knowing Austin couldn't do anything but get riled up.

Austin tried to remind himself that the only reason Donnie did it was that he was hurt their father had left Austin the shop. It had to be hard on Donnie to see the bad son—the son who'd always messed up everything—end up with the place he'd put his heart into and dreamed of owning one day. Still, Donnie sometimes pushed far past the limits of anyone's patience with the exception of maybe Job. Those were the times they had it out and those times usually ended in a punch or two being thrown. Austin hated it because he knew how it upset his mom. But sometimes, he just couldn't take Donnie's ribbing any longer.

Donnie was obviously pushing for a punching. He wanted Austin to take a swing at him in front of Melody so she would think of Austin as a Neanderthal jerk. Not that Austin knew why Donnie wanted Melody to dislike him so much. Except for maybe the fact that Donnie didn't want anybody at all to like Austin. Donnie would have probably danced with joy if Mom kicked Austin out of the house. As it was, Donnie had moved to the third floor when Austin came home. However, both of them knew Mom would never make either of them go anywhere.

After dinner, everybody headed out to the porch to wait for Regan. She was bringing over some watermelon for them. Austin touched Melody's arm, and she stiffened. He moved closer to her. "Thanks for dinner. It was really good."

"You're welcome," she said in a shaky tone. He wondered if he had an effect on her similar to the one she had on him. "I want to ask you something," she said, "but I don't want to seem like I'm prying."

"Ask away," Austin said, leaving his hand at her elbow. He hoped she would let New York and the notebook she'd found go. If not, he'd just have to find a way to distract her. He caressed her neck with his eyes and wondered how it would feel under his lips.

"Did you really steal the shop from Donnie?" Her brown eyes were soft and sweet, as if she didn't want to believe such a thing.

He chuckled. "Is that what he told you?" He pushed a wisp of black hair out of her eyes.

"Did you?" She leaned closer to him.

"I guess it depends on how you want to look at it. Dad left it to me. In the will." The heaviness of those words wiped all traces of mirth from him.

"Why would he make it sound like you stole it then?"

"Here's a little secret that might not be so secret. Donnie pretty much hates me for everything I've ever done. Leaving town. Coming home. The shop. He blames me daily for ruining his life." He left out the part about Donnie blaming him for Dad's death because he blamed himself for it, too. He didn't want to get into all of that with her. "Avery can stand me a little better, but we're not close. Not anymore." His sister had definitely taken Donnie's side.

"Oh. Austin. I wish I had siblings, and you and yours barely talk. That must hurt. Especially with Avery being your twin."

"Fraternal."

"Still."

He shrugged. "Hey, Regan's here. That can only be her truck rumbling up the driveway. Let's go meet her."

They stepped off the porch and sure enough, Regan's truck rolled up and came to a stop near the cars parked at the end of the driveway. There was more than enough watermelon for all in the back of her truck. Austin and Vernon helped Regan unload and cut it while Mom and Nina collected plates from the kitchen and then distributed them. After they were all happily eating, talking, and laughing, Regan pulled Austin to the side.

"You like her," Regan said with a knowing smile before taking a bite of watermelon.

"She seems like an okay person." It would have been uncomfortable to talk about his developing feelings for Melody with anyone, but it was especially uncomfortable to discuss them with Regan, his former somewhat lover. So instead of adding anything else about Melody, he took a deep bite of watermelon from the slice of it he held. Juice dribbled down his chin.

She wiped the juice away with her thumb. "It's okay, Austin. I'm a big girl. I don't regret what happened between us, but I know that it's over, and it was never meant to be forever.

"I'm so sorry I hurt you," Austin said, the words swollen with sincerity. He thought about it, guilt-laden thoughts, almost every day.

She snorted. "Who's hurt? You know my horses always come first. I don't have enough time for a real relationship with a man. I'm too set in my ways and devoted to my horses for all that." She looked toward Melody as she spoke, so he couldn't see her face. She said, "But Melody. I think she could be good for you. So answer my question."

Austin stalled. "What question?"

"Austin. Come on now. I've known you most of your life. This clueless routine doesn't work with me, hon."

"She'll be gone as soon as her car's fixed. A week or so from now at the most."

"That doesn't answer my question."

"The answer to your question doesn't matter if she's leaving soon, does it?"

"Doesn't it?" Regan flipped her red hair over her shoulder and looked up at him with sparkling green eyes. She was beautiful, and working with the horses kept her in great shape. Still no doubt looking as good in her tight Wrangler jeans at forty-two as she had at twenty-two. Why did he have to hurt everything precious in his life? That was another good reason to leave Melody alone.

"I don't want to hurt her. Look at her," he said. Melody had one arm around Avery and the other around his mom and all three of them were doubled over with laughter. "She's something special. Everyone's seemed happier in the few days she's been here. I don't want to bring her down like I did—like I do everybody."

"All I have to say is...don't let fear make you throw away everything. You're not a bad person. You just can't get a break. Partly because you won't open yourself to any opportunities for one." She patted his shoulder.

"But if she's going to leave soon, what kind of opportunity is that? For either of us?"

Regan shrugged, shifting a piece of green and pink rind from hand to hand. "Just be open. That's all I'm saying. Now." She patted his shoulder. "I'm going to get some more of this melon. This thing is just as sweet... If I have to be the one to say so, I've outdone myself. I'm going to have to keep on making my own fertilizer if this is the result."

He watched her walk back over to the group, thinking about her words. It wasn't that he wanted to keep the distance between himself and Melody. It just wasn't a good idea to get any closer. After all, everything he touched so far in life had turned to dust.

His mind went back to Isadora, skin cold, lying on the floor of their apartment. He'd come out of a drug haze to find her sprawled out on the carpet in the living room. Empty eyes staring at the ceiling but seeing nothing. He should have never helped spring her out of rehab early.

He'd known then, even as he screamed into the phone for the medics to hurry after dialing 9-1-1. He'd known she was gone and that he was doomed to crush everything he cared about.

CHAPTER SIXTEEN

That night, possibly the hottest night of the summer, the air conditioning decided to conk out. It hadn't been working right since the first night Melody moved in—the night of the huge thunderstorm. Even with the three windows in his room up and two box fans plus the ceiling fan on their highest speed, the night was hot and sticky. After tossing and turning for he didn't know how long, Austin slammed his sheet aside and rolled out of bed. He slipped his running shorts over his boxer briefs, just in case he ran into Melody or Nina in the hall, and went down to the kitchen.

He stumbled into Melody, and she stifled a shriek. He grabbed her shoulders to steady her as their collision had knocked her off-balance. Her dark eyes, widened with surprise, were luminous in the moonlit kitchen.

"Oh. Sorry. I didn't think anyone would be in here," he said, his hands cupping her perfect shoulders. He couldn't stop his eyes from roaming over her thin nightgown. As his eyes adjusted to the dark, he could appreciate more, but not as much as he wanted to. His hands slid lower on her arms.

"Too hot to sleep," she said.

"Tell me about it," he said.

"I came to get something to cool myself off with." She held up a popsicle. "Grape. Want some?" She held it up to his lips.

"Sure," he said. In that moment, with her body so close to his, he probably wouldn't have refused a vial of poison from her. She slid the cool, sweet treat past his lips. He took a bite, and she pulled it back.

"Don't bite," she said.

Realizing that he hadn't let go of her yet and very aware of the proximity of her body, he stepped back and dropped his arms to his side. He hoped she wouldn't see just how aware of her he'd become. After all, it was pretty dark in the kitchen. Only the silver light of the moon cut through the shadowy darkness of the room.

He took a seat at the kitchen table, and she sat on top of the table in front of him.

She said, "Have you heard of a woman named Blanche Leroux?" She licked the popsicle in a way that had to be illegal in at least forty states and probably a few territories, too.

"The crazy woman who lives in the woods? Sure. Everybody knows her," he said. He was much more interested in her naked legs and the way that popsicle looked against her full mouth than he was in talking about Blanche.

She pressed the popsicle to his lips again. "Don't bite this time," she said.

He obeyed. Sucking at the popsicle, he thought about what it would be like to press his mouth to her skin instead.

"So people think she's crazy?" She drew the popsicle back.

He sat back in his chair. "I mean, everybody's nice to her, we all humor her, but come on. She lives in a cabin in the middle of the woods, and some people say she thinks she knows magic. She just showed up here one day from Louisiana, moved into that abandoned shack on the edge of town after claiming it belonged to some of her kin, and nobody said much about it. We just let her be."

"You don't believe in magic, Austin Holt?"

He snorted. "No. Why? Do you?"

She slid into his lap and slipped an arm around his neck. Her fingers tickled the bottom of his earlobe. With her free hand, she held the popsicle between their lips. He barely noticed the cool, sticky juice dripping onto his stomach.

"I dunno. It'd be nice if it did exist," she said.

"Uh-huh," he grunted. He didn't have enough blood left in his head for coherent thoughts let alone words. Her thighs shifted against his, and he came to full attention. If she moved one inch in the wrong direction, she would know what she'd done to him.

She wrapped her lips around one side of the popsicle and he wrapped his around the other side. Lips touching, they devoured what was left of it. He tossed the stick onto the kitchen table and pulled her close. Pressing his lips to hers, he tasted her mouth the way he'd wanted to every since she'd pulled her long legs out of Regan's truck Friday afternoon.

Her mouth was cool and sweet. It tasted like grape popsicle. She gave a soft moan, and he pulled her closer, massaging her waist through her thin nightgown. He then moved his massage lower, right over her hipbones, his fingertips playing into the side of her perfectly round bottom.

Her fingernails dug into his neck before she moved her hands up over his hair. Her hands moving over his bristles of hair gave him an almost hypnotic pleasure. He lost himself deeper in the kiss. He wanted to stay there, locked with her all night, showing her without words how much he wanted her and wanted to fall for her and use his mouth for anything but talking. He moved his hand under her nightgown and groped her thigh, massaging his fingers into it.

She moaned against his lips, and he deepened his caresses. He moved his lips over her chin, down to her throat. Nibbling at her neck. He slipped his hand farther

HIS MELODY

under her nightgown. His fingers played lightly over the heated flesh of her inner thighs.

He didn't want to think. He probably couldn't have if he tried. All he wanted was her. Under his fingers, his tongue. Touching her was the only thing that mattered.

Melody pulled back with a gasp. "What was that?"

"Huh? What?" Austin murmured, still in a fog of desire. He started to pull her in for another kiss when he heard it, too. Someone was crashing around in the living room. "Shit." There was only one person who could sound like a heard of elephants moving through that house even when he was trying to be quiet.

Donnie entered the kitchen just as Melody was climbing off Austin's lap. Melody rearranged her nightgown and hugged her arms over her chest. Donnie looked at them for a moment. Austin sent him a glare that dared him to say anything. For a moment, it seemed as if Donnie would comment on the situation. Then he headed for the breadbox on the counter nearest the refrigerator. He reached into the fridge for meet, cheese, and mayo. He brought everything over to the island in the center of the kitchen.

All he ever did was eat, but he remained skinny as a rail. He'd never been able to put on weight no matter how hard he tried. He took that off Mom.

"Y'all couldn't sleep either, huh?" he said as he began making his sandwich.

"Too hot," they both said at the same time. She looked away from him, but he caught a grin at the corner of her lips.

"Yeah." Donnie slapped his sandwich together. "Wish I had some fried taters to go with this," he muttered.

Austin looked at Melody. She kept glancing at him and then looking across the kitchen in the direction of the large window above the sink whenever she knew she was caught. He had a feeling she was having just as much trouble with words as he was at the moment. His mind was nowhere near conversation about sandwiches and potatoes.

"How about that watermelon Regan brought over?" Donnie rubbed the spot where his belly would be if he had one. "Mm, mm. I wish I had some more." He paused for a minute, maybe thinking about the watermelon, maybe not. Then he said, "I reckon me and my knucklehead brother helped that watermelon come to be, didn't we?"

"Yeah," Austin said. He wondered why Donnie was being so friendly. Especially after the way he'd tried to get Austin's goat earlier. It had to be a trap.

"Yeah. We help Regan out when we can." Donnie looked straight at Austin when he spoke his next words. "We owe her a lot."

Austin couldn't disagree with that. "We sure do."

Donnie went into a story about a watermelon seed spitting contest that ended with him getting chased clear across town by the mayor's ornery dog. Melody couldn't stop laughing. Austin barely listened. For one thing, he'd heard the story more times than he cared to count. For another, he was wondering what Donnie was up to. He was sure Donnie wasn't done sticking his nose where it didn't belong yet.

Donnie put the bread and mayo away after making a second sandwich. Knowing Donnie, he'd take that one back upstairs. "I'll see y'all in the morning. Well, later this morning, I guess." He headed upstairs with his second sandwich.

Austin turned to Melody, trying to think of something to say. With one look at her, he could tell the moment they'd shared earlier was over.

"I guess I should go up to bed, too."

"Okay." He stroked her hair as a substitute for stroking something lower on her body. He had to get his mind on something besides her. And what she would look like completely naked. Only that little scrap of a nightgown kept him from finding out.

She pressed her forehead to his for a brief moment. "I'm leaving in a few days. This...It's not a good idea."

"I know," he said, desire making his voice husky.

She moved his hand from her hair to her lips and kissed his fingertips.

He clenched his teeth, it taking all his strength not to pull her back in for something that maybe neither of them would have been able to stop. "I thought you said it was time for bed."

"It is," she said, but she didn't sound any more ready to leave than he was to see her go.

Their eyes met. When he saw the expression on her face in the semi-darkness, the same kind of longing he felt, he nearly grabbed her to finish what they'd started.

"Are we still going running in the morning?" she asked. "Well, in a few hours now, I guess."

"Yeah," he said. He could have done with a few miles right then. "Six o'clock sharp."

"I'll be there."

"It's kind of cool that early in the morning," he said, hoping she wouldn't show up to run in a sports bra and itty bitty shorts. He was having enough trouble behaving. As it was, he'd already broken his promise to himself to keep his hands to himself. If he didn't get away from her soon, she might find herself minus a nightgown.

"I can barely imagine that right now," she said.

She surprised him with a hug.

"Good night, Austin," she said, letting her hands linger on his lower back.

"Night, Melody." He backed away so his hard-on wouldn't press into her stomach.

She ran her hands up and down his torso and then over his sides. Sheer torture, but in a good way. Then she headed for the stairs.

He hoped that engine for her car would hurry up and get to Sweet Neck because he had to get her out of there before they did something she'd regret. He'd already ruined enough lives. He couldn't add her to that list of unfortunate people.

If something started up between them, it could only end badly. There was no way he was getting in another serious relationship or leaving Sweet Neck again. Not even for Melody.

CHAPTER SEVENTEEN

Melody was on the phone with Jen, trying to explain why she couldn't come home yet. She'd been in Sweet Neck for over a week, and Jen was getting antsy about it. She kept trying to convince Jen that she was fine, and that she'd be home soon, but Jen wasn't having it.

"Okay, obviously you've temporarily lost your mind or something, so I have to come down there and rescue you," Jen said. Melody could hear her fidgeting with something in the background. It sounded like tiles plinking. Jen was probably working on a new mosaic collage. They were a hobby of hers. She knew a guy who specialized in bathroom renovations, and she was always getting discarded tile from him. Sometimes, she went to art stores and even hardware stores, but she liked making recycled art much more. She called it her artistic and environmental contribution to the world rolled into one.

In fact, art was how she'd met Jen. They'd been in a pottery class together held at a local community college in the evenings. Melody had taken it for fun and out of curiosity. Jen had real talent for visual art, though.

"No, Jen, really. I'm fine," Melody said.

"You've been down there for two weeks. That's not okay. I'm coming this weekend."

"Don't you have your dance class?" she asked, trying to derail Jen's plan. Jen taught a dance class on Saturday mornings.

"I'll cancel the class. This qualifies as an emergency. I'm coming to get you, and we'll figure out how to get that scrap metal you insist on clinging to back to Atlanta later." Under her breath, Jen added, "You should have kept the Range Rover."

"You know I heard that, right?"

"Oh. Did you think I didn't want you to? You should have kept it."

Melody rolled her eyes even though Jen couldn't see her through the phone and said, "I'm fine."

"You keep saying that, but I can't figure out why you're staying there, Mel. Some weird sense of duty to this guy who's fixing your car? Some kind of post-losing your job melt down? I have no clue."

"When you say it that way, it sounds crazy."

"That's because it is. I'm coming. You can't stop me."

"I'll be home soon. The car is almost fixed."

"What, you trying to keep Grayson Meadows all to yourself or something?" she teased.

Melody bristled. "His name is Austin. And no."

"Oh. Oh Melody." Jen paused for dramatic effect as she often did when she was about to say something inflammatory. "You like him. Don't you?" Her tone was both accusatory and teasing.

"C'mon, Jen," Melody said, her ears on fire. "Don't revert to grade school. What are you going to do next? Sing about us kissing in a tree?" But as she reprimanded Jen, she thought back to the kiss she and Austin had shared the night the air conditioning had gone out. Over a week later, they hadn't come close to another moment like that. It was like he went out of his way to avoid her. They went running in the mornings in near silence and then lifted weights in an outbuilding behind the main house in the same kind of quiet. At work, he'd spend as little time as possible in the office. Most of the time, when a customer needed ringing up or when one of the three mechanics needed something from the office, Austin would send Donnie or Avery into the office to do it or get it.

"...Melody? Earth to Melody?"

"Oh. Sorry, Jen. What did you say?"

"Girl, I know you. Okay, I'm definitely needed there. I have to see what the deal is down in Sweet Neck," Jen said with an exaggerated—and really bad—version of a Southern accent.

"There's no deal, Jen."

"Saturday morning. Ten A.M. I'll be there. You can't stop me. Now, you gonna give me the address of Grayson's garage for my G.P.S., or do I have to look it up online? 'Cause you know I'll do it. I know how to use Google, and I know it's called Holt's Garage."

She knew. Although there'd be no website for Holt's, Jen could probably find an online listing with the garage's address. With a resigned sigh and a smile at the thought of her tenacious little friend, Melody gave Jen Leigh Anne's address as well as the address for Austin's shop where she would most likely be Saturday at ten.

#

Melody ran outside Saturday morning when Donnie told her that Jen had arrived.

She ran over to her petite friend and grabbed her, not realizing just how much she'd missed her until that moment.

"When you said you were in the sticks, girl, you weren't kidding," Jen said once they were done hugging and saying their hellos. Jen wore a red and white print dress. She held her favorite pair of oversized sunglasses up near her forehead as if she couldn't believe what she was seeing while looking through them. Her silky dark chocolate brown hung loose over her shoulders. She wore strappy gold sandals on her tiny feet. She'd painted her toenails red to match the dress.

"I know," Melody said with a grin. "But it's really not that bad." She thought of Austin as she said that.

"So where's Grayson?" Jen asked in an exaggerated whisper. Her big brown eyes grew even wider.

As if on cue, Austin walked out of the garage, wiping his hands on his trademark dirty rag and squinting against the sunlight.

"You must be Jen," he said. "I'm Austin. I would shake your hand, but I don't want to get you all dirty," he said.

Jen was clearly star struck. "Grayson, I mean Austin, I mean nice to meet you. I already met your brother." She was babbling just as she did any time Melody introduced her to the up-and-coming hopeful future music stars their label had snagged or that they were courting from other labels.

Austin smiled and nodded. "Yeah. Donnie. I have a sister, too. She's in the middle of a battle with a busted carburetor right now. Otherwise, I'd introduce you. You'll meet her later on, I'm sure. You're staying with us, right? Mom mentioned something about that."

Jen's red and gold dangling earrings swung wildly as she nodded, her face still lit up with celebrity love.

"Well, I should get back to work. Mel, why don't you knock off for the rest of the day and go with Jen?" He looked at her in a way that made her heart thud so hard it hurt. This was the most he talked to her all week, but so what? Why was she acting so love struck? No. She wasn't going to use that word. Not even in a seemingly harmless way like that. Not a word to be thrown around—or even in her vocabulary—when it came to Austin Holt.

"You sure?" Melody wanted to draw out this conversation for as long as possible. She wanted to hold his gaze, hear his voice. The irrational part of her that'd gotten her into all the trouble she'd ever been in over her short, young life so far was at work. She had to give that part credit for one thing, though—it'd also been responsible for most of the fun she'd had so far in life. Her ex-husband was the exception that proved the rule, though.

"Of course," Austin said. His eyes bore into hers for a moment before he turned to walk back to the garage.

Melody turned back to Jen who mouthed, he is so hot!

Melody grinned. "Did you bring the clothes I asked you to? And were you able to sell that Birkin online?" Melody's heart dropped at the thought of losing her favorite handbag, but she needed the money.

"I did both, but I still want you to come home with me tomorrow. I see why you're reluctant to, though." Her gaze lingered on the door Austin had walked through on his way back into the garage.

"What?" Melody laughed off her friend's words. "Austin? There's nothing going on between us. I told you that."

Jen snorted. "Girl, you are smitten. Don't forget how long I've known you. And he was giving you a kind of hungry greedy look, too."

"Hmph," Melody said. Austin had hardly looked at her since the night of their kiss. Still, she wanted to believe her friend's words. "Let me get my purse. I'll be right back."

When she went in to get her purse, Austin was in the office. He looked at her like he'd been caught doing something wrong even though it was his office.

"Sorry, I was just leaving," he said.

"Sorry for what? It's your office. I don't know what I did to you to make you hate being around me, but I might be leaving with Jen when she goes home. Then you won't have to worry about me sticking around, being in your way," she said, hand on hip.

"You know why I'm trying not to be around you?" he said, fire in his eyes.

"No, not really. You hardly talk to me, so how would I know anything?" she said, lifting her eyebrows.

"Because I've been trying to resist with everything that I am doing this," he said, hooking his hands into the waist of her jean skirt and pulling her close. He smothered her lips with his, and she gave a little moan. Backing her against his desk, he pulled her skirt up to her waist and squeezed her bottom. "A thong?" he murmured against her lips. "Why do you do these things to me?"

In answer, she wrapped her legs around his coverall clad ones. He lifted her onto his hips, gripping her bottom to hold her there. She grinded her hips against his. The whole time, they put everything they wanted to do to each other into their deep, long kisses. His hands went from cupping her bottom to caressing the sensitive skin where it met her thighs. Locking her arms behind his neck, she kissed him harder. It wasn't possible to get close enough to him. Drunk with desire, she never heard the door open.

"Austin, what's taking you so—" Donnie's voice started. "Oh."

Austin twisted his torso toward the door, and Melody yanked her skirt down as best she could with Austin still between her legs.

"Oh," Donnie said again. "We talked about this." He gave his brother a look of pure hatred. "Dammit, Austin." Donnie backed onto the walkway and slammed slammed the door.

Melody put a hand on Austin's arm. "You know I wanted that, too, right?" In fact, she wanted some more of it right then.

Austin rubbed his finger over his bottom lip, seeming to think for a moment. Then he said, "He's right. That's why I've been trying to stay out of your way since we, um. Since last week."

"He's not," Melody said, reaching for his arm again. He stepped out of range.

"Yeah, he is. There's so much you don't know about me, Melody." His beautiful green eyes hardened. She could tell that he was determined to keep her shut out of knowing it.

"So tell me, Austin. Please. I want to know you. Everything about you." She reached out again, and this time, he didn't pull away from her touch. Knowing it was probably a bad idea, but also knowing she'd never get anywhere if she didn't press, she said, "I want to know about Grayson, too. He's a big part of you."

He pulled away and rubbed a hand across his forehead, leaving a grease smudge behind which made him look like a grime and grease covered Catholic on Ash Wednesday. "Jen's outside waiting for you. And I need to get back to work."

"Don't push me away," she said. "Please."

He gave no indication he'd heard her. He just walked out of the door and back to the garage bay.

Melody started to leave the office when remembered there was a box of stuff she'd found behind the file cabinet that morning that Austin had told her to trash. She decided to take it out to the dumpster before she left with Jen. She picked it up and, still discombobulated from the kiss, tripped over her own feet. The box fell, and its contents scattered over the floor. Mumbling a curse, she bent down and began stuffing things back into the box. She stopped when she came across a CD in a blue plastic jewel case.

She read the words printed across the face of the CD in magic marker to herself. "Rhyme M.D. Demo CD." After stuffing the CD in her purse, she put the rest of the spilled stuff into the box and carried it out to the dumpster. On her way to Jen's car, she thought about that CD. Demo. Whose demo? The same person who'd written in the notebook she'd found? Had to be. All she had to do to fix all her problems was find the Rhyme M.D.

CHAPTER EIGHTEEN

Austin went straight to the shed behind the house when he got home from work. There were two small buildings behind the house. One contained tools, and Austin had remodeled the other old outbuilding and now used it to house his weight lifting equipment other than the free weights in the basement that everyone used.

He needed a good workout when he got home from work Saturday. Maybe by pumping some iron, he could pump the images of Melody out of his head. Get rid of the memories of how it felt to hold her in his arms. Taste her. Eliminate those dangerous fantasies of what could come next from his mind. She was off-limits, and that was that.

It felt good, bench pressing, working on his lats, and going through the rest of his upper body routine. Sure, it was hot as a sauna, but that helped keep him from thinking about Melody, so he didn't mind too much.

She wouldn't want him if she knew the truth anyway. He'd destroyed every single woman he'd tried to love. He was sick of trying—and that was the best thing for him and especially for any poor woman he might develop feelings for. Or who could see himself being attracted to for more than one night.

HIS MELODY

He thought about what Melody had said about strange old Blanche Leroux. Huh. Magic. If only it was real. If so, maybe he could've had Melody in his life and everything would've been automatically better. Maybe he wouldn't have to be so afraid of her knowing the truth. Heck, maybe he could erase the ugliness from his past altogether.

Austin stretched his legs out in front of him, put his hands on the bench behind him, and dipped down so that he could work his triceps with some bench dips. His breathing was the only sound except for that of the wind rustling through tree leaves coming through the open windows and door that he'd left cracked open. The silence was nice. He concentrated on counting his reps so that he wouldn't have too much freedom to think.

When he was done, he walked over to the full-length mirror that he used to watch his form when he was working with free weights. He ran his hands over his head and looked down at his sweat stained shirt and then back up into his own eyes. He didn't want Melody to go back to Atlanta with Jen, but maybe it would be best if she did.

He mumbled, "I can't let this happen." He wasn't good enough for her. Never had been, never would be.

Even if that weren't true, she was going back to Atlanta. He would never leave Sweet Neck again. He'd learned his lesson. City life wasn't for him.

#

Austin showered after his workout and then wandered downstairs wearing basketball shorts, a T-shirt he'd cut the sleeves off of, and nothing on his feet. Not ready to get into alcohol quite yet, he grabbed a Mason jar from a cabinet in the kitchen and filled it with sweet tea. Gulping down tea, he wandered outside to find Donnie drinking with some of his buddies and his girl, Nina, in the backyard. Vernon, who was home for the weekend only, was setting up an impromptu barbeque. He'd fired up the grill so that the charcoal could start heating up. Austin breathed in the smoky smell, similar to that of burning wood. His stomach rumbled.

Donnie had already started in on a six-pack, and from the proximity of Donnie's infamous red cooler, Austin was sure that plenty of reinforcements lay nearby. Great. Austin would have to work double-time to keep his temper in check now.

Vernon came over to him. "Austin, how are you, buddy?" He clapped Austin on the back.

"Great, man. How was your run?" Austin clapped him back.

"Good, good. Just a small run down to Florida starting Monday, though. Too hot to be going to Florida this time of year. I'd rather be going cross-country again, strange as that may seem. It's a longer haul, but at least you don't have the humidity to deal with in Arizona. L.A. Reno. Places out there," Vernon said.

"I hear you," Austin said. "I see you 'bout to cook us up something good." He glanced in the direction of the grill.

"Yeah. In honor of Melody's friend being here, and to give Leigh Anne a break from that hot kitchen, thought I'd throw some ribs and steaks on the grill. And some chicken 'cause that Melody don't eat much real meat you know. She don't know what she missing."

Austin laughed. "Yeah." Only Austin was the one missing something worth having when it came to Melody. But he wasn't allowed to say—heck, he shouldn't have even been thinking about—that.

Vernon and Austin talked for a few more minutes about meat and then Leigh Anne called Vernon into the house for something.

"Bro," Donnie slurred. "Come over here."

Austin took a deep breath. It was about to begin. The epic and all-too-often-fought battle of dealing with Donnie's bitterness.

"Yeah, Donnie," Austin said, looking to the heavens for patience as he approached the picnic table where his brother sat. Austin drank some more of his tea while he waited for his brother to get started.

Nina sat on Donnie's lap, wearing bleached cut-offs and a button-up with the shirt tails tied together, exposing a little midriff. A typical outfit for her.

"Bro. Pretty boy," Donnie said. "You got a thing for Melody, huh? She your next victim?"

Austin dug at the ground with his big toe, concentrating on the movement.

"I asked you a question, boy. What, you too good to answer me? Oh, I'm sorry, can't just anybody talk to my brother, Mister New York." Donnie turned to one of his friends and sneered. "That's Mister New York there. Too good for any of us. I don't know what in the world he's doing here among us lowly hick folk anyway. Oh that's right." Donnie turned a glare on Austin, and Austin didn't back down from it. "He's a thief, too."

"I never stole anything from you, Donnie." Austin set his jar of tea down on the ground, near where he stood.

"You a damned lie," Donnie stood up so quickly that Nina nearly toppled off of his lap. After catching herself with his help, she took a seat on the bench of the picnic table. "You stole the shop. You stole Kristen from me, and you ruined her. You've ruined so many people. Regan. Mom. Hell, you killed Dad. Fuckin' New York. Grayson Meadows. What the hell kind of name is that? I'll tell you. It's the name of a liar and a killer."

Austin clenched his teeth and fists in tandem. He closed his eyes briefly and then he said, "I'm gonna see if Mom and Vernon need any help."

"Go on. Run. You never fought a day in your life for anything or anyone. You don't care enough or you're a coward. Or both." Donnie spat chaw juice near Austin's feet. It hit the side of Austin's jar of tea.

"I'm done having the same old fight with you. You don't like me. You wish I was never born. I get it."

"Then get out of my house." Donnie had been inching closer, and he was now close enough to push Austin. He shoved Austin's shoulder.

"This isn't your house."

Another shove. "Ain't none of yours, either," Donnie said. "The smartest thing you ever did was leave, and if you had any sense, you'd pick up and do it again. This time for good. Nobody wants you here, not even Mom who's yet another person you claim to love who you tried to destroy. She just won't say it. Nobody wants your worthless ass around, Grayson."

That was it. Austin snapped his fist back and caught Donnie full in the mouth with it before he could stop himself. The next thing he knew, the two of them were on the ground punching, wrestling, and shouting. Someone was screaming for them to stop it, but Austin was too intent on beating the crap out of his brother to think about who it was.

Finally, someone pulled him off Donnie. One of Donnie's friends helped Donnie to his feet. Donnie held his bleeding nose and cussed at Austin. Austin tasted blood and figured he'd gotten a busted lip out of the fight, if it could have been called that. Donnie had never been as good of a fighter as Austin was and knowing that, he usually tried to hold back. He should have laid off him that time, too. He shouldn't have allowed himself to get provoked at all, but Donnie kept at him. He'd been digging away at Austin's patience more than usual since Melody came to town.

"You see, Melody? You see what an asshole he is?" Donnie shouted. So his brother had accomplished his goal. Good for him.

"Well. That was real adult. Real mature," Melody said from his left.

He didn't have any defense for himself so he stood there, fingers pressed to the side of his mouth, watching Nina make a fuss over Donnie and try to get him to hold his head back. Avery was holding packs of frozen peas out to the two of them.

Melody stepped in front of him. She took a bag of the peas from Avery and handed it to him. "That's gonna bruise."

Austin took his fingers away from his mouth and stared at the blood on them. "You think?" Donnie had gotten him with that damned class ring of his. Why couldn't he ever walk away from a fight with his brother? He tried, but he never succeeded.

"C'mon." She nodded toward the house.

"Huh?"

"What, did he knock your brain loose?" she cracked with a little laugh. "Let's get it cleaned up. See how bad it is."

He followed her into the house. He couldn't help but watch the way her short cotton skirt clung to her hips as she walked ahead of him. She led him to the half bath near the stairs. He leaned against the sink, and she wet a cloth and pressed it to the corner of his mouth. He winced a little in anticipation at first, but relaxed at the gentleness of her touch.

"Just a little cut," she murmured, close enough that he smelled the vanilla scent on her skin. He leaned in closer to get a better sniff, barely aware he was doing it.

"You're not mad?" Austin asked.

"About what? You and your brother playing Neanderthal games? That's between you two, I guess. But can I ask you a question?" She concentrated on his cut and avoided his eyes.

"Shoot." He shifted the pack of frozen peas a little higher on his jaw.

"What is it between you two?"

"He likes to provoke me." He shrugged. And a girl. Some lies. A few disappointments. Nothing he wanted to tell her.

"Why do you let him?"

"I try not to."

She rinsed and wrung the cloth out in the sink, and he watched his diluted blood chase water down the drain. "Well. I don't think it'll need stitches. It's already starting to clot, I think." She put her fingers on his jaw and turned his face toward the mirror above the sink. "See?"

He put his hand over her and ran his thumb over her knuckles. "Thanks," he mumbled. He thought that night in the kitchen as he often did. The cool sweetness of her mouth. Her soft, warm body under his hands. That flimsy nightgown. And then earlier that day in his office. He couldn't get the things he'd wanted to do to her out of his mind. Probably because he still wanted to do them.

"Sure," she said, pulling her hand from beneath his. "Austin, I—I want to ask you about that notebook I found. It doesn't belong to Avery or Donnie. And there's a—"

"No." He walked to the door of the small room. "Would you drop it already? Throw that thing away and forget you ever saw it. I don't know whose it is, and you need to quit bugging me about it. Dammit."

She looked stunned, but all she said was, "Okay." Her eyes hardened. "No need to yell at me. I was just asking a question."

"About something that I already told you I don't want to talk about."

"Well, I guess I'll get back outside then." She pushed past him.

He sighed and let his head rest on the doorframe with a dull thud. He had some apologies to make when he got the energy up to go outside and make them. He hadn't meant to snap at her, and of course she would be curious, but she kept trying to dredge up a past better left forgotten. He wasn't going to let that happen.

CHAPTER NINETEEN

When Melody got back outside, Jen grabbed her, ready for a full report.

"Well?" Jen's eyes were wide and she made a flurry of gestures indicating that she should spill. Melody guessed she would be curious, too, if she hadn't spent the past couple of weeks with the Holt brothers.

Vernon chose that moment to turn the volume up on a Mariah Carey song, so Melody was pretty sure they could talk without being overheard, especially since they were sitting in a couple of chairs off to the side, away from the picnic table where most everyone else was.

"Well, Austin and Donnie basically hate each other," Melody said.

Jen snorted. "No kidding."

"No one will give me the whole story on it, but I think it has a lot to do with Austin going away to New York and even more with him coming back here," Melody said. She filled Jen in on what little she knew about Austin.

Jen pulled her long, dark hair away from her face and settled it behind her shoulders. "So Donnie's not happy about the shop being left to Austin."

"Yeah and I get the feeling that's not the half of it. Especially after what we saw just now."

"I'd say you're right about that my little amateur detective friend."

Melody raised an eyebrow. "I'm the little one, eh? You're what... five feet with those platforms you have on?"

"Ha ha." Jen grinned, bumping Melody's shoulder with small, pale one. "Funny girl."

Melody slumped in her chair.

"What's wrong?"

"I dunno. I just wish they got along better. They're family."

"Aw. I know how important family is to you." Jen rubbed her shoulder.

Melody had never had a big family. It was just her and her mother after the divorce. Her dad hadn't had the will to live after his family and his music career were taken from him. He'd pickled his liver with cheap whiskey a few years after the divorce. He never even got to see Melody graduate high school. She didn't have any brothers or sisters. Her parents had been only children, so no aunts and uncles. Her paternal grandparents lived in California, so she didn't see them much, and her maternal grandparents lived in Jamaica, so she saw them even less often. "There has to be something I can do," she said, thinking of Blanche.

"If anybody can figure it out, it's you," Jen said. "I'm pretty much convinced there's nothing you can't do."

She laughed humorlessly. "Except keep my job."

"Hey." Jen playfully swatted her shoulder. "Stop that. You know that man's an unreasonable jerk. Besides, you know what I'm going to say."

Melody rolled her eyes. "Oh yes I do."

"And I'm still going to say it. It's way past time for you to strike out on your own."

"Maybe."

"You know the money thing is just an excuse. A weak one."

Melody didn't respond to this one. She picked at the chipped polish on one of her pinkie nails instead. She needed to fix that. Maybe she should escape upstairs right now and fix it.

"Look," Jen said. "Let's go have a good time, you're not allowed to sulk. You're over here in the corner and Grayson—"

"Oh yeah. I'm not talking to him."

"What happened?"

"He was an ass. Again."

"Nope. Unacceptable. C'mon. We're dancing." Jen stood and reached for Melody's hands.

"Stop, Jen." She made no moves toward Jen.

Jen didn't listen, not relenting until she got Melody on her feet. "I know one you can't resist," Jen said in a devious tone. She called over to Vernon. She could really project her voice for such a little person. "Vernon. You have some Al Green for me? Love and Happiness."

"Sure do."

"Throw it on and turn it up loud." Jen turned to Austin who was nursing his pride and a beer at the same time it seemed. She beckoned to him. He just looked at her. He was soon to learn Jen didn't take "no" for an answer. From anybody.

Jen went over, grabbed him, and wouldn't relent until he was out there with them, dancing with his beer still in his hand. Before the first refrain, she had everybody up and dancing.

#

That night, Jen insisted they go out to karaoke once she found out the bar—the one and only in town—had karaoke on Saturday nights. She was able to talk everyone into it except Vernon and Leigh Anne. They needed some quality time because Vernon had been on the road for so long and would soon be leaving again. Avery, Donnie, Nina, and their friends had come along and were behaving themselves for the most part. Donnie even got up and sang a Toby Keith song. Jen had a magic touch.

Jen was addicted to karaoke. She had a great voice, and she enjoyed the attention. The problem was Jen almost always conned Melody into singing, and Melody was less than confident in her own voice even though Jen tried to convince her she could sing. Yeah right. Jen just wanted someone to karaoke with.

Melody watched Austin whenever she thought he wasn't looking while Jen sang Gladys Knight's "Midnight Train to Georgia." Nina sang Bonnie Raitt's "Something To Talk About." Melody thought about how nice it'd be to give people something to talk about, all right, when it came to Austin. Then again, he was secretive and guarded those secrets furiously. What was so great about getting involved with someone like that? Not that getting involved was really an option. She was leaving town soon. Possibly as soon as less than twenty-four hours from that moment.

Still, he wasn't easy to ignore and probably wouldn't be easy to forget. She'd known that from the moment he'd come out of his shop, wiping his hands on that filthy rag of his. And part of her wanted to force her way through that tough shell of his and take away whatever it was that was hurting him. Show him that some people could be trusted and that opening up could be a good thing. A healing thing.

"Feel at home back in the spotlight?" Donnie snickered and looked around Nina and the others.

"Sure," Austin said. The way he said it was pretty neutral, but his green eyes hardened, and his angular jaw locked.

Melody glanced at the bruise on his cheek and was glad he didn't take the bait again.

"What, you ain't gonna throw another hissy fit?" Donnie feigned shock. "Oh, I guess you still want to pretend you can fool Melody. That she hasn't figured you out yet."

Jen jumped up. "I think it's time for another song."

Melody groaned when she heard the opening bars of "Try a Little Tenderness." That was Jen's favorite song. Jen always got into that song like no other; for the length of that song, she thought she was Otis Redding. Jen gestured wildly for her to come up. Melody shook her head, but she knew it wouldn't do her much good to protest.

After dragging Melody to the front of the bar, she said, "You know I was never going to let you out of this."

Melody laughed. "Wishful thinking." She took the mic and Jen told the guy manning the karaoke machine to start the song over again. He did.

Nodding and moving her hips in time with the slow rhythm of the song's beginning, she tested the opening words to the song. She was tentative and shaky as usual at the beginning, but as people started to clap along at the chorus, she gained more confidence. Then her eyes found Austin's, and her voice became stronger. She realized she was singing to him from that moment on.

At the end of the song, she barely heard the applause erupting around her. Her heart raced when Austin stood, starting a standing ovation. She dropped her eyes away. Handing the microphone off to the host of the karaoke night, she hurried back to her seat.

"I guess it's my turn." Austin stood and stretched.

She watched the muscles flex in his arms as he stretched. She just couldn't help herself. "I didn't know you karaoke," Melody said.

He chuckled. "I'll bet there's a lot you don't know about me."

Not from lack of trying, she thought.

As Austin was walking to the stage, Melody caught a wink and a nod between Donnie and the guy manning the karaoke machine.

For a moment, Austin stood motionless as "Rapper's Delight" by The Sugarhill Gang came on. Then he frowned at the screen in confusion before looking at the karaoke guy who only shrugged. The beginning of the first verse rolled by before a glint of understanding lit up his eyes. He glared in his brother's direction. Donnie grinned, stood up, and took a bow. Cupping his hands around his mouth, he called, "M.C. in the house!" Then he guffawed at the top of his lungs.

In answer, Austin smoothly picked up in the middle the second verse of "Rapper's Delight" as if he'd written the song himself and knew every word inside out.

At the end of the song, Melody was stunned and convinced. If Donnie's comment hadn't done it, Austin's performance would have. She felt the CD through the skin of her leather clutch, still staring at Austin. He pulled his chair up next to hers and sat down. Looking straight ahead, he said, "So now you know."

She turned to stare at his profile and nodded. "I guess I do." Pulling the CD from her purse, she handed it to him.

He laughed tonelessly. "Where in the world did you find that?" He flipped it over in his hands a couple of times.

"Found it while I was cleaning your office. It's you?" She was unsure of whether he would tell her what she wanted to know, but she was completely certain if she listened to that C.D., she would hear Austin's voice.

"It's a demo C.D. my agent had me make. She wanted to branch out into music in addition to modeling. She found out I was into music and…" he trailed off and gestured toward the karaoke stage which one of Nina's friends had just taken.

"The notebook really is yours," she said. "The one I've been asking you about."

He scratched his jaw, still looking straight ahead. "It's mine."

"You're good."

He shrugged and moved his head, but not to look at her. He looked down at his hands. "I'm done with all that. My music is just for me these days."

"That's selfish of you." She tapped the C.D. "This needs to be shared with the world."

"What? You heard me do a karaoke cover of 'Rapper's Delight.' You saw a few of my stupid rhymes in a notebook. What does that mean?"

"From one musician to another? Everything." She touched the back of his hand and used her other hand to turn his head toward her. "Doesn't it?"

He took her hands in his, pressed hers between his and gave her a look that was sex and sadness all at once. "Whatever else it could have been? Is over. This is me now, Austin the mechanic. I have everything I want." He pressed her hands to his cheeks. "Almost everything."

She had a very difficult time swallowing since her mouth felt like it was full of cotton.

"Melody, I'm not Grayson anymore for a reason." His voice was soft, and she barely caught his words in the noisy, crowded bar.

"But it doesn't have to be that way this time, Austin. I work for a small label." At least she would be working there again if she could convince Austin to come back with her. She was almost sure of that. "You'd have a lot of creative control and—"

"I know you mean well, but once you put yourself out there in the public eye? You never have control. Besides, I couldn't do it to—I owe…a lot of people," he said.

"What about what you owe yourself? What about your own happiness?"

"Some day, I'm gonna get the nerve up to tell you everything." He kissed the backs of her hands before putting them on her lap. "And you'll understand."

She wanted so badly to reach for him, to kiss him right there in that crowded bar, which was sure to cause a scene. Austin the notorious town celebrity and the out-of-towner getting promiscuous at karaoke. But she wouldn't. What was she doing anyway? And she always accused Jen of getting carried away when it came to guys and falling too hard too quickly.

"I'll be right back." He stood.

"Where you going?"

He ran a hand over his head and the bristles of blond hair on top of it. "Outside. I need some air." And he was gone.

Jen dropped into his chair and handed her smart phone to Melody. "Look what I found. Googled him."

Jen had pulled up a website that hadn't been updated in ages that had photos of dark-haired Grayson, all danger and sex appeal. She clicked on a tab at the top of the page and saw a tall man in a hooded sweatshirt. "Rhyme Doctor" was scrawled across the top of the page in a graffiti-type font.

"So you two were steaming over here," Jen said. "What were you talking about?"

"This." Melody handed the phone back to her. "He has to listen to me." She truly did want to help him pursue his dreams. She could tell music was important to him, no matter what he said. She'd heard it—seen it—when he'd been on-stage earlier. But she also couldn't help but thinking that if she brought him back to Atlanta with her, Saeed would let her back in the door of New Face Records.

"About?"

"Didn't you hear him up there? New Face Records needs him, and he needs New Face. You know we've been looking for a new artist who can take us places. Austin could save New Face." The company had been on the verge of going under for the past few years. That was one of the reasons they were being so militant about expenses.

"'We'?" Jen frowned. "Weren't you fired?"

"Maybe not anymore."

Jen pushed her dark hair away from her face. "Don't push him, Mel. I don't know what all happened, but it has to take something big to make a person leave New York for a place like Sweet Neck, Georgia. And whatever he has going on with his brother... I mean, going back to the spotlight might be the last thing he wants or needs."

They looked across the table to where Donnie, Nina, and the others sat. Donnie wore the smug smile of someone who'd won a battle. There was a glint of hurt in his eyes, though, that made her think being estranged from his brother bothered him more than he cared to admit.

Melody shrugged. "Might be." But she was already thinking of how to bring her idea up to Austin.

CHAPTER TWENTY

That night, Melody dreamed of Austin, which wasn't new. Bare-chested and doing some raunchy things to her with chocolate sauce. But then, to her disappointment, the image of Austin faded away and to her shock, it was replaced with Blanche Leroux.

Suddenly, she was in a darkened room that reminded her of a cave, and Cajun music blared from a phonograph. Psychedelic colors splashed on the walls in patterns that indicated they were coming from a strobe light.

"You can fix the Holt brothers. You know what you need to do. Austin is your destiny, and he is yours, chère."

"What's going on?" Melody looked all around, but she couldn't find the source of the voice.

"Up here."

Melody looked up and saw Blanche suspended from the ceiling of the cave like a bat.

Blanche broke out into a maniacal cackle and Melody gasped. Her eyes flew open, and she sat up ramrod straight in the bed.

"But Mom, I want to feed the ponies," Jen murmured, stirring next to her. Melody dropped her feet to the side of the bed and hugged herself. "Wait, whoa, what's happening?

What are you doing up? It's..." she heard Jen picking up her phone from the night stand. A moment later, a soft electronic glow partially lit the room. "Four in the morning? Ugh, Mel, no good."

"Just a dream," Melody said. "Go back to sleep."

She heard Jen sit up, and a moment later, she felt a hand on her back. "Must have been a bad one."

She shrugged. "Not the most pleasant one I've had."

"Mean to tell me you're not dreaming about Mister Sex on a Stick? What's wrong with you?"

Melody laughed. "Must have been that glass of wine I had at karaoke." She didn't want to say anything at all about the dream. Jen already thought the Blanche thing was crazy. She'd told her as much when Melody told her about it while they were getting ready for bed. "Let's get some sleep," Melody said. She lay down and patted the bed next to her. "You have a long drive back soon."

"We have a long drive back." Jen lay next to her.

"We'll see," Melody said. She pretended to fall back asleep, but she was wide awake. She knew she wouldn't be able to sleep anymore and she'd just lay there until it was time for breakfast since she and Austin didn't run on Sundays. She kept thinking about the dream and Austin's performance at karaoke. Which led to more thinking about Blanche and what she'd said in the dream.

Later that morning, when she told Jen she was staying, Jen pouted. Melody laughed. They stood next to Jen's car. Jen had on her favorite get-comfy-for-the-long-drive traveling outfit—Juicy Couture sweats—and she'd pulled her dark brown hair back into a ponytail.

"You knew there was a possibility I'd stay," Melody said.

"Yeah, I guess I can't blame you considering you haven't gotten your, uh, tune up from your sexy mechanic yet." Jen cast a knowing glance in the direction of the house.

"Hey. He's not the reason I'm staying. Or at least that's not the reason I'm staying." Melody felt her cheeks burning. "I mean, I want him to come back to Atlanta with me, but for business reasons only. Until I can convince him to do that, I'm staying."

Jen narrowed her eyes. "You haven't even mentioned it to him yet, have you?"

"I have to find the right way to bring it up."

"See? That means you know it's a bad idea."

"No, I don't because it's not. You know how much that job means to me, and once Saeed hears Austin, he'll be glad to take me back. Plus, Austin deserves this chance even if he doesn't know it yet. You heard him last night. Tell me with a straight face that you don't think he's good, and I'll get in that car and go back to Atlanta with you." Melody just knew that if she could get everything and everyone in the right place at the right time, it'd all work out.

"I can tell you I don't think he wants this, and it's a bad idea. But you tend to be stubborn, so…" Jen said as Melody slid her bag into the back seat of her car for her.

"Would you love me if I was any way but how I am?" She shut the car door and leaned on it.

Jen leaned her head to the side and tapped a finger against her cheek. "Hm…let me think about it…"

"Hey!"

They laughed, and Melody pulled Jen in for a hug. "It was so good seeing you. I'm gonna miss you."

"Not for long you won't. Or else…you'll make me come down here on another rescue mission. I plan to make the next one successful even if I have to drag you back kicking and screaming."

Melody grinned. "Okay."

Jen got into the car, and Melody waved to her until she was out of sight. She missed Jen already.

She jumped at the sound of Austin's voice. "You staying then?" he asked.

She turned to look at him. "I didn't hear you come out here. Yeah, until my car's ready."

He stared down the lane at Jen's disappearing car. "Shouldn't be too much longer. We can probably have you out of here by Wednesday."

"Sounds like you're in a hurry to get rid of me," Melody said, half-joking, half testing the waters.

He stuck his hands in his pockets and still looking down the empty lane, which now contained only a cloud of dust, he said, "Gonna storm tonight. Might be bad enough to flood the creek. I'm gonna go see if Regan needs any help before it hits. So I won't be here for dinner."

"I could come with you," Melody offered.

"No offense, Mel, but a city girl like you? Wouldn't be much help," he said with a forced smile. He then walked away without giving her a chance to respond. He was avoiding her, and she had a pretty good idea of why, but what he didn't know was that she didn't scare off easily. Especially when she knew she was right.

One day, he would thank her for what she was about to do. She walked back into the house and saw Donnie in the kitchen talking to Leigh Anne. She shook off an uneasy feeling as she recalled the dream she'd had as well as Blanche's earlier words about the Holt brothers.

#

That night, after dinner, Melody called Saeed on his private number, knowing she was taking a big gamble by calling him on his personal cell on a Sunday night, but she had a trump card. And she let him know as much as soon as he started in on her.

He stopped mid-tirade and there was a pause after which he said, "What are you talking about, hip-hop artist?"

"It's more of a jazz-hip-hop fusion, but he's really good." Melody repeated the story of going to the karaoke bar the night before. She then told him about the notebook she'd found and the demo CD. She'd listened to the demo the night before, and she told him how she'd never heard anything quite like it and how it was better than any of the demos she'd heard since they signed Aphrodisia, a German hip-hop artist they'd picked up a couple of years ago. Good thing they had because Aphrodisia was the only thing keeping the company afloat at the moment.

"Bring him to Atlanta then," Saeed said as if this was the obvious next step. Natural for him to assume so.

"Um...it's not going to be that easy." She shifted her phone to her other hand. "You see, he doesn't know he wants this yet." He would figure it out. He just needed some time to realize how incredible the opportunity she offered him was.

"What?" He scoffed. "You're wasting my time with crazy talk again. This is another one of your half-baked schemes that has us halfway into bankruptcy court, isn't it?"

Sure. Blame her for all of upper management's mistakes that had led the company down that road. She had to keep her temper in check this time, though. She was already in enough trouble with Saeed. "It's not like that," she said. "Just listen—"

"There's a showcase at The Spot, Saeed said. "Three weeks from now. That's your last chance. You get him to show up there? You might save your job."

"Okay." Melody knew of the club. She would go to their website or call the club's manager and get the details. Saeed wasn't in the mood for details.

"And send me that demo you have."

"But it's—" she started and then realized she was talking to a dead line. "At least five years old," she muttered to her phone after removing it from her ear. Ah well, at least she had a chance. She had one more shot at her dream, and she wasn't going to waste it.

Music was in her veins. Ever since she was little, every good memory involved music. She remembered watching her father play saxophone with a local jazz band. He'd always let her sit in on the practices even though they usually ran way past her bedtime. In school, the easiest way for her to study for tests was to make songs out of the material. It worked for every subject, from English to history to physics.

Her mother hadn't wanted her to get too carried away. She was to be practical unlike her father who'd landed them in bankruptcy court twice before the divorce. Still, Melody had found a way to make a career out of music. She wasn't about to let all that go now.

She also wasn't going to let Austin ruin his chance at having his dreams come true. He didn't know how he'd regret this if she let him, but he wasn't going to have to worry about that. He'd never have a chance to regret it because she wasn't giving up on him the way she'd given up on herself and her own dreams of being first a songwriter and now a music manager.

CHAPTER TWENTY-ONE

Austin walked into his office late Monday morning and found Melody at his file cabinet, a stack of papers in a box next to her feet.

"I'm gonna start on your car this afternoon if we don't have any priority jobs come in today. We should be able to get you out of here by the end of the week," he said. "I'm shooting for Wednesday."

She turned to him, placing a hand over her chest. "You startled me."

His eyes lingered on the hand and her low-cut tank top for a minute before he forced them away. "Sorry."

"You have a few minutes?"

"Anything older than five years can be shredded," he said, repeating what he'd told her earlier that morning.

"It's not about this." She gestured to the box at her feet.

He'd been afraid it wasn't. He sat on the corner of his desk and looked in her direction, waiting for her to say something.

"You've been ignoring me again," she said, coming closer. Too close. But he couldn't move away without being obvious about it. "Ever since we kissed Saturday," she added.

"You had your friend here. I assumed you wanted to spend time with her."

She shook her head. "No. I don't think that's it. You were tense all day Saturday. I guess Donnie was part of it. I think there's more, though. Especially after what I found out—what I heard—at karaoke."

"I didn't mean to be rude. I just don't see the point in us getting..." he searched for the right word, but nothing came to him. "I'm not looking to get involved with anyone, and it wouldn't make sense for us to even if I were. You're leaving soon." The sooner the better because he was having trouble convincing himself of the veracity of the part about him not wanting to get involved. If she wasn't there, he couldn't get himself into trouble. "And we're not even going to talk about music."

"I just want you to talk to me." She put a hand over one of his, and he shifted but didn't pull away from her.

"About?" He rubbed his free hand over the back of his head.

"Everything. Why you're afraid of me."

"I'm not afraid of you."

"Tell me about Donnie and the rest of your family. New York. Just...everything."

She kept pushing like she was personally invested. "Why does it matter so much to you?" he asked.

"Because you matter to me." Her face was so open and honest. And dangerous. Like a bear trap lined with honey.

"You've only known me a couple weeks." He pulled away from her and stood, walking across the office. Maybe his music mattered to her the way it had mattered to his agent. But he wasn't going to get fooled into thinking he mattered to her. He wasn't stupid. The only thing more dangerous than an A&R exec was an A&R exec looking for a job.

Maybe she was curious about Grayson like all the reporters who'd tried to hunt him down after he left New York. But he couldn't imagine anyone outside of his mom,

Vernon, and Regan—and maybe Avery—caring about him. Much less someone who barely knew him. Besides if she knew him, if she really knew him and what he'd done, she wouldn't be throwing words around about him mattering to her so eagerly.

"And I've been trying to get you to tell me what happened to you that whole time," she said. "I want to know more about you. You're the one holding out on me."

He looked up at her briefly before returning his attention to the floor. He said the words slowly, thinking about each one before saying it, "Because there's no point. You belong in Atlanta, and I belong here. There's no point in going into a whole bunch of stuff that doesn't concern you."

"So our kiss meant nothing to you? You didn't feel anything at all?" She moved in front of him as if she were trying to force him to look at her. He turned away.

He had to lie. If he didn't, he was opening himself up to a whole world of trouble and hurt. He shook his head. "Nope."

"I see." Her voice changed.

"I mean it was nice, but it's not gonna lead anywhere or change anything." He stared at a poster advertising synthetic motor oil without really seeing it. "Sorry."

"I'm tired of hearing you say that, sorry."

"S—I'll be in the garage if you need me."

She didn't answer him. Instead, she went back to the file cabinet and grabbed an empty banker's box sitting next to it. She carried the box over to his desk and plunked it down.

"You need help with those before I go?" Austin asked as she moved across the room to retrieve another box from the stack.

"Nope." She lifted a second box.

He started toward the boxes.

"I said I don't need any help," she snapped. "Besides, you're wasting time. The quicker you get to the garage, the quicker you can get me out of your hair forever, right?" Her tone was bitter. She'd gone from pleading with him to sounding like talking to him was the last thing in the world she wanted to do.

"I didn't mean any harm. And you're better off, believe me."

"That seems to be the case." She slammed a third box down on the desk and ripped off the lid.

"Yeah, so...I'll be in the garage. Like I said." He walked out, not expecting an answer and not getting one. Why was he feeling guilty? She'd provoked him into it. She kept picking when he'd made his feelings clear about his past and about romantic relationships from the beginning. And his music career was out of the question. It was like the rest of his past—dead and gone.

Besides, all she wanted was what she could get out of him. She wasn't the first one. Ignoring the fact that she'd done nothing to provoke that thought really, and throwing out all rational thinking and all thinking about her at all, he went into the garage to throw himself back into his work. He had an alternator to replace. That's what he needed to focus on.

He was poking around in his tool chest, trying to remember where he'd last left his socket wrench when Donnie started cackling.

Austin glanced up at him. "What?"

"It's the music man," Donnie said, wheeling himself from under a Dodge Dakota. He lay back on the long wooden board of his creeper and looked up at Austin, a satisfied grin on his face.

"The stunt you pulled at that bar wasn't funny at all," Austin said. Nothing he did was ever as funny as he thought it was.

"What?" Donnie feigned innocence.

"I know it was you who changed my song at karaoke."

"What? You didn't want your new friend to know about your musical side, Rhyme Doctor?" Donnie asked. He arranged his face into a mask of confusion.

"It should've been up to me to decide when, how, or even if I ever wanted to tell her. That had nothing to do with you, but yet again, you came butting in where you weren't needed or wanted." Austin banged his fist against the side of his tool chest.

"What you want don't amount to a hill of beans to me." Donnie snickered. "I just thought Melody should know what she's dealing with is all. You're a liar and a washed-up loser, and I wanted her to know about the mess she's getting herself into."

"Nobody's 'getting into' anything or anyone," Austin said.

"Hey, whoa, whoa. Calm down now."

"You know what? Fuck you, Donnie. You don't know what you're talking about, and you don't know who you're messing with. You have no idea what you've done," Austin said. "Because you're just that stupid."

Donnie's goofy smile finally faded. "I guess that's why Dad left you the shop, huh? I was too stupid to run it."

Austin glared at him. "I don't know why he left it to me any more than you do, but you need to let go of things that aren't going to change." He balled his hands into fists at his sides.

"You won't even let me read that damned letter he wrote you." Donnie sounded like a sniveling child.

"It's none of your business what's in it."

Donnie stood and leaned against the truck he'd been working on earlier. "None of my business? You have no business even being here. Nobody wants you here. You ruin everything you touch. Gonna add Melody to that list now?"

"You know what? I'm not going to put up with this shit today. Not today," he said. He needed to get out of there before he did or said something he would regret. He needed to be away from all of them, even Melody and especially Donnie. He headed toward the washroom at the other end of the garage so he could clean up and get out.

"Where you going?" Donnie asked.

"I don't know. Away from here," Austin called over his shoulder. "You and Avery are on your own for the rest of the day. I'll be back tomorrow."

"What about Melody's car?" Donnie asked.

"I said I'll be back tomorrow. I reckon it'll still be here then!" Austin snapped. He then turned his back on his brother, ignoring anything else he had to say.

CHAPTER TWENTY-TWO

Melody had Vernon drop her off at the bar where she'd gone to karaoke over the weekend. She walked in and spotted Austin right away at a small table near the back. The table was littered with empty glasses. He was nursing an obviously warm beer as there was no longer frost or even condensation on the glass and glaring at no one and nothing in particular. She took a seat at the table.

"Leigh Anne said you'd probably be here," Melody said.

His green eyes glittered with smoldering anger when he turned them on her. He answered her by drinking from the half-empty glass of beer. She glanced to the left where a considerable number of empties sat.

"Drinking your dinner?" She raised her eyebrows.

He slowly pushed the glass of beer back and forth between his hands. "What are you doing here?" He slurred his words, but he didn't sound as incoherent as that number of beers would have made Melody. He could have had more than there was evidence of; she didn't know whether the server had taken any empty glasses away yet or not. Then again, he was a lot bigger than her so he could probably handle a lot more alcohol than she could.

A dark-skinned woman with her hair pulled back from a pretty oval-shaped face walked up to them. "Anything for you, hon?"

"I'll take a glass of water for now," she said.

She nodded and moved her eyes across the table. "Another beer for you, Austin?"

"You know it." He winked at her.

She smiled and then murmured to Melody, "You're not letting him drive, right?"

"Definitely not," Melody murmured back.

After she left, Austin said, "You're here to harass me or lecture me about Donnie again."

"I'm just here to have a drink," Melody said.

"Of water?" He shook his head slowly. "No you're not. You're here for information. You know what? I don't even care anymore. I'll give you what you want. I'll give you everything," he gave her a lecherous scan, and she knew he was drunk and hurting but she couldn't deny she was hot for him, "you want."

"And what do I want?" she asked, hoping her tone didn't give away the fact that she wanted to crawl across the table and get it. She'd been feeling that way especially since the kiss they'd shared Friday.

Austin slurred his words. "You want to know about Grayson. Well, let me tell you about fucking Grayson Meadows. You wanna know about him? Fine. He was a murderer and a cokehead. So I did what had to be done. I killed him."

"What do you mean a murderer?" Both were hard to wrap her head around, but murderer edged out coke addict. She didn't remember hearing about either in the news and couldn't imagine how either could be true. Granted, she didn't follow celebrity gossip closely, but Grayson had been a pretty big deal and Jen did follow it pretty closely. It seemed she would have heard something about either or both of those things.

The server brought over Melody's water and Austin's beer. He pushed what was left of the warm beer aside and grabbed the cold one.

Austin's face drooped with sadness. He clenched the glass the server had brought him, but didn't lift it to his lips. "I watched her die. I could have saved her, and I watched her die. I killed him, too. It was my fault he had that stroke. Both the first one and the one that killed him." The glass shook in his clenched, trembling fist. A little beer sloshed out of the top and dribbled over the side of the glass. The dark amber liquid ran over his fingers, but he didn't seem to notice.

"Austin, I don't understand. What are you saying?"

His eyes met hers dead on. "My girlfriend, Isadora Lampkin, died of an overdose. We were both hooked on coke at the time. God, she was beautiful. She didn't deserve that. And my dad? I was such a knucklehead. I gave him that stroke. And he—he left me the shop anyway. Despite all I did to him? He still loved me."

She did have a vague memory of hearing about former supermodel Isadora Lampkin, who she remembered being connected to Grayson as a love interest, dying of a drug overdose. And he blamed himself for killing his dad, too. What an awful burden to carry. "Oh, Austin."

"Don't 'oh Austin' me. I screwed up. I know it. And that's why I had to leave that life behind. Don't you see? Nothing good ever came out of me leaving Sweet Neck, and I don't plan on doing it ever again. First off, I owe too much to the people who saved me. Second? What do I need with that kind of life? People always thinking you're something you're not. Always trying to push you farther from everything real—everything that matters. It's all about money and one-upping and fighting to not be yesterday's news. It's a brutal, deadly popularity contest. All materialism. Nothing of substance. I don't want it. None of it." He downed half his beer.

"It doesn't have to be that way. It isn't always," she said quietly even though she was becoming unsure of her words as she spoke them. If she was meant to be the one to save him, how was she supposed to do that? Blanche hadn't shared that part with her.

Melody leaned forward in her chair. "Tell me more about Grayson. Tell me everything."

To her surprise, he did.

He leaned back in his chair and tapped his glass against the table as he spoke. "After high school, I wanted out of here. The last thing I wanted was to end up stuck in Sweet Neck, married, and taking over the family shop. So I hitchhiked to New York, looked into modeling, tried to find an agent. Finally, I lucked up on one." He laughed. "We met in a strip club. She was there with some of her clients who wanted to go to the club. That and she's discovered a few girls at strip clubs. She's always working." He shook his head. "She was my only one-night stand that turned into a relationship—my longest relationship. Bianca White."

"Isn't she one of the top modeling agents?" she asked. "She founded Modeling Elite, right?" She had this knowledge courtesy of Jen.

Austin downed some of his beer before nodding. "That she is. She's ruthless but effective. She changed my name, changed everything about me so that I wasn't even sure who I was. Helped me cover up a coke addiction. Introduced me to Isadora. We had a lot in common, Isadora and me. No. Jane. Jane was her real name." He paused and a sad, little smile creased his face. When he looked up at her again, he said, "Jane was from a small town, too. Her parents were farmers in Iowa. We hit it off, but the only thing Bianca cared about was how good we looked together and that the match was good for both of our careers. She helped the two of us cover up more than she should have." He finished off his beer. "Like the fact that we were killing ourselves."

She put a hand on his arm. "That's terrible."

"I had a good run, but I was hollow. And high for most of it. I barely knew what was happening from day to day. I don't even remember half of it. I remember Jane going in and out of rehab. Trying to convince me to go. I never did." He gulped more beer.

She tried to think of something to say, but she couldn't. She rubbed his arm again instead.

"That show about the male models?" He snorted. "I got kicked off it for going on a coke binge, beating the hell out of one of the models and leaving him in an alley behind a club."

"I don't remember hearing about that."

"Bianca's good. She kept it as contained as possible. Kept it out of all the major media circles anyway by feeding them more 'exciting' stories about ex-clients she decided to throw under the bus. She even 'convinced' some of her media contacts that a vagrant beat that guy up and robbed him. That helped confuse things so no one knew what to believe."

"Really?"

"I told you she's ruthless. And she can be very persuasive when she wants to be." He looked down at his empty glass. "After that, she hired the image consultant. The image consultant wanted to go with a 'darker' image. He wanted to make me 'edgier' or something. That gave Bianca the bright idea that I should become some stereotypical gimmick white rapper. She found out I was into music, and she saw dollar signs." He laughed bitterly.

She nodded. So that was where his refusal to even consider a music career came from.

"She came up with yet another name for me, Rhyme Doctor." He sneered at his beer. "She decided she wanted to get into representing musicians, too, and I would be her first. She wanted to market me as some Paul Wall-Bubba Sparks knock-off. I went along with it for a while, but my heart wasn't in it. It's not what I wanted to do. She wanted to change my sound, my image, everything about me."

"And what happened to the Rhyme Doctor?" Melody asked.

"I got Isadora out of rehab early." He heaved a shuddering sigh. "One last time. We celebrated getting high and. And. She went to sleep and didn't wake up. I was too high to realize what was happening until it was too late. After Isadora died...my dad got sick not too long after that. I came back here, and he was dead within a couple of weeks. I didn't want to go back to that life in New York." His face hardened. "I should've never left here. I asked my mom and Regan to help me. They put me in rehab, and that's that."

"And the shop?" She folded her hands around one of his.

He considered the remains of the warm beer for a moment then pushed it aside. "My dad left it to me in the will, to my surprise and everyone else's."

"Austin, I think you've probably had enough," she said when he tried to signal the server again.

"No. You've had enough."

She moved her chair next to his.

"Weren't you listening?" he asked. "You should get on out of here. If you had sense, you'd get as far away from me as you could." He grabbed the warm beer and finished it in a few desperate-seeming gulps.

"We all make mistakes. Doesn't mean we have to pay for them for the rest of our lives."

"Don't you understand? I'm the one who sprung her out of rehab early. Me. She told me she wanted to come home. I'm the one who put the poison right back in her hands. That wasn't the first time. I didn't know it would be the last..." He ran a hand over his face. "I killed her." He choked out the words.

"That's an awful burden to carry," she said, pulling his head onto her shoulder. "You didn't kill her, Austin. You happened to be in a bad place like she was. Her path of self-destruction ended less fortunately than yours did. That's all." For a long moment, he sat there, unmoving. When he moved, she thought it would be to push her away, but instead, he put his arms around her waist.

"I don't want to be alone tonight. I have bad dreams when I drink like this. About her. And Dad," he said.

"Okay." She moved the backs of her fingers from the back of his head to the nape of his neck over and over again.

He sat up and put his fingers under her chin. Bringing her lips close to his, he traced his thumb over her lower lip. She closed her eyes and leaned forward. Taking her face between his hands, he nibbled at the corners of her mouth before kissing her lips fully and slowly. His tongue pushed over hers, demanding a response. She sank into the alcohol-soaked kiss. She hadn't realized just how much she missed the feel of his lips against hers until that moment.

She moved her fingers over bristles of his hair and then the skin of his neck. She pressed against the hard wall of his chest, feverish for more.

His fingers pressed into her waist. His thumbs slipped just inside the waistband of her jeans. She started to climb into his lap, but then stopped herself, realizing she how carried away she was getting.

He pulled back slightly. "We better get me home before I pass out. I'm kind of heavy to carry, you know," he mumbled over her lips.

She laughed. "I noticed."

"I didn't scare you off. Hm," he said in a musing tone. She didn't know if he was talking to her or to himself. Before she could decide if he wanted an answer or not, he said, "I snore."

She grinned. "So do I. C'mon. Up we go. If you can still walk."

Somehow, he made it to his feet, and they made it out to his truck. He dropped the keys into her hands and managed to pull himself in on the passenger side.

Once they were in his room and she'd helped him change into sweats, she went back to her own room to change and then came back to his. She thought he was already asleep when she leaned over to check on him and almost left, not sure if she should really stay based on a plea he'd made in a moment of drunkenness. Right as she was about to leave the side of the bed, he reached up and grabbed her around the waist, pulling her into bed with him. He said, "You came back."

"Yeah." She snuggled against him. He wrapped his arms around her and pulled her close. Something had changed between them that night. She'd finally gotten him to open up to her. Now that she knew his story, she was less sure she'd be able to convince him that her plan would be good for them both. She was also less sure that she was right about it being the right thing for him.

With his eyes closed, he mumbled into her shoulder.

"Hm?" she nudged him gently.

He lifted his head from her shoulder, but his eyes remained closed. "I said, I lied to you earlier."

"About what?"

"When I told you kissing you meant nothing to me. Every time I kiss you, touch you, I feel a whole hell of a lot. I need to stop."

"Why?" she barely whispered.

"'Cause every time just makes me want more of you than I have any right to take."

Her heart thudding, she sank back against the mattress and pillows. She didn't know what to say or think. With her wrapped in his arms, he was fast asleep in minutes. It took her a lot longer to fall asleep because she couldn't shut her mind off. All she wanted to do was replay his words in her head. She wanted so badly to call Jen and tell her all that happened that night, but there were two problems with that. The first was, she was afraid to move a muscle. He might wake up, regret asking her to sleep in his bed, and send her away. The second was, two in the morning was not a good time to call anyone.

#

The next morning, she woke before Austin and watched him sleep for a while until he blinked and squinted at her. He rubbed his eyes and took a deep breath. "Hey," he said.

"Hi," she said.

"You stayed all night. That's gotta be a good sign I wasn't too awful last night."

"Yeah. You asked me to. So I did. Remember that?"

"Unfortunately? I remember everything," he said with a humorless laugh. "Mmph, my tongue feels like it's made out of fur, and I could use about two bottles of aspirin."

She propped herself up on one elbow and looked down at him, eyes roaming over him, comparing what she saw with what she remembered of Grayson.

"What?" he asked, stifling a yawn.

"I had a dream about you last night," Melody said. He was in too good of a mood that morning, especially amazing after a night of drinking, for her to bring up Grayson.

"Oh yeah?" Austin stretched and gave her a sexy smile.

She let her eyes move over the flexing of his muscles as he stretched, not shy about appreciating. After all, she might not get many more chances to appreciate them. She was going to enjoy looking at every inch of him that she could see while she could. "Mm hm. It was a dirty dream." She didn't mention that she'd been having a lot of those lately.

"Oh yeah?" He slipped his fingers under the strap of her camisole.

"Yeah."

He trailed his fingers just under her bottom lip, and she leaned in closer to him, desperate for more of his touches. "I would ask you to act it out for me, but I don't guess that would be too appropriate," he said.

"What if I wanted to act it out for you?" she whispered.

"No," he said, but he sounded reluctant about it.

She pressed her forehead to his and sighed. She was afraid sex with him would make her too attached, so she didn't push it any further. After all, she was already starting to feel too much for him. He'd needed her the night before and being there for him had felt good. Just felt right. Too right. She needed to keep her head on straight.

What kind of business relationship would they have if she was falling all over him? And they were going to have a business relationship. She was determined about that. She could show him that it didn't have to be like in New York. She wasn't his former agent. And he didn't need to be afraid to follow his heart. Him coming to Atlanta could and would be good for both of them. She wouldn't allow herself to lose sight of that. She could show him that not everyone outside of Sweet Neck was like Bianca. That she'd never do anything to hurt him, no matter how much money or prestige was at stake. She knew what it was like to put all your trust into someone and be betrayed. She wouldn't do that to anyone, and she wouldn't let anyone do that to Austin.

"So...you should get out of my bed." Austin pulled away from her. "Because I can only take so much temptation," he said, drawing out the last word.

She brushed against him in a very suggestive way as she got out of the bed.

"That was just cruel," he said.

"No more cruel than you kicking me out of bed after what you did to me in my dreams," she said.

"And what exactly did I do? You never said," he said, following her with his eyes.

"I wouldn't want to be any crueler." She left the room, wondering how she was going to make it through the next few days without giving into what she wanted to do with him. And not really wanting to resist.

CHAPTER TWENTY-THREE

Tuesday after work, on the ride home, Austin looked over at Melody before looking back at the road.

"What?" she said.

"Your car will be all ready to go by tomorrow afternoon. I'll probably finish up with it by lunchtime," he said. The job had gone faster than expected, faster than he'd wanted it to. He'd thought about drawing it out, but why prolong the torture? The sooner she left, the better chance there was he wouldn't fall completely for her. He'd already gone too far. He cringed inside, thinking of how he'd all but fallen to pieces in front of her the night before. Had he really asked her to stay with him because he was scared to sleep alone? The answer to that question was a tragic yes, he had.

"Okay," she said with a heavy sigh. She sounded just as reluctant about her leaving as he felt.

"There's somewhere I want to take you tonight," he said. He watched her turn toward him from the corner of his eye. Took in her curious stare.

"Where?" she asked.

"Just this place. It's a surprise," he said.

"Okay," she said.

After all he'd put her through over the past couple of weeks, and especially after last night in the bar when he'd been at or near his lowest, he felt that he owed her this one last thing before she left town. He owed it to himself, too. He needed to stop shutting things out and refusing to deal with them in hopes that they would go away. Certain things were a part of him, whether he liked it or not, and trying to ignore them wasn't helping him or anyone who had to deal with him.

#

Austin knew he was in trouble when she met him at the truck in a low-cut red number. It clung to her perfect shape, curved in all the right places, ended just high enough on the thigh to put his imagination in high gear. He tried not to stare, but she'd made that damned near impossible.

"I'm ready," she said in a low voice that connoted she meant more than she was ready to get in the truck and go with him. "Wherever you want to take me."

"Um, let's go then," he said, barely able to watch where he was going because he couldn't take his eyes off her. His eyes trailed over those perfect shoulders, moved down the naked skin of her back exposed by the skimpy dress.

"Am I overdressed?" she asked as they climbed into the truck.

He looked down at his dark jeans and button-down and then smiled up at her. "You're perfect."

She returned his smile.

He drove them to Glennville, to a place called Myrtle's Catfish and Beer. He hadn't been there in almost a year, and he could only hope he wouldn't make a fool of himself. He walked over to her side of the truck and opened the door.

"I don't understand. We already had dinner. And it's past nine," she said.

He grinned, nodding in a gesture indicating she should hop out of the truck. "You will. C'mon."

He walked her into the dimly lit restaurant with his arm around her shoulders. She spotted the "Open Mic Poetry

Slam" notice scrawled on a chalkboard in the entry way and her eyes darted between it and his face at lightning speed. His grin widened as he watched her figure it all out.

"Oh Austin," she said, her voice a low, sultry murmur that made him want to kiss her right there in the entry way with people moving in and out around them.

"I haven't done this in about a year and if I suck, you brought the ear pain on yourself. And I fully plan on embarrassing you by letting everyone know you're with me," he said.

"I'm with you?" Her words were a near-whisper.

He looked deeply into her eyes, lost in their brown depths. "You're with me." Before he could do any more damage, he walked her into the restaurant proper and up to the bar.

"Austin Holt! Am I seeing things?" A fortyish, black-haired, brown-skinned woman placed a hand over her large chest.

"Hey, Myrtle," he said.

She hurried around the bar and gave him a huge squeeze.

"And who's this?" Myrtle asked. "You've never brought anybody with you and such a pretty thing." Myrtle turned to Melody. She was certainly right about that.

"This is my friend, Melody. Melody, Myrtle. Myrtle's the proprietor of this fine establishment," Austin said.

The two women greeted each other.

Austin then said, "You have room for me on the schedule tonight, Myrtle?"

"Oh, I always have room for you, baby," she said in her naturally smoky, sultry tone. "You can go on at eleven, right after Big Boy Leroy as he's decided to refer to himself this week." Myrtle rolled her eyes. "Y'all have a seat. I'll bring you drinks. On the house. Austin at open mic for the first time since I don't know when? Cause for celebration. Austin, I got you, Jack right? And Melody, what you drinking, darling?"

"Vodka tonic," Melody and Austin answered at the same time. Melody locked a look on him that was caramel and sugar and everything warm and good. "That's right," she said. He didn't even notice Myrtle leave. He was too busy noticing the way her brown skin seemed to glow under the low house lights. When he was able to tear his eyes away, Myrtle was behind the bar again.

"Let's grab those seats she mentioned," he said, putting a hand on her lower back and guiding her to an empty table. He took a seat across from her. She was smiling at him. "What?"

"I never expected this." She looked around the dimly lit restaurant. "I'm glad we're here, but I just—never expected this. Thank you," she reached across the table and put her hand over his, "for bringing me here."

He put his other hand on top of hers, stroking her knuckles with the side of his thumb. He hadn't expected to come there. He hadn't expected to do a lot of the things he'd done since meeting Melody. All of a sudden, he wanted to share everything with her.

"That's Shawn up there now. He's good, huh?" Austin turned his attention to the stage to distract himself from her. It was a good thing she was leaving soon. Whenever he started to have these kinds of feelings, things went downhill from there. He'd devastated Kristen and Donnie along with her. The whole thing had been a huge tangle of mistakes. He'd killed Isadora. And poor Regan had done so much for him, and he'd given her so little besides grief in return. He'd never be able to make up for that. For any of it.

"Austin, about last night..." Melody's voice trailed off and Austin looked up to see Myrtle at the table with their drinks. Good. He needed one. The dark liquid burned in a good way going down. He held Myrtle at the table a moment, starting up a conversation with her to avoid a difficult one with Melody. They talked about the restaurant and how well business was going. After a while, he turned the conversation to Melody.

"She's A&R." His eyes landed on Melody. "You have any cards you can give Myrtle? She gets some real talent in here every now and then."

Myrtle squeezed his shoulder. "Like this one right here."

He chuckled.

"No. Sorry." Melody smiled up at her. "I'm between jobs right now anyway. So I'm not sure how much I could do for anybody." She gave Austin a look he couldn't quite read. Turning back to Myrtle, she changed the subject to something about interior design and color schemes. Austin lost interest and turned his attention back to the stage.

When it was Austin's turn, he listened to the soft neo-jazz music in the background on his way up front, thinking of what to say. He had it by the time he grabbed the mic. Smiling, he said, "I'm Austin Holt. Some of y'all know me." He paused for shouts. "Yeah, I'm back. You can blame this one right here. My friend, Melody." He nodded to Melody and he could see the brown skin of her cheeks redden from where he was. She earned a few wolf whistles and a lot of clapping. "So everything I do up here tonight, I dedicate it to her. This first one is called…" he hadn't named it yet and came up with a title while staring at Melody. "So Beautiful."

Austin had eyes only for Melody all the way through the three pieces he performed. He noticed no one's reactions but hers. No one's applause but hers. He made love to her with his eyes in front of a bar full of people.

When his time was up, and he walked back to the table, she stood and hugged him, murmuring against his ear, "You were a hit."

"Really?"

"Didn't you notice your standing ovation?"

He moved his fingertips between her shoulder blades. "What did you think?"

"You scorched me. In a good way." Her cheek brushed his. "A very good way. Tease." She grinned. She should be talking what with her wearing that dress and all.

"I take that as a personal challenge." His hand slipped down her back. He let his fingers brush against a place that elicited a sharp gasp from her. Then he grinned and took a seat, clapping as the next act took the stage.

CHAPTER TWENTY-FOUR

By the time they got in the truck for the long drive home, he could barely sit still. It was going to be a long ride. He tried to keep his hands to himself, but she wasn't having it. She linked her fingers through his almost as soon as they got in the truck. Once they were on the road for a few minutes, she brought their hands to her lips. She pulled his index finger into her mouth and sucked it long and slow, grazing her teeth along it as she finally released it from her mouth.

He groaned and shifted in his seat. Tried to think about something, anything else but ripping that little red scrap of fabric off her body. Then she held their fingers up to his chin. No. He wasn't going to get pulled into this trap, this sexy little trap of hers. She grazed her index finger along his bottom lip. Then she did it again and again, over and over. He sighed without thinking about it and her finger found its way to his lower front teeth. Fuck it. He wasn't made of steel. He sucked her finger, letting his tongue do all the things to it he wanted to do to the rest of her. She finally pulled it away from him with a rich moan.

"You're gonna pay for that," she said before pulling his middle finger into her mouth. She made good on her threat. He almost let the truck drift onto the shoulder.

By the time they'd worked their way through each other's fingers and ended with the thumbs, he realized they weren't going to make it home without a pit stop. When he spotted the dark path he'd been looking for that he remembered from his high school days, they were over halfway home. By now, she was practically sitting on his lap, and he didn't know how he was still able to drive with her busy hands all over his heated body.

He drove down the path a little ways and then pulled over to the side. Turning to her, he unleashed all the kisses and touches he'd wanted to give her while driving—wanted to give her since the last time they'd kissed. He backed her against the passenger side door, and her long legs wrapped around his waist. Her dress had ridden up her hips and his jeans pressed against her panties. He reached down and touched the fabric between her legs. Silky. His fingers moved lower and she arched her back, moaning out his name. Wet silk.

"Austin, please," she whispered the words against his ear, fumbling with her dress until she pushed it down to her middle. It looked more like a bunched up red belt now than a dress. He stared down at the plump round mounds she'd just exposed and the chocolate drops at their apexes. Cupping her breasts with his hands he gave her mouth another hard, wet kiss before moving down to her breasts. Pulling one of her nipples between his teeth, he rubbed his thumb in circles against the other. She clamped her legs tighter around him.

He moved her panties to the side and pressed his fingers past the wet curls of hair, moved them against the sensitive, slick skin inside. He moved his fingers lower, pushing them inside of her briefly. She moaned in protest when he moved them out again. He made up for it by pinching the sensitive skin of her clitoris. While his fingers worked, his mouth went to hers and then her breasts and back again until she came with shuddering breaths. He wanted so badly to be inside her when she did, but he settled for pushing his fingers back inside her, stroking her until she came a second time. Afterward, she lay limp and happy against the passenger side door.

He then kissed his way down her body, stuffed her panties into his back pocket, and put his mouth to work, letting her know he wasn't done without saying a word. After she came a third time, he pulled the skirt of her dress down and helped her slip the straps back onto her shoulders.

On the rest of the ride home, she nestled her head into his chest and wrapped her arms around him. They didn't talk about what had happened or the fact that her car would be ready to go back to Atlanta in a few hours or Myrtle's or anything else. He wanted her in his bed again that night, but he didn't trust himself, having her be that close all night, after the heated time they'd just spent together. Driving home with her wrapped all around him was hard enough. He wouldn't have wanted her any place else, but still, it wasn't easy.

She yawned and shifted against him. He stroked her hair, using only his left hand to drive. What in the world was he doing? It was best not to think about it. Yes, she'd be gone soon and at least he had one helluva memory and a lot of other good ones from her being there. But it was best not to analyze or think and he was so glad they weren't talking. It was the best and most comfortable silence he'd ever shared with anyone. He kissed the top of her head without removing his eyes from the road and then slipped his hand to her shoulder, trailing his fingers over the fine hairs there, raising goose bumps on her skin.

Her hand slipped between his thighs and unzipped his pants.

"What are you doing?" he asked.

"Will you be able to concentrate on the road if I do this?" She gently bit at his earlobe as her hand reached past his zipper and into his boxers.

"Sure," he said, his breathing shallow.

She pulled out his penis and stroked it in a way that gave him tortuously slow, sweet pleasure as her lips nibbled at his neck and jaw line. Her strokes became faster, more insistent, and his breathing matched the pace.

It didn't take long. It'd been so long since anyone else had touched him like this, and he'd never been touched by her like this. Outside of his head anyway. Still, he came so quickly that he surprised them both. Tucking him back in and zipping up his pants, she gave him a quick kiss before snuggling against him again.

Her eyes had burned into his all night. She was something special. She had to get out of there and it was good she was going, but he knew he'd never forget about her. Never forget one thing about her or her red dress.

CHAPTER TWENTY-FIVE

Melody paced her room Wednesday morning—well, the room she'd come to think of as hers—while talking to Saeed. She didn't go into town to work at the garage that day because it was ostensibly her last day in Sweet Neck. She had sent Saeed the demo, sneaking off to the post office one day at lunchtime to do it. He'd called her to tell her he'd listened for once. Thankfully. He'd Googled the Rhyme Doctor and had been curious. Also thankfully, he liked what he'd heard.

"I know, Saeed, but getting him to come to this showcase might not be all that easy." Melody nibbled her lower lip. The showcase was now less than two weeks away. "My car is fixed now, and I've burned through all my excuses to stay here and if I brought it up to him now...I think he'd just get upset and refuse to come." She'd racked her brain for excuses to stay in town, but couldn't think of any that Austin might buy. No matter what she said, he'd probably be suspicious of her true motives for delaying her return to Atlanta.

Saeed's tone changed immediately. "Melody, I did not say anything about you being in the clear. This showcase is still your last chance."

"I know, I know." Melody pressed a hand against her forehead. Austin had trusted her last night. He'd opened up and shared things with her in ways that couldn't have been easy for him. She still hadn't processed what had happened the night before at Myrtle's or in Austin's truck. Now she was being asked to get Austin to do the impossible. She'd brought it on herself, sure, but still. "I just, I need some time to think."

"You do not have a lot of it."

"Thanks." Like she didn't realize that.

"Well, I have to go. Busy day ahead of me. I will see you at the showcase, and this Austin, or else I do not plan on seeing you again. We understand each other?"

"Perfectly." Melody flopped down onto the bed.

"Good. Because I will have some very important people with me. And if you make me look like an idiot in front of them, losing your job will not be the worst thing that has happened to you," he said. Like he needed any help making himself look like an idiot.

It took a lot of strength to hold back the smart aleck remark he'd begged for with that one. "Yeah."

She wrapped up her call and tossed her phone onto the bed. Pressing the heels of her palms to her forehead, she tried to think of ways to dig herself out of the mess she'd made.

#

Austin walked into the house, and she heard him clunking up the stairs in his heavy work boots. Her heart thumped harder with every step he took. She went out to meet him, and he grabbed her in the hallway near her room and wrapped his arms around her waist, lifting her off the ground. She forgot all about her conversation with Saeed and the stress it'd caused.

"Hi," he said, burying his face in her neck; his voice was muffled by her skin. He set her down, but kept his arms around her waist. Nothing had ever felt better than being this close to him did.

She laughed. "Hi." She turned to face him and pressed her forehead to his. "How was your day?" *What are we doing here? This can't possibly end well. I don't sleep with the label's artists.* She thought as his lips closed over hers, and her stomach quivered. She sank into his arms. All she knew was that his touches turned her into melted butter. They made her forget everything else in the world.

"It was good." He moved his hand slowly up and down her back. "Your car is all fixed up. New engine is in and ready to go."

"Oh." She tried to hide her disappointment.

"Does that mean you're leaving?" he asked.

"I don't want it to. At least not yet." She pressed her body against his. He groaned and shifted a little, but not before she felt the hard ridge of his erection against her stomach.

He pulled back a little. "You're going to have to eventually, though."

She kissed his lower lip. "I don't want to talk about that."

"This isn't a good idea."

Yeah. She knew that. Reaching up, she gave him a full kiss on the lips. "I don't want to talk about that, either."

He wrapped his arms around her and gave her a long, deep kiss. "You're incredible," he said between kisses. "This is all I think about ever since the first time we kissed."

She reached for him again, drunk on his kisses and touches. She had a problem. She was never going to be able to get enough of him.

He pushed one hand into her hair, and the other slipped under the hem of her skirt. His hand crept up her thigh while he smothered her in kisses. Pushing her head back slightly, he moved his lips down to her throat. She let out a low moan and pulled him closer. She wanted to take him into her room right that moment and bend her over, but everyone would be sitting down to dinner soon. As if to prove her point, Leigh Anne called up the stairs, telling them dinner would be ready soon and she could use some help getting it on the table.

They walked down the stairs side by side. She said, "You know, Donnie's not that bad of a guy."

"Yeah, maybe not to you."

"I hate seeing how you two treat each other. You're lucky to have each other, you know that? Family is important," Melody said, thinking of her own family.

"Speaking of families, you don't talk about yours much," Austin said.

"There's not much to say. It's been just me and my mother since my dad died. I was an only child, and my parents were only children, so I don't have aunts, uncles, or cousins." She stopped at the foot of the stairs, and he stood next to her.

"Tell me about your dad."

"He was a musician, too." She gave him a sad smile. "Jazz."

He squeezed her hand and kissed her forehead.

"Then I was married, and that obviously didn't work out. So I've always wanted a big family more than anything, but I've never gotten to have it. You have one, but at the same time, you don't. And it's because you're stubborn, both of you," Melody said.

"I'm sorry, but that's just the way things are between Donnie and me. Ain't never gonna change."

"Don't you want it to?" Melody asked as they walked toward the kitchen.

He shrugged. "Not particularly. If he wants to be an ass, fine with me. I don't care."

"The problem is this. I think you do care about your relationship with your brother. You may not want to, but you do." She slipped into the kitchen and left him outside of it, staring at the dining room table.

At dinner, they all talked about Melody's car being fixed and ready to go.

"So I guess you'll be leaving us soon, huh?" Leigh Anne asked, looking the way Melody felt about it. "We'll be sad to see you go. We've really enjoyed having you here."

"Thank you," Melody said, picking at her green beans. "I've enjoyed being here just as much if not more."

"When do you think you'll be heading out?" Leigh Anne asked.

"I don't know," Melody said truthfully with a sigh. She'd made a rent payment to her apartment complex online and transferred the money from savings to checking to cover it the other day, so she didn't have to rush back. She could live off her savings for a month or two to go before she really started to put a dent in her New Career reserves. Still, she needed to get back and start looking for a new job. Besides, she missed her mom and Jen. But leaving Sweet Neck meant leaving Austin. Or did it?

She glanced at across the table at him, and her face warmed when she realized he was staring right back at her. "I'll be leaving in a few days, I guess," she said. "I wish I didn't have to, though."

"So do we," Leigh Anne said, giving her a knowing smile. "So do we."

"Yeah, there's a lot to Sweet Neck I'm gonna miss," Melody said, looking across the room at nothing in particular, hoping she wouldn't give herself away if she didn't look at Austin while she spoke.

After dinner, Melody and Austin made out in her room like horny teenagers. He stripped her down to her panties, and they were dangerously close to finishing what they'd started last night. They would have to stop soon. No sleeping with the label's artists—no matter how sexy. Plus, there was still something they needed to talk about.

She pulled back for air and said, "What if you came with me?"

"What if I what? Huh?" Austin asked before pressing his lips to her neck. He teased her nipple with the pad of his thumb.

"I'm an A&R exec. You're a musician. It makes sense," she said, trying to warm him up to the idea of the showcase.

He stopped kissing her neck. "Ex-musician. Besides, there's the shop. My mom. The fact that I have no desire to ever leave Sweet Neck again," he said. He pulled away from her and sat up straight in the bed.

"You don't understand what I'm trying to say."

"I know perfectly well what you're trying to say," He laughed humorlessly. "I wasn't going to say anything, but I've heard of New Face records. That's the label Aphrodisia's signed with, right?" Aphrodisia was a German rapper who'd taken her name from the Greek goddess Aphrodite and the word "aphrodisiac."

Melody sighed. She'd hoped that wouldn't come up. "For now." Aphrodisia was threatening to break her contract, and unfortunately—for many reasons—she was the only thing keeping New Face afloat at the moment.

"So you want me to be a gimmick just like Aphrodisia, huh?"

"She's not a gimmick. The media's trying to make her into one because she's a novelty."

"Say whatever you want, I told you what I went through before. I don't want to be anybody's marketing ploy ever again."

"She's more than a marketing ploy. You don't see a female rapper of South American descent from Germany every day, sure. But she's got talent."

"Yeah? Well, novelty wears off. Trust me. I know." Austin ran a hand over his face.

"Austin, this won't be like before." She put her hand on the side of his face.

He chuckled. "The funny part is you actually believe you can control something like that. It's not something you can promise because it's not something you can know. You can't promise the world in a contract, Mel. No matter how much you'd like to."

"That's not the way I look at things." She moved closer to him on the bed. "For me, it's all about good music. Not genre or sub-genre or flash and dash or flash in the pans." She kissed his shoulder. "I want you to come back with me. We can build something great together. Just the two of us."

"Just the two of us, huh?" He gave her a disbelieving look. He slid off the bed and stood in front of it. "I think it's about time I go to bed."

"Just think about it, please."

"Good night, Melody."

"Night," she said, shaking her head. Yeah, this was going to be just as hard as she'd thought it was going to be.

CHAPTER TWENTY-SIX

Thursday, Melody convinced Austin to shut the shop down at noon because business was slow. She told him she wanted him to take her fishing because she'd never been. They headed out to the parking lot and got in his truck. He wasn't shy about glancing over to appreciate her calves and shoulders. She wore a pale pink cotton halter-top and jeans rolled partially up her calves.

Once they got into the truck, Austin plunked a straw hat over her head. She laughed and reached up to adjust the hat.

"It's good for you," he said, grinning. His hand lingered on the side of the hat. "Keep the sun off."

"Thank you." She put a hand on his arm. He'd left his coveralls back at the garage. He now wore khaki shorts and a blue T-shirt along with a beat-up pair of old loafers and a baseball cap.

"Welcome." He kissed her cheek before pulling the hat low over her forehead. "We'd better get down to the river." He ran his fingers over the side of her face, touched the backs of them to her collarbone.

"What's the rush?" She wanted him to move his fingers lower, but he took them away from her instead.

"If we don't get going now, we might not make it there," he said, giving her a hungry look as he put the key in the ignition and turned it.

She scooted closer to him on the bench seat. "Is that a promise or a threat?" Maybe she didn't want to make it there. She started to lose sight of her goal while sitting so close to him, breathing in the strong, clean scent of the soap he'd used to clean up a little while earlier.

He put the truck in reverse and backed out of his spot. "Little bit of both." He put the truck in gear before resting a hand on her knee.

"Good," she said.

He moved his hand halfway up her thigh.

When they got to the river and saw Donnie's SS low rider, Austin exhaled slowly through his nose. "You're not gonna let this thing alone, are you?"

"No, I'm not going to give up on you two if that's what you mean," she said. "Now, you gonna teach me how to fish or not?"

"Let's go," Austin said. He hopped out of the truck. Melody hopped out of her side. Before she could offer to help, Austin had grabbed both poles and the tackle box. They headed down a dirt path from the parking area to the river.

Donnie was sitting on the riverbank with his own fishing supplies when they got there. He leaned back on the rock he was sitting on and said, "Well, well."

"Thought you were getting rid of me for the rest of the day, didn't you?" Austin said. He reached behind him for Melody's hand, and she gave it.

Donnie lifted his eyebrows well over his black sunglasses. "You invited him." Donnie had enlisted in the marines for his first few years after high school, and he said that now he couldn't stand to wear any kind of sunglasses except for plain black ones because that was all he'd ever worn while in the corps.

"I did," Melody said.

HIS MELODY

"I should have known," Donnie muttered.

"You two need to stop shutting each other out. Do you know what it's doing to your family? Your mother?"

"Look, Melody," Donnie said. "I know you mean well, but what happened between us…it's done, and there's no going back." Donnie snapped the line on his pole from the water. "There's just no 'fixing' us up and letting bygones be bygones. He's a snake, blood or not, and I'd just as soon as not have anything to do with a snake."

"What if we just sit here and fish together? You two don't have to say anything to each other. We'll just all three fish."

Donnie stopped reeling his line in. "Yeah, well, I guess too much talking'd scare the fish off anyway."

Melody turned to Austin. "So show me how to do this."

He grinned. "First, you'll need one of these." He handed her the rod. Then he showed her how to bait the hook and cast the line. After that he said, "Now, if you actually catch anything, I'll show you the rest."

"Ha ha." Melody rolled her eyes, but she was laughing as she did it. She sat on the broad, flat rock next to Donnie. Austin sat on her other side. The three of them sat there, waiting for something to bite and listening to insects buzz by and birds chatter off in the distance. Occasionally, Donnie took a swig of beer; he'd brought his red cooler down to the river with him. He offered a beer to Melody, but she declined it. Austin sat hunched over, watching the river, with his mouth set in a firm line. She would've loved to know what he was thinking, but didn't dare ask.

"I think I got something," Melody said. The rod started vibrating in her hand.

"Hold the rod steady," Donnie said.

"Start reeling it in. Don't give him too much slack," Austin said.

The two men started firing directions at her about how to reel in her catch in between arguing with each other, and she couldn't make sense out of any of it because they were both jabbering at the same time and often saying contradictory things.

Austin had moved behind her after she stood in order to get a better grip on her pole. He put his strong arms on the outside of hers and guided her as he spoke. Together, they reeled in a decent-sized, extremely slimy catfish.

"I did it!" Melody shouted. "Gross," she said after getting her first close up look at the bug-eyed gray-brown fish.

"Be careful of the whiskers," Austin said.

"I'm going to let you handle the whiskers and everything else," she said, handing him the pole.

He laughed. "I thought you wanted to fish."

"Yeah, well, it's all fun until you actually catch one," she said.

"Is that your philosophy about other things as well?" he asked. He took the fish off the hook. It flopped around on the ground.

"Throw it back. Please," she said.

He did as asked.

"To answer your earlier question, not always," she said.

He wiped his hands on his shorts. "Good to know."

"That's the question she should be asking you, stud," Donnie said from where he sat on the rock. Austin remained standing, but cast his line back into the water. He clenched his rod, and his jaw locked.

They fished in silence for a while. Eventually, Donnie said, "You never told her about Kristen, I reckon," Donnie said.

"Not really," Austin said quietly.

Melody remembered the name going with the cashier with the sad eyes in Zip's Supermarket. Austin had mentioned her that night in the bar, too.

"So why don't you tell her?"

"Donnie was crazy about Kristen, but she had eyes for me."

Donnie mumbled something unintelligible under his breath.

Austin continued with the story like Donnie hadn't made a sound. "He asked her out, and they went out a couple times. Then she asked me to one of those Sadie-Hawkins dances."

"We dated, and you stole her," Donnie said. "If you're going to tell it, tell it right."

"I didn't steal her."

"Yeah, go right on telling your lies like you have for the past twenty-nine years." "Oh, Lord." Austin continued, "Just so we can get on with this, let's say I stole her."

"You did." Donnie jerked his line from the water. "And you broke her heart by cheating on her with Lil and then you ran off to New York City and left them both behind," Donnie said, nostrils flaring.

Austin looked down at his hands.

"She was never the same after that." Donnie shook his head in disgust. "I loved her with everything I had, but—didn't matter. Wouldn't even look at me after he broke her heart." Donnie glared at Austin before continuing. "She married the first guy who came along after Austin. She has four kids and a husband, but she ain't happy. She's miserable. I hear she's a drunk, I don't know if that part's true, but whether it is or not, all her misery is 'cause of you," Donnie said. He glowered at his brother.

Austin stared into the river, still grasping his fishing pole.

"I don't know why Dad left you everything. You're such a fuck-up."

"I don't know why, either, but he did."

"You know you should have given me and Avery our due and gotten the hell out of here. Why'd you come back here and mess everything up for everybody?"

"Funny. I came back here to try and fix everything. Obviously, that didn't work out." Austin glanced at his brother, his upper lip curled in a sneer.

Melody said, "Donnie, are you happy with Nina?"

Donnie glanced at her sideways. "That's a strange question to ask. And the answer is yes of course."

Melody nodded, looking down at the sun glinting off the red metal of her rod before turning back to Donnie. "Do you love her?"

"The answer, once again, is yes. Of course."

"Then would it be fair to say that things worked out for the best?"

Donnie didn't say anything.

Melody reeled in her line and set her pole on the ground beside Donnie's. "I'm a firm believer that everything happens for a reason." A shiver went through her spine as she remembered her conversation with Blanche yet again. Either the woman was really wise as well as a little crazy or she really did have the gift of foresight. In any case, Melody had a feeling she'd been right about Melody being there to help heal old wounds.

Donnie pulled her out of her reverie by speaking. "Are you now? You really believe that? So you're telling me to turn the old cheek, huh? So he can do something else shady to me? Steal from me yet again? Who knows what he'd steal this time?"

"I don't want to steal anything from you, Donnie," Austin said quietly. "I also don't want to feel like I'm paying for the same dumb old mistakes over and over. You know." Austin whipped his head around so that he was facing his brother. "You act like you've never made a mistake, never done anything dumb in your whole life."

"Have you?" Melody asked. "Ever made a mistake, Donnie?"

Donnie grinned, sat back on the rock, and popped open a fresh beer that he'd taken out of the cooler a few moments earlier. "There was this one time. During basic training. I got the bright idea to sneak a girl back to my room at the barracks even though we were pretty much on lockdown at the time." Donnie laughed to himself. "Whew, boy, did I pay for that one."

Melody grinned. "You're done paying for it now, though, right?"

"Yeah, yeah, I see where you're going with this one, Mel." Donnie stood up and stretched. "I gotta take a whiz. I'll be back in a sec." He walked off toward the woods.

Melody scooted closer to Austin on the rock. He put down his pole and put his arm around her shoulders. She turned his face up to his. He gave her a gentle peck on the lips.

"I done good, huh?" she asked.

He laughed. "I reckon." He pulled her closer. "I'm going to miss you like crazy, you know that?"

"You could always come with me," she said. "Have you thought any more about what I said?"

"And live in Aphrodisia's shadow?" he said in a joking, good-natured tone that had a bit of an edge to it. "Nah. No thanks, babe."

"But you wouldn't—"

"Don't ruin the moment," he murmured before capturing her lips in a full, searing kiss. He moved his hand under the hem of her shirt, pressing his rough, calloused hand to the hot, soft skin of her flat abdomen. She moaned and leaned into the kiss. All coherent thought left her brain. She was going to miss him like crazy, too. All because he was still being stubborn. At least she got him to budge on one thing. Maybe that was a sign of things to come. She could only hope.

CHAPTER TWENTY-SEVEN

After they left the river, Melody and Austin took the long way home. She watched the trees and farms passing by the window on her side of the truck.

Ahead, she saw a shed-like building with a low roof. A hand-painted sign on the side of the road leading toward it advertised fresh produce for sale.

"Austin, can we stop there? At the produce stand?" Melody asked. She loved visiting the huge farmer's market back home in DeKalb. There were no farmer's markets in Sweet Neck—no need for them when almost everybody who wasn't a farmer had at least a small vegetable garden patch in their backyards.

"Sure," Austin said, slowing down the truck. He pulled off the road several yards away from the building, which wasn't far from a gas station.

"I want to pick up a few things for your mother and the house," Melody said, opening her door. She hurried over to the stand.

"Hello," an older man with a shock of white hair and a weathered face gave her a partially toothless smile.

"Hi," she said, returning the smile. Her eyes roamed over the bright oranges, yellows, reds, and greens of the tomatoes, squash, peppers, cabbages, and other vegetables on display. Over to the side were watermelons, cantaloupes, strawberries, and even a few bunches of grapes.

"Hi, Gene," said Austin, walking up behind her.

"Austin Holt! Good to see you, boy!" Gene said, holding out his hand. Austin grabbed it and shook. "How's your mom and them?"

"Everybody's good. How are your wife and Beverley?" Austin said.

"Good, good. I don't know who's more stubborn is all."

Austin laughed. He leaned in and murmured to Melody, "Beverley is his goat." Melody nodded and laughed, loving having him so close.

"Who's your friend?" Gene asked.

"I'm sorry, don't know where my manners went. Gene, this is Melody. She's from Atlanta, but she's staying here for a while. Melody, this is Gene. One of the best farmers there ever was and all-around good guy. Knows his way around a tiller motor, too," Austin said.

Melody smiled and shook Gene's hand. She chatted with him while she picked out her fruits and vegetables, but something kept nagging at the back of her mind about the way Austin had introduced her. It made her feel like her time there was so temporary. Well, she guessed it was, but still. Was he in a hurry to get rid of her?

Back in the truck, Melody set her paper bag full of squash, collard greens, and peppers between her feet. Austin set the cantaloupes they'd bought on the seat between them. She reached across the seat for his hand. He took hers and brought it to his lips, kissing it. She smiled as he started up the truck.

"Austin, what's gonna happen between us when I go back?" She chose not to bring up the music again yet. She had to mention the showcase soon, though. She was running out of time.

He dropped her hand and gently patted it before pulling onto the road. "Melody, I'm grateful for what you did today.

I want you to know that. But it's best if you forget about me when you go. Leave me behind in Sweet Neck where I belong. Forgotten." She could almost hear the, "by everybody" he left off the end of that statement.

"Why?"

"Haven't you been listening? I'm poison to the things I love. I destroy everything I touch."

Her heart pounded at his choice of words. Did that mean he loved her? Regardless of what he'd meant, he had no problem letting her walk out of his life. Ignoring her unsteady, sweaty palms, she said, "Is this about Kristen? Or Isadora?"

"Both. Everybody. Just—I'm done making a mess of things, okay?"

"So you plan to die old, shriveled up, and alone."

He smiled and shrugged. "I dunno. I might get a dog."

"Very funny, Austin. I'm trying to be serious here."

"So am I."

"You know you're not responsible for what happened to Kristen, right? She made her own choices she has to live with just like you did. Like everybody does." She reached across the seat and patted his knee. "What happened to Isadora isn't your fault, either."

He didn't say anything, but he did put his hand over the hand she had resting on his knee.

CHAPTER TWENTY-EIGHT

Friday evening, Austin and Donnie went over to Regan's after dinner to help her bale hay and make some repairs to her shelving and hooks in the tack room.

Donnie laid claim to the brand new John Deere as soon as they got there. Austin, ever the patient older brother—or at least he tried to be—walked alongside and kept watch over the baling.

Back in the barn, while they were putting away the bales, Donnie said, "You and Regan get along okay, huh?"

"Yep," Austin said with a grunt as he hefted a bale of hay above his head. Donnie grabbed it and stuck it in its proper place in the loft. Austin climbed down so that he could go get another one.

"I guess if she can forgive you, I can, too."

"Huh?" Austin almost dropped the bale of hay he was carrying.

"I've been thinking a lot about what Melody said when we went fishing," Donnie said.

"Yeah?" Austin tossed the bale up to his brother who grabbed it and stuck it up there with the rest of them.

"Yeah, well, I guess she's right about a lot of things." Donnie peered down at him from his perch in the loft. "You shouldn't let her get away from you."

Austin ran the back of his hand across his forehead, wiping sweat from it. "You're just saying that because you want the shop."

Donnie laughed. "All a part of my plan." He sat so that his legs dangled over the edge of the loft. "Seriously, though, she's good for you. Even I can see that. You've been happier—more peaceful or something—since she showed up than you have in a long time."

"Yeah, well, she's from a different world than I am." A fast-paced, public world. One he had no desire to go back to. The part of him that wanted any of that—the Grayson part—was dead. And good riddance.

"Not so different," Donnie said.

"It'll be better for everyone if she goes." He carefully chose his words, avoiding the phrase, If I just let her go.

"You'll regret it," Donnie said.

"How do you know?"

"Oh believe me. I know a lot about regret," Donnie said with a small grimace. His eyes fell away from Austin's. "There's so much I didn't say to Dad at the end."

"I think he knew all the important things. Y'all were best friends." Donnie had a much better relationship with their father than he ever had.

"He wanted so much for us to make up at the end. You and me," Donnie said. "You know our last fight was about that? The last one before he had the—before he went to the hospital that last time."

"Oh," Austin said.

"Yeah."

It was silent in the barn for a while, each brother lost in his own thoughts.

Then Donnie jumped to his knees and clapped his hands. "Let's get a move on. These bales ain't gonna walk themselves up the ladder and into this loft. And we haven't even gotten to the repairs in the tack room yet."

"Right," Austin said. He climbed down the ladder and went to fetch another bale. His brother's words stuck with him for the rest of the night. He made a mental note to re-read the last letter his father had written him when he got home.

#

There was an orchard behind the Holts' house. Peaches had been grown there long ago, but nobody had planted anything there in years besides a couple of junk trucks. Leigh Anne and her mother and her mother's mother had planted signs of magnolia trees back there over the years as well, and they were scattered throughout the land where peach trees used to grow. Leigh Anne wouldn't tolerate the junk trucks anywhere near her yard, so her boys compromised by keeping them toward the back of the old orchard.

That was where Melody found Austin at dusk. He hadn't come inside after he'd gotten home from baling hay. Apparently, he'd gone straight out to the truck.

Austin sat in a rusted out Ford Bronco that had been red at some point in its long life. It was up on cinder blocks. He was staring out into the reds and purples of the sky at the place where the sun had set earlier.

"Hi," she said.

"Hey," he said before swigging his beer.

"I didn't hear you come in the house. How'd you get a beer?"

"Donnie and I stopped at the gas station on our way home," Austin said.

Melody stared at the frame of the truck. It was missing its driver's side door. "What happened to the door?"

Austin shrugged. "Was like this when we got it."

"How do you keep the rain and," she shuddered, "critters out?"

"Tarp." Austin grinned and pointed at the tarp that he'd rolled up and flung over the roof of the truck.

"Oh."

"Wanna sit with me a minute?" He set down his beer between his legs on the floorboard and held out his hands. She put her hands in his, and he pulled her across his lap and into the truck. He tucked her next to his side and picked up his beer again.

"Hm." She picked at the cracked vinyl on the dashboard. "Talk about vintage."

"Dad and I were fixing this thing up when I was in high school," Austin said, shocking her with information about his past that she didn't have to pull out of him. When I ran off…he just parked it out here in the old orchard and forgot about it. Gave up on it." He gulped some of his beer.

Melody put her arms around him and hugged him to her. They sat there for a while, holding each other. The only sounds were the chirps of crickets and the calls of bullfrogs from a nearby pond. She closed her eyes and breathed in the cool yet heavy evening air.

"I've been thinking a lot about what all you've said." Austin rested the side of his face against hers. "And all you've done for us since you've been here."

"And?" She pulled back a little and looked at him.

"Thanks." He kissed the tip of her nose, and she inhaled the beer on his breath. Then he kissed her mouth. Beer had never tasted so good. When he pulled back, she put a hand on his thigh and leaned across his lap. Resting her back across his thighs, and propping herself up slightly on her elbows, she looked up at him. He stared down at her. She tried to memorize his face. The strong, angular jaw. Long, slightly crooked nose.

She missed home, but she couldn't imagine being in a place where Austin wasn't.

"You didn't have to do any of that," he said.

"But I wanted to."

"One of the many great things about you." He searched her face with his perfect green eyes. It seemed like he was looking for something he couldn't quite find.

"What?" she asked, nestling her head against the thick, muscled wall of his chest. She felt his hand move to her hip. His fingers slipped under her shirt and inside her jeans to caress the skin just under the waistband.

"I had a good talk with my brother while we were baling hay for Regan." He pulled her closer. "I think Donnie and I are going to be okay now. Thanks to you." He said, "I've spilled my guts and all my family drama to you, but you haven't done the same."

"What are you talking about?" she asked.

"Tell me about your parents," he said, his thumb moving back and forth over the skin at the base of her spine. "You don't talk about them much."

They listened to the bullfrogs chirp as she tried to get her thoughts together, decide what she wanted to say. She smiled. "My dad was a saxophone player. He was really good, too. He played with his band in this jazz band in the late seventies and early eighties. That's how he met my mom. She was in the audience one night and…they couldn't keep their eyes off each other. He asked her out afterwards. They dated for a few months before getting married." She wondered briefly if her mom had felt the same thing she felt when she looked at Austin. Funny, she'd never felt this with her ex. She'd thought she loved him at the beginning, but maybe she was wrong about that. She certainly hadn't loved him at the end.

Wait. Did that mean she loved Austin?

"So they knew right away, huh?" Austin said.

"Yeah." She snuggled closer to him. "Dad was great. He used to play for me almost every night when he was home and not out on the road touring. He let me sit in on the band's practices even though mom fussed because it was past my bedtime." She tried to laugh, but the sound got stuck in her throat. "I was a Daddy's girl. That's for sure." That was enough. It was still painful to go back into those memories even though years had passed. Her dad died when she was a senior in high school, but talking about it made it seem like it'd happened yesterday.

He kissed the top of her head and rubbed her shoulder. "So he had his own band, huh? What was the name?"

"Rapture," she said faintly.

"Oh yeah. I heard of them."

"Well, not too many people did," she said bitterly. "Dad got angry that the band wasn't taking off the way he wanted it to. The way they deserved to. They were really good. The angrier he got, the more he drank." She took a deep breath. "Another group started copying their style and sound. A group that already had a recording contract with a major label. Dad wanted to fight them in court, but the rest of the guys didn't think it was worth it. So the band started to fall apart, and so did my parents' marriage."

"I'm sorry." He pulled her close her and stroked the center of her back.

"They got divorced when I was twelve. By the time I was seventeen, he'd drunk himself to death. Mom never really got over it. She loved him even if she couldn't stand the way he acted. She told me to never fall in love with a dreamer and that becoming a dreamer was even worse." She sighed and looked up at him. "She wanted me to be safe. To her, that meant practical. Do something that's going to bring you a sure paycheck, she says. Find a man who can provide you with security. That's who she thought my ex was. She was devastated about the divorce. Her number one favorite thing to remind me of is, dreams don't pay bills."

"That's why you're afraid to go into business for yourself as a music manager."

"No, it's not," she said, resenting the fact that he sounded like he had her all figured out. "I told you. I'm just not prepared for that financially."

"It's funny." He chuckled. "You keep telling me how it's a waste if I don't follow my dreams. But fear paralyzes you from following your own."

"You're a sure thing," she said. "Bianca saw it. You're sexy, talented. You have everything it takes to become a star. Anybody who knows anything about music would be able to see it. It's not the same thing."

"Hm," was all he said.

She was about to let him have it for sitting over there all smug, acting like he had all the answers, when he kissed her again. With his lips moving over hers, she forgot to be angry at him. He pulled back, and they sat there smiling at each other in what was left of the day's light as twilight faded into dusk. He was all she wanted in so many ways. After the past few days, she couldn't understand how he couldn't see things the way she did. She could barely force herself to think the most horrible thought—that maybe the days they'd spent together hadn't had the effect on him they'd had on her.

"I don't want to go back without you." She put her hand low on his jaw. He pulled her to a sitting position on his lap.

He covered her mouth with his, and soon she couldn't think of anything besides him and how good it felt to be in his arms.

CHAPTER TWENTY-NINE

Saturday evening, Austin and Melody went back to the shop after eating dinner at Rose's Diner because he'd left some papers there that he wanted to look over that weekend.

Austin had wanted to take her out to dinner, just the two of them, because she didn't have many nights left in town, and they wouldn't get time alone during all of them. The Holt family wanted to take her out to a farewell dinner Monday night because that was Vernon's last night in town for a while; he had to leave for a run on Tuesday. On Tuesday night, Melody's last night in town, everyone wanted to throw her wanted to throw her a small going-away party. Leigh Anne, Avery, and Nina were doing most of the planning for that. It was top-secret apparently. She couldn't get many details out of them about it.

On Wednesday, she was supposed to be heading out of town. That would put her at home just in time to meet with Saeed and prepare for the showcase—or showdown as she'd been calling it in her head—on Saturday night.

She didn't really know what she was preparing for anymore, though. Austin seemed pretty dead set against going back with her, and he was definitely against the idea of a music career, and so the showcase was most likely out of the question. Still, she had to try. Maybe there was some way she could persuade him to see things her way.

"Thanks for dinner," Melody said as they walked into the office. "The food was really good."

"I wish I could take the credit, but Rose's is always good," he said. He picked up the folder. "Well, I guess that's it."

She walked over to him and trailed her fingers up his bare arm, tickling his skin. He tossed the folder back on the desk and put his arm around her waist; his touch was hot through the thin fabric of her sleeveless blouse. She shivered even though the air conditioning had been turned off hours ago and the day's heat lingered into dusk.

"I want to ask you something," she said. "But I'm afraid of how you might react."

In answer, he covered her lips with hers and pulled her closer, squeezing her waist. She moaned, responding enthusiastically to the kiss. He left one hand on her waist and ran the other through her hair. She pushed her knee between his thighs and he backed against the wall behind the desk, bringing her with him.

"This is what I want all the time," she said between kisses.

"Then stay," he murmured while moving his lips from her mouth to her neck and then to the border between her low-cut blouse and her skin. He made his way up to her neck again before pressing slow, sweet kisses against her collarbone.

His hands found their way under her blouse. He cupped her breasts through the lacy fabric of her bra while his tongue explored her throat. She threw her head back, wrapped a leg around his waist, and enjoyed the slow, sweet torture of his touch. Putting her hands on the back of his head, she directed his kisses lower until she felt his teeth close gently around her nipple through two layers of fabric. She moaned his name softly. His hand dipped into the waistband of her skirt. She pressed against him, and he pulled his hand free and jerked the skirt up to her waist.

He rubbed small circles against the front of her panties, pushing the fabric into skin that had been wet for him since dinner. She gasped, pushing closer, grinding herself into his fingers, needing to feel his touch.

"Don't leave," he said before biting at her ear lobe.

At that moment, she couldn't imagine being anywhere but there. She pushed closer and closer. Soon, she felt waves of pleasure washing over her. When it was over, she slumped against his chest. He started to move, but she shook her head and slipped her hands down to his belt.

"We have to get back," he said reluctantly, but made no further attempts to move toward the door.

"Do we?" She unfastened his belt and unzipped his pants.

"I guess we have a few minutes," Austin said, his voice low and husky.

She pulled out his rock solid penis. She still hadn't felt it inside of her. She wanted it so badly she was aching and wet with desire. She slid down his body, massaging his balls as she did so. He let out a low, guttural groan.

She slid her mouth over the hot shaft of skin, sucking on it rhythmically. He grabbed the back of her head with one hand and braced himself against the wall with the other.

"Where did you learn to do that?" he whispered before encouraging her to do more of it. Pushing the head of his penis against the back of her throat, she moaned, knowing the vibrations would drive him crazy. She grabbed his butt with one hand and used the other to cradle and stroke the fleshy, vulnerable skin under his penis until he surrendered to the strokes of her tongue and hand with a strangled cry and a shudder.

She stood and tucked him back in before zipping up his pants.

"Now, what did you want to talk about?" he asked, his eyes unfocused; he looked and sounded dazed.

Figuring it would be hard to catch him in a better mood, she said, "There's a showcase in Atlanta next week." She kissed him, but he didn't kiss back.

"And you want me to go," he said.

"I want us to talk about it," she said.

He adjusted his pants and buckled his belt. Grabbing the folder off his desk once again, he said, "You ready to go?"

She followed him from the office. "If you would just let me tell you about it, you'd see that this could be such a huge opportunity for you."

"For you, you mean," Austin said. He didn't say anything else until they were back in the truck. Then he turned to her with a mixture of hurt and anger in his eyes. "That's the only reason you want me to come back with you, isn't it? I'm a commodity to you." He leaned in close enough to kiss, but he clearly didn't have kissing on his mind. The sallow glow from a nearby streetlight cut across his chiseled jaw line. "You're just like Bianca."

"No, Austin. That's not the only reason. Over these past few weeks, I've come to care about you so much." She put a hand on the side of his face. He pulled away from her and started up the truck.

"If that were true, you'd understand why I don't want to go to that showcase or have anything to do with your record company or anyone else's."

"I don't have a record company," she said, thinking of how nice it would be if she did—how different everything would be. She wouldn't run her company anything like New Face was being run because New Face was being run right into the ground.

"Well, the one you represent, sold out to, however you want to put it," he said.

"Okay, Austin, okay," she snapped. "Fine." She had no idea what she was going to tell Saeed. Worse than that, she had jeopardized what might be her last few days ever with Austin.

She looked across the seat at Austin. Everything she wanted was so close that she could reach out and touch it. Instead, she was going to have to watch it all slip through her fingers.

CHAPTER THIRTY

Sunday, after church, Melody went with Leigh Anne to run errands in town. When they got out of Leigh Anne's truck at the grocery store, Melody saw Blanche across the street, outside of the bank, weeping loudly and dramatically. A much younger man—the tall, dark, and handsome type—stood next to her gesturing in a way that indicated he was trying to reason with her about something.

Leigh Anne followed her gaze and said, "Well. I wonder what it is this time."

"Do you know that man who's with her?" Melody asked.

"That's her grandson, Remy." Leigh Anne put a hand on her hip and rocked back on her heels. "Every so often, he comes into town from Louisiana to check on her."

"I'm going over there for a minute," Melody said. "I'll meet you inside."

"You don't want to get involved in all that."

"I'll just be a second."

Leigh Anne gave her a wary look.

"I won't be long," Melody said. "Promise."

"Okay," Leigh Anne said with a labored sigh. "I'll see you in a few minutes." Leigh Anne put extra emphasis on the last couple of words.

"I'm right behind you."

Leigh Anne threw her a look.

"Almost," Melody said.

Leigh Anne headed for Zip's, and Melody went across the street to Blanche and Remy.

"Blanche, what's wrong?" Melody asked.

"Oh, ma chère. It's terrible. This old brute wants to take me away from here." She smacked at the young man's hand as he attempted to take her arm.

"I'm not an old brute," the man said in a Cajun accent that was almost as thick as Blanche's. "I'm Remy, her grandson," Remy said, sticking out a hand for Melody to shake. He smiled, exposing dazzlingly white teeth.

Melody took his hand and returned the smile. "Melody."

"It's not that I mind the going, no not that at all. It's where he's taking me. Ask him where he taking me, chère," Blanche said. She grabbed fretfully at the light blue scarf she wore over her gray hair. "Go on, ask him."

"I'm taking her back to Louisiana," Remy supplied without further prompting. He leaned close in a conspirator-like way and said, "Grand-maman is getting a little too old for all this nonsense, and I think she's gettin' a little senile, too."

"He gonna put me in one of them old nursing homes, chère. A home! Don't nobody last long in one of them things." She sniffed indignantly before laying a cold look on her grandson. "To think." She started muttering under her breath.

"You see..." Remy let his voice trail off and stared helplessly in his grandmother's direction.

"You don't care nothing at all about me, you don't," Blanche said. She stared up at him as his height required her to. She balled her small hands into fists at her sides.

"I'm taking you home with me because I do care," Remy said in a tight voice; his strained patience was evident in his tone. "It's not a nursing home, grand-maman. You know that. It's an assisted living facility close to where Marie and I live."

"Marie is his wife," Blanche said. "She's a nice person. She don't go around terrorizing her elders." She shook her head at Remy. "Should be ashamed of yourself is what you ought to be.

"Grand-maman, I can't leave you here," Remy said, running a hand over his face and letting it rest at his mouth. He looked as if he were at the end of his rope.

"Aw, get on out of here. Wait for me in the car, and I'll be over in a minute." She pointed to a burgundy sedan. "I gotta say goodbye to my friend here first." She nodded at Melody.

Remy didn't look so sure.

Blanche gave him a little tap on the arm. "Well go on. It ain't like I can run. You catch me before I get out the parking lot good. You just grabbed all my little money out the bank. Where would I go if I could run?"

"Grand-maman—"

"I know, I know. Go on now. You leave me alone for a minute, and I'll go with you after that and won't even put up a fight."

Throwing his hands up in resignation, Remy said, "Okay." He turned to Melody. "It was nice meeting you, even if briefly and under these..." He glanced at his grandmother. "Circumstances."

Melody smiled. "Nice to meet you, too, Remy."

Remy walked to the car, and Blanche put a hand on Melody's arm.

"The reason I say I don't mind the going even if that old brute is taking me away." Blanche squeezed Melody's arm. "The reason I say that is my work here is done."

"Oh?" Melody glanced over at Remy. He sat in the car, shaking his head and gesturing wildly while talking into his cell phone.

"You brought them brothers back together." Blanche nodded. "I was here for you, and you were here for them," she said. "You still are."

Melody looked down at Blanche, and the older woman winked at her.

"You know it's true." Blanche nodded slowly. "There's only one thing left to do. You know what that is, too."

"I'm not sure I do," Melody said.

"Don't you give up on dat boy. He still needs you. In here." Blanche put a small, papery hand over her heart. "You know that well as I do."

Melody was going to miss this woman. Odd but unforgettable. "Okay, Blanche."

"Oh, of course you'll never forget old Blanche. Nobody ever do."

Melody gave her head a little shake. Surely the old woman couldn't read minds?

"Now I got to get out of here now before that old brute grandson of mine has a fit."

"I'm glad I got a chance to meet you," Melody said.

"Of course you did. That's what I was doing here the whole time, I keep trying to tell you. Waiting on you to show up," Blanche said. She hobbled forward a little.

"Let me help you to the car." Melody offered her arm.

"Naw, chère, I'm gonna be just fine. I ain't that bad off yet." She took a few more steps forward before turning to face Melody once again and saying, "You two have a safe trip back now."

"Two?" Melody echoed, slightly confused. Maybe Blanche really was becoming senile.

Blanche's face turned grave. "If you don't take that boy away from here with you, I fear the future for both of you. I see a terrible storm headed your way." She shook a warning finger. "Some kind of terrible."

Melody nodded. What could she say to that?

"Bye now. Remember what I said to you. All of it."

"Bye. I will," Melody said. Not like that would get it to make any more sense to her. She watched as Blanche hobbled toward her grandson's car. Remy got out of the car and opened the passenger side door. He tried to help his grandmother into the car, but she slapped his hand away and settled into it at her own pace.

Once Melody found Leigh Anne in Zip's, Leigh Anne asked what had taken so long.

"Just saying goodbye," Melody said with a shrug.

"Oh, is she going somewhere?" Leigh Anne asked as she studied the label on the back of a can of refried beans.

"Her grandson is taking her back to Louisiana with him."

"It's about time." Leigh Anne tossed the can of beans into her basket.

"He thinks she's senile."

Leigh Anna frowned a little. "He's probably right. That poor dear."

Melody followed Leigh Anne down the aisle, trying to decide if she agreed with that assessment of Blanche's mental state or not. Blanche might have been a little strange, but everything she'd said had made a great deal of sense, and she'd ended up being right about a lot of things in the end. What if Blanche continued to be right? She'd mentioned something about a storm headed Melody's way.

She didn't need another storm in her life..

She felt a small shiver; Blanche's last words stuck in her mind. Those and thoughts of Austin.

CHAPTER THIRTY-ONE

Monday night, Melody, the Holts, Nina, and Regan went to a small diner for her farewell dinner. It was no Rose's Diner, and it didn't quite compare to the meals Leigh Anne cooked either, but the food was still very good. Especially the chicken fried pork chop, which Nina had insisted she try. Austin shared a piece of his steak with her, and it was so tender, it melted in her mouth.

She and Austin had come to an unspoken and fragile truce. The number one rule of it was that she wasn't allowed to mention one word about music or record labels. The fact that she was running out of time made things worse. She dreaded the phone call she had to make to Saeed the next day. She'd promised to call him on Tuesday, and she knew better than to break that promise. That and her last conversation with Blanche kept nagging at her.

"I want to take you somewhere tonight, after dinner," Austin whispered from where he sat next to her.

She grinned and whispered back, "You do, huh?"

"I have a going-away present for you." His green eyes locked on hers in a blazing gaze.

"Okay." She managed to keep the smile on her face, but the words "going-away" made her stomach sink. He really wasn't coming with her. "You sure my car is fixed? You really don't need more time to work on it?"

"What, you doubting my automotive skills?" Austin asked, eyebrows raised in a playful fashion.

"No. Just wishful thinking."

He reached over, grabbed her hand, and gave it a squeeze.

From across the table, Regan said, "Melody, I remember you saying something about wanting to learn how to ride when you first got here. I know you don't have much time left, but how about you come over tomorrow morning and I'll give a crash course? Horse riding 101."

Melody nodded. "I'd like that. Thanks, Regan." She hoped no actual crashing would be involved. But she was active. She weight trained. How hard could it be?

"I'll drop you at Regan's place on my way into the shop tomorrow morning," Austin said.

"Okay," Melody said. So she was finally going to get to learn how to ride a horse. Everything felt so final all of a sudden. She put her hand on Austin's thigh as if keeping physical contact with him could keep her from losing him in just a few short days. She'd never fallen for someone so quickly. The thought of being torn away from him was nearly unbearable. Austin slipped his hand beneath the table and squeezed hers.

She knew falling for one of the label's artists was forbidden, but none of it really mattered. She was almost certain she'd never convince him to come to Atlanta. She was leaving, and he was staying. Nothing going on in her melting heart mattered one bit.

Across the table, Regan started talking about one of her tractors and something that was wrong with it. She gestured across the table with her fork and said, "Hey Austin, you know anything about tractor motors?"

"Little bit," Austin said.

"You think if you came by and took a look at this one, you could do something with it?"

"Might could," Austin said.

"Thanks," Regan said.

Melody grinned.

He grabbed her side and then let his hand rest on her hip. "What?"

"I'm going to miss the way you talk," she said, a smile hovering at the corners of her mouth. "That's all."

"You better miss more than that about me." He pulled her chair closer to his.

"Of course I will," she said, squeezing his knee. Her smile faded.

CHAPTER THIRTY-TWO

After dinner, Austin drove Melody to an inn on the edge of town. He drove to the back of the property where a row of small cottages stood and parked in front of one of them. The red door had a gold number three on it. When he killed the headlights, the walkway in front of the bungalow remained illuminated by hanging lanterns that'd been placed on either side of it.

"What is this?" she asked.

"You'll have to come inside and see." He got out of the truck, walked around to her side, and opened the door. She stepped out, standing next to him in the small parking lot facing the cottages. The distant, quickly fading rays of the sun gave everything a dusky golden glow. He slipped a big, strong hand around her waist and guided her up the walkway and over to the red door. He took a key out of his pocket, unlocked the door, and shoved it open.

"Austin," she murmured.

He left her to admire the room while he struck matches and lit the candles that had been strategically placed around it. She noted an ice bucket with a bottle of champagne in it. A silver bowl full of chocolate covered strawberries sat next to it. She wandered from the living room to the bedroom of the suite. The dark silk duvet was covered in rose petals. The room smelled like vanilla and coconut. An open bottle of massage oil sat on the nightstand. She picked it up and read the label. "Coconut," she said to herself and smiled. The vanilla scent seemed to be coming from the candles.

She went back to the living room where Austin sat, shirtless, on the arm of the loveseat.

"I don't even have an overnight bag here," she murmured as she drank in the sight of his pecks and perfectly sculpted abs.

"Sure you do." He pointed to a corner. A small, black carry-on suitcase rested there. It looked brand new. "Everything you need should be in there."

"But how'd you pack that without me noticing anything missing?" She should have noticed. She'd been packing for her trip back to Atlanta—albeit slowly and reluctantly—earlier that day.

He chuckled. "I went to the store." He stood and stretched; a delicious ripple moved through the muscles of his shoulders and arms. "I'm nothing if not thorough."

"I see," she said. She bit her bottom lip as he started toward her.

"After tonight, there never will be a way you'll be able to dream of such a thing as." He ran his hands up her arms. "Doubting." He brushed her neck with his lips. "My." One hand dipped to the small of her back while the other caressed the nape of her neck. "Thoroughness." He mumbled the last word against her neck before giving it a moist kiss. He trailed his tongue from her neck to the corner of her lips. She hungrily pushed her lips against his, melting into the kiss that she craved—the touches that were always on her mind.

"I've wanted this all day," she whispered hoarsely.

"I've wanted this since the moment I first saw you," he said. Kissing her again, he pulled her onto his hips without ever separating their mouths. She wrapped her legs around his hips and locked her arms around him, bracing her hands against his strong, muscular back. She ground her hips against his as their kiss deepened. This won a small groan from him.

He carried her to the bedroom with her legs still wrapped around him and their lips still locked together. He tangled his hands in her hair. She needed that—needed him.

"Slow down," he whispered between kisses. He set her down and she started to protest. "Sh." He laid a finger against her lips. Backing away a few steps, he adjusted the crotch of his pants and licked his lips before running a hand over the short bristles of his blond hair. She moved closer and rubbed her hands over the back of his head.

He groaned and gave her a hooded look that made him look hypnotized and wild with desire at the same time. He pulled back a little with obvious effort and unbuttoned her short-sleeved blouse, running his finger lightly over every new inch of skin he exposed. When he was finished with the buttons, he pushed the shirt away from her shoulders and placed a hot wet kiss between her breasts before probing the skin there with his tongue.

She gasped, not having known it was possible to want one person so much. She would've done anything—given up anything—in the world just to have him keep touching her. She shrugged out of the blouse, and he planted those searing kisses over the top of her breasts, over her collarbone, and upwards until he was at her mouth again. His tongue moved over hers, tasting every inch of her mouth at a slow yet intense pace. He seemed to be restraining himself. He didn't have to on her account.

"More," she murmured, pressing her body against his. He deepened the kiss and slipped her bra straps down from her shoulders. Unhooking it, he let it fall to the floor. She whimpered softly at the sweet, pleasureful yet tortuously slow circles he traced over her nipples. She reached for his belt buckle, but he took her hands away, shaking his head. She pulled his hands back to her breasts and wrapped her arms around his neck.

He moved his kisses lower until he was kneeling in front of her. He unbuttoned her shorts and unzipped her zipper slowly while stroking her inner thigh. When he finally slid the shorts down her legs, she eagerly stepped out of them. He removed her panties at the same maddeningly slow pace.

Burying his face between her legs, he breathed in deeply and groaned against her skin, caressing the backs of her thighs with his thick, sure fingers. His hands moved up to cup her bottom and she grasped the back of his head. "Austin, please."

He placed teasing, hot kisses along the sensitive skin where her thigh met her hip before blowing on it. Her legs weren't going to let her keep standing. She was weak with pleasure; her knees trembled.

He made his way back up the length of her body, his kisses and touches leaving a heated trail as he did so. He lifted her up and placed her on the bed.

"On your stomach," he said while stroking her hair away from her temple.

She rolled over, and he straddled her. The fabric of his jeans was rough, but in a not unpleasant way, against her naked skin. He leaned over and she watched lazily from the corner of her eye as he grabbed the bottle of massage oil from the nightstand. She heard him rub his hands together, slicking the oil over his palms, before his strong, oiled hands began massaging her neck and upper back. Every inch of her screamed out for his touch. His expert hands kneaded into her sore, overworked muscles.

"You're too good at that," she said breathlessly.

He answered by taking the movement of his hands lower and deeper. She melted into his big, strong, capable hands. She went into a trance-like state as his fingers worked into her muscles, relaxing and thrilling her at the same time. She craved his touch.

He worked his way down her body. When he kneaded his hands into her buttocks, she let out a rich moan.

"I need you inside of me," she said. "Please."

He continued massaging her rear. "Yeah?"

"Now." She writhed under his hands and repeated the word, shouting it this time.

He raised himself up so that she could flip over. She tore at his belt buckle, fumbling with it, frustrated at not being able to get it open quickly enough. He helped her, and together, they pushed his pants down and through his boxers, she saw the erection she'd felt against her legs earlier. She ripped at his boxers until he was naked.

He reached into the nightstand and pulled back with a condom. She impatiently tugged at his earlobe with her teeth until he had it on. He settled his hips above hers and rested his elbows near her ears.

"Melody," he said as he slid his hot, huge hard-on into her. She moaned as he filled the place she'd ached for him to fill so completely ever since they first kissed. She arched her hips toward him and slid her hands over his back as he pushed deeper. They locked eyes, and she knew she was done for. She was completely his, whether she wanted to be or not. Whatever happened after that night, no matter how far apart they were physically, a part of her would always be his.

CHAPTER THIRTY-THREE

Austin gritted his teeth, looking down into her deep brown eyes. Holding back was proving difficult, but he was determined to make sure she wasn't cheated out of one moment of pleasure that night.

She lifted her head from the pillow and he dipped his, meeting her for a soft slow kiss that quickly became hungry and urgent. He sucked gently at her lips between kisses. Her nails grazed the skin over his hips, lower back, butt, the backs and sides of his thighs. Shifting his weight to one elbow, he reached down for the soft, firm mounds of her breasts, fondling her nipples. He needed to make her come. He wasn't going to be able to hold back much longer.

She gasped, grinding her hips into his even more urgently. He flipped her over to have better access to her body. He entered her wet, soft body from behind. She whimpered with pleasure while one of his hands stayed on her breasts and one went to the bud right above where he was inside of her, pinching, squeezing, and rubbing gently yet insistently until her breaths were short gasps and her hips trembled and writhed against him with every move up and down. She cried out for him over and over as the soft, wet vault of skin clenched and released around his penis.

Knowing it was almost over, he groaned, giving into his own need for release.

She collapsed against the bed. He lay next to her and pulled her into his arms. Holding her close, he stroked her shoulder.

"Again," she said.

He laughed and said into her hair, "Give me a minute."

"That was amazing." She peered up at him, and he kissed her chin.

He felt so good with her in his arms. It felt right, natural. There was no way he could describe it other than to say he felt that he could relax for the first time in his life. Running his fingers from her collar bone to the tops of her breasts and back again, he almost told her how she made him feel.

He caught himself just in time and compromised with what he'd been about to confess. He said, "I was thinking I might go back with you. For a few days."

Her eyes lit up, and she snuggled closer. "Really?"

"Yeah. Donnie and Avery would get a kick out of being in charge for once—especially Donnie," he said. "And I'd get to spend a few more days with you." He kissed the corner of her mouth.

"I'd love that," she said, giving him a look that warmed every inch of him right down to his soul.

"I'm not making any promises about that showcase or anything else having to do with music," he said.

"I don't care about that. I just want you." She grabbed the back of his neck and kissed him softly.

"I'm not making any promises about anything at all," he said for his own benefit as much as hers.

"I know," she said between kisses. "I know." She threw a leg across his hips. "I'm just glad for every moment I get with you."

He felt the same way, but he wasn't about to say that either. Instead, he turned off all thought and focused on holding and kissing her and the way that felt.

#

Tuesday morning, Austin dropped Melody off at Regan's as promised. She was lost in a fog of thought about the incredible night they'd spent together. Earlier that morning had been good, too. Really good. They'd barely made it out by the eleven o'clock check-out time. She couldn't concentrate on much besides her memories of being in Austin's arms. Regan had to keep repeating herself. Finally, Melody apologized for her distracted state.

"It's fine." Regan gave her a knowing smile. "I understand completely."

Regan led her out to a paddock where a giant brown horse with a white streak down his nose stood. They were so much bigger up close. The thing was a giant. He stood there quiet and patient as if he'd been waiting for them.

"This is Thorn," Regan said, patting the horse's side. "He's a Palomino."

"How am I supposed to get up there?" Suddenly, the saddle looked imposing.

Regan nuzzled the horse's nose and fed him some bits of carrot she'd pulled from her pocket. "Don't worry. He's the gentlest horse I have, and all my horses are sweet-natured. Aren't you, boy?" Regan lapsed into baby talk, and the horse snorted softly, obviously eating up the attention.

"O-okay. But that doesn't solve the mystery of how I get up there," Melody said.

"You could use that." Regan pointed to what looked like a small, white footstool nearby. "Or I could give you a leg up."

Melody looked between Regan and the stool.

"C'mon, you can't be that heavy, and I'm a pretty strong gal. Get over here." Regan waved her over.

Melody took a few tentative steps toward Regan. Regan pulled her the rest of the way and gave her a good-natured pat on the back. She showed Melody where to hold on to the saddle. Then she bent down and braced her hands for Melody to step into. Melody followed Regan's instructions.

With a little struggling, and no grace at all, she finally made it into the saddle.

I have to tell Jen about this. She'll get such a kick out of it, Melody thought. She really missed her friend. She couldn't wait to see her mom and Jen. She was still sad to leave Sweet Neck, though. At least she'd have Austin with her. She wasn't going to allow herself to think about the fact that him coming back with her was only temporary.

While Regan helped guide Thorn around the paddock—Melody refused to let the woman out of her sight even though Regan insisted she was doing really well for a first timer—they talked about Sweet Neck. Somehow, it came out that Austin was going back to Atlanta with Melody for a while.

"Good," Regan said. "This is what he needs."

She sounded so sure of it. "I'm sorry. I know you probably don't want to talk about this. I know you two…"

"We what? We're friends. Whatever happened between us is in the past."

Melody shifted in the saddle, trying to get more comfortable. She was already a little sore from last night—and that morning. The horse riding was only going to add to that. "You sure?"

"Yes. You're good for him, and he needs to move on. He needs to put himself out there again when it comes to being in a relationship. He hasn't in so long." She sighed sadly. "I'm tired of watching him just sit around here brooding, wasting away."

"It's gonna be quite a long-distance relationship. If we try to have one, I mean." Melody hadn't even thought that far ahead.

Regan looked up and gave her a mysterious smile. "Maybe, maybe not."

What was it with everybody? "He's never going to leave Sweet Neck, and my job—my career—is in Atlanta." There was nothing in Sweet Neck for a music exec even if the place was charming, bucolic, and seductive even.

"Austin isn't as happy here as he's trying to convince himself he is. Guilt is keeping him in Sweet Neck more than anything else. That and fear," Regan said.

"Yeah?"

"Mm hm. Don't tell me you haven't picked up on that."

"I guess maybe I have," Melody said, thinking back to the few times she'd gotten Austin to open up about his past.

Regan smiled. "Okay, I'm going to leave you and Thorn to it."

"Don't," Melody said, but Regan was already backing away.

"You'll be fine. You'll see."

And amazingly, Regan was right. Melody didn't fall off the horse or do anything else disastrous. She started to think, to hope, Regan was right about other things as well.

#

Tuesday evening, Austin walked into the house with a bunch of flowers in one hand and a C.D. in the other. After saying hello to his mother and finding out that Melody was upstairs in her room, he tip-toed up to her room in hopes of surprising her. He stopped right outside the door. From the crack in it, he could see that she was pacing back and forth; he caught a glimpse of her every few seconds. She was also having an intense phone conversation with someone.

"I know, Saeed, I know."

Saeed. Her old boss. His heart sank.

"He's coming back with me," she said. "Just let me— would you let me talk please?"

There was silence for a moment.

Melody stopped walking and tapped her foot against the floor. "I know." Another pause. "I know that, too. You're not listening to me, though...Yes, I know it's Saturday. You tell me that every day. I just need you to hear me when I tell you that this is a very delicate situation."

Austin clenched the cellophane around the flowers, crushing the stems in his hand.

"He doesn't want to," Melody said. She was quiet for another long stretch. She shook her head and held the phone away from her ear a little. Holding the phone close to her ear again, she said, "I need more time. That's all I can tell you."

As soon as she ended the call and dropped her phone onto the bed, Austin pushed the door wide open.

"So that was Saeed," Austin said.

Melody turned to him, eyes wide, and put a hand over her chest. "Austin. I didn't see you there."

"Yeah," he said. "I'll bet."

"I was just telling him—"

"I told you I couldn't make any promises. But you keep pushing. And pushing. And pushing."

"No, it's not like that. You don't understand—"

"You're right I don't understand. I thought you were listening when I told you all those things about me, but I don't see how you could've been when you just as good as sold me to your boss."

"I didn't," Melody said, but she wouldn't look him in the eye.

"Oh yeah?" He raised his eyebrows. "You know, I blame myself. I'm the fool who hoped and thought you might be different. But you're just like all of the rest of them." He shook his head in disgust. "All you see is money and power and what I can do for you and your career. You don't see me. You don't give a damn about me at all." Austin dropped the flowers on the floor and snapped the C.D. in half. "I never want to see you again." He walked out of her room and out of the house without saying a word to anyone. He got into his truck with no idea of where he was headed.

He refused to think about anything at all. He shut down because shutting down was the only way he could be sure he wouldn't do something stupid like go back to the house before she left for Atlanta.

CHAPTER THIRTY-FOUR

That night, Melody tried to remain upbeat at her going-away party, but she was miserable. Austin's absence was notable, but no one said a word about it. She knew they were all ignoring the fact that he wasn't there for her sake. She appreciated it, but at the same time, it irritated her. It was like they thought she was so fragile, she couldn't even handle hearing his name.

The party was held in the back dining room that could be reserved for private parties at a local restaurant. Everyone sat at a long table that was covered with dishes such as spare ribs, fried chicken, gravy smothered pork chops, collard greens, fried potatoes, and cornbread. There was food everywhere. It all looked and smelled great. She would have been stuffing herself if she hadn't completely lost her appetite earlier that evening when Austin stormed out of the house. No one had seen him since.

After everybody ate, they went outside to the patio where there was a table of desserts and music. A few people danced. Most people stood around, watched the dancers, and talked.

Melody spent most of the night talking with Regan, Nina, Avery, and Leigh Anne. She mingled a little, and Donnie would occasionally flit over, but being social was exhausting for her that night. Every time she played the last twenty-four hours back in her mind, they overwhelmed her.

"Melody? Are you listening?" Regan asked.

"Sorry," Melody said, realizing that Regan must have been trying to get her attention for a while. All conversation in the group had stopped.

"She spaced out again," Avery said. She gave Melody a sympathetic look.

"And I bet I know where she went," Nina said. She patted Melody's shoulder.

"I can't believe he's being like this," Leigh Anne said, her face hard. "I didn't raise him this way."

"I know," Melody said. She stared across the patio at the paper lanterns that hung in a line at the far edge of it. "He wouldn't even let me explain." She shook her head. "I keep bringing this up, and I'm sorry." She looked around. "I'm sure you guys are tired of hearing it."

"No, Melody, it's okay. Really," Nina said, patting her shoulder again.

"I was trying to tell him." She took a deep breath. "I was telling Saeed that going to the showcase was a decision that Austin had to make for himself, and I couldn't promise that Austin would be there Saturday night even though I wanted him there. I want him there for himself first and foremost, but he's never going to believe that now." She took a long sip from her glass of port. "I know it looks bad now, but I wasn't trying to trick him. I just wanted him there with me because I want him. Not because I want to use him."

"I know," Regan said, nodding sympathetically. "He'll come around." She wouldn't look Melody in the eye when she said it, though. Melody couldn't blame Regan if she had trouble believing her own words. Melody had trouble believing them too. If there was one thing she'd learned about Austin over the past few weeks, it was that he was stubborn as hell.

"I hope so," Melody said. "Lord, how I hope so." Even though she didn't think there was much of a chance that it would actually happen.

"We'll talk some sense into him," Leigh Anne said. "Don't you worry."

Melody smiled and nodded. The problem was she couldn't help but worry.

#

True to his word, he didn't risk ever seeing her again. When Melody came down for breakfast Wednesday morning, there was still no sign of him.

"He didn't come home last night," Avery said in an apologetic tone when Melody sat down for her last breakfast with Avery, Donnie, and Leigh Anne. "He called Mom early this morning and sent me a text. Said he'd see us at the shop." She made a sour face. "I tell you, that brother of mine is a complete fool."

"I didn't really expect him to be here." She'd hoped he would be, though. She forced a smile and poured herself a glass of orange juice. "It's fine."

"No it's not," Leigh Anne said, shaking her head. "I apologize for my heathen son's poor behavior."

"It's okay, really. You don't have to do that," Melody said, but they were wooden words on a wooden tongue. Everything felt so unreal that morning. It seemed almost impossible that just two nights ago, she and Austin had shared a bed and more passion than she'd ever shared with anyone.

"Did you have fun at your going away party last night at least?" Avery asked.

"Yes, thanks," Melody said automatically because it was the polite thing to say. And because it had been so nice of them to throw her the party. It wasn't their fault that she couldn't be anything but miserable. He'd told her he would come back with her. She'd been so close to having him take the trip back to Atlanta with her. Now, she was about to take that long drive all alone with plenty of time to think about how much she missed him.

Screw the showcase, screw New Face. Screw it all. All she wanted was him.

Leigh Anne gave her a sympathetic smile, patted the back of her hand, and passed her the pancakes and butter. Leigh Anne had made all Melody's favorites for breakfast that morning. At least she had plenty of comfort food if she couldn't have Austin.

"I can't believe that fool," Donnie grumbled.

"This isn't anybody's fault," Melody said. She didn't want everything she'd tried to do while in Sweet Neck to be a failure. She hadn't brought Donnie and Austin back together just so that she could be the one to tear them apart again.

"Sure it is," Donnie said.

Avery gave him an elbow to the side and a meaningful look. Donnie muttered under his breath and piled his plate up with eggs and bacon, but didn't say anything else about Austin.

After breakfast, they all walked her outside and hugged her goodbye. Leigh Anne had gotten her address and promised to write and maybe even visit one day. Melody looked at her shabby red car and took a deep breath.

Austin had driven the car to the house Monday evening, but Melody hadn't bothered to drive it herself yet. She wasn't crazy about the idea of being close to the thing that would take her away from Sweet Neck forever—the same thing that had brought her there in the first place. Finally, Melody slid into the car and turned the engine over for the first time since the day she'd discovered Sweet Neck. The car started right up. It sounded better than it ever had since she'd bought it from those crooks at the so-called Used Car Shopping Mall. She smiled faintly. Austin did good work.

Smiling sadly, she pulled out of the driveway, waving to Leigh Anne, Donnie, and Avery in the rearview mirror. She hated leaving this way, but she had no choice. Austin should have been leaving with her, but he'd made his choice, and that choice didn't include her. She needed to get used to that fact. And maybe if he was going to go jumping to conclusions and not let her explain, she was better off.

CHAPTER THIRTY-FIVE

Austin slid from under a car when he heard his brother and sister enter the garage.

"Austin, you're an idiot." That was his brother's greeting to him.

Austin slid back under the car. He watched his brother's feet coming toward it.

"You can hide underneath there all you want, but you know it's true." Donnie laughed. "Just like you to hide behind your work, huh?"

"She lied to me," was all Austin said without sliding from under the car. He was already having a hard enough time trying to forget about her. He didn't need Donnie mouthing off and making it worse. Unfortunately, those were Donnie's two greatest talents.

"You didn't even hear her out, man."

Austin slid from under the car again and stood. "Isn't this what you wanted? You kept telling me to stay away from her. Well, I'm far way from her now." He didn't even want to think about how many miles there were between Sweet Neck and Atlanta. And how many of them Melody had covered by then.

"At first," Donnie admitted. "Yes, at first before I saw how good you two were for each other. You were different when she was here. And it don't take a genius to see that she's something special."

Choosing not to take the easy shot at his brother even though Donnie had practically handed the ammo to him, he said, "That's what I thought, too, but she's no different." He thought back to his days in New York and his agent. Bianca. He'd thought he was more than dollar signs to her once, too. He'd been wrong about that, and it'd cost him more than anything ever should have. He wouldn't be making that mistake again.

He'd told Melody about New York, too. It was something he didn't share with many people. Dammit, she knew everything and she'd still gone and done what she did. That proved she didn't care. That she was no better than those slimy creatures he'd known in New York. She was just better at hiding it.

"You don't know what she was saying to that man on the phone," Donnie said. "Her boss or whatever," Donnie said.

"Neither do you." Austin snorted. "What, you think she can't lie?" She'd lied to him more times than enough. "I heard her end of the conversation. I know all I need to know."

"You jumped to conclusions like you always do. You've always been hotheaded. You got the nose to prove that." Donnie pointed to Austin's nose.

He touched his nose where it was slightly crooked. He'd gotten in a fight with some members of the rival team at the homecoming football game one year because they kept at him. Then they started in on his girl. The guys on the other team had gotten the worst of it, though.

"Think about it," Donnie said. "Think about all she did for you that she didn't have to do. Do you really think she did all of that just to trick you into working for her?" He shook his head sadly. "How full of yourself are you?" He started to walk away, and then he turned around and said,

"Did you ever stop to think that it was because she cared about you? That maybe, just maybe, she was trying to do this for you as much as for herself? If not more than for herself?"

Austin stared at his brother for a moment. Then he turned to Avery who gave him a disappointed look before heading over to a minivan that needed an oil change and a state inspection.

Austin turned on his heel and headed for his office. He threw the overhead light switch and looked around. The office was cleaner than it'd been in years. Damn, who was he trying to fool? It looked great. He could actually move around in there. Thanks to Melody. Everywhere he looked, he saw her.

He sat down behind his desk with a sigh, put his elbows on the wooden surface, and steepled his fingers together.

If things had been different, he'd be on his way to Atlanta with her right now. Had she passed Glennville yet, where he took her to the open mic night? What was she thinking about? Maybe the fact that he could've gotten her job back for her, and he hadn't. If she was thinking about that, could he really blame her?

You expect too much from people. That's your biggest problem, bro. That was what Avery said to him sometimes when talking about Donnie. Austin stood and went over to the safe, which was built into the wall next to the bookcase in the office. He spun out the combination, opened the door, and reached in and grabbed the envelope labeled simply, "Austin" in the shaky handwriting that had been his dad's near the end.

Shutting the safe, he went back to the desk. He sat down again and put the envelope on the desk. Smoothing his hand over the surface of it, he thought about the man who'd written the letter. Both of them had made mistakes, but that man still had it in his heart to write this letter.

His father had never talked much. The letter reflected his spare use of words. It consisted of three short paragraphs. It basically said that everyone makes mistakes, and it's how we choose to pay for them that matters. It also said that he wanted the shop to do for Austin and his brother what their dad had never been able to. All he wanted was for his family's wounds to heal and for everyone to be close again like they had been when the boys and Avery were younger.

Folding up the letter, he stuck it back in the envelope and carried it out to the garage bay in which Donnie was working. He stood next to his brother who was bent over under the hood of a 1975 Chevy Scottsdale. That old truck had seen better days, but the owner would never give up on her. Whenever he couldn't figure out what was wrong with her himself, he brought her to the shop.

Donnie looked up. "What is it?" He wiped at the sweat on his forehead with the shoulder of his coveralls.

Austin held up the envelope. "I've been thinking about it, and…Dad would've wanted me to let you read this."

"Really?" Donnie looked at him as if he thought this might be a trick.

"Yeah."

Donnie stared at the envelope for a moment before saying, "Give me a minute to wash up a bit."

Donnie went to the back of the shop, and when he returned with clean hands and without his coveralls, Austin handed him the envelope. He went into the office with it and closed the door behind him. Avery wandered over to Austin.

"What was that about?" Avery asked, her dark blue eyes filled with concern.

"I guess you're right. Maybe I do expect too much of people sometimes," Austin said. "He's reading the letter Dad left for me."

Avery clapped him on the back. "Well. Maybe your head ain't completely full of rocks after all."

He laughed. "Only half?"

She grinned. "Yeah, maybe about half."

Later, when Donnie walked out of the office, he grabbed Austin's shoulder. "Thank you," he said, looking his brother in the eye. He handed him the envelope. "You're all right, I guess. For the most part."

"For the most part?" He quirked an eyebrow. "I'll take it." Austin tucked the envelope in the inside pocket of his coveralls.

"Yeah," said Donnie. "For the most part. You're still hardheaded as the devil, bro. You know it's true."

"Yeah, yeah. Everybody back to work," Austin said. "These cars ain't gonna fix themselves while we stand around gabbing all day." He went back to the car he'd been under earlier that morning when Avery and Donnie walked in. He stared down at it for a moment and glanced back at the office.

He shook his head as if that would help him clear out all thoughts of her, crouched down before laying on his back on the creeper, and backed himself under the car again.

He couldn't shake the feeling, however, that he'd made a huge mistake. Possibly the biggest one he'd ever made in his life. And that was saying a lot.

CHAPTER THIRTY-SIX

Austin spent the next day moping around the house. He'd sent his brother and sister to the shop without him. He couldn't sleep. Every time he closed his eyes, all he saw was her. All he could think about was the way her skin had felt under his—the softness of it. The taste of her lips. Why couldn't he get her out of his system? A woman hadn't had an effect like this on him since...Isadora.

When Leigh Anne came downstairs, he was on the couch in the same sweats and T-shirt he'd slept in, staring at the television.

"Well, you came home last night," Leigh Anne said. "I guess that's an improvement." She put herself between him and the television. When he tried to look around her, she grabbed the remote from its spot beside him on the couch and turned it off.

She put her hands on her hips and said, "Son, you know I love you, and anything I say comes with the guarantee of the best of my intentions."

He nodded.

"Right now, you are being the biggest fool I have ever seen you be. And I have seen you do some quite foolish things. Do you know what you're doing?"

He knew, despite the pause, he wasn't supposed to try and answer that.

"You are blaming other people's mistakes on that poor woman. You are making her pay the price for the scrapes you've gotten into because of other people's stupid choices, including your own."

"Well, if that's the case, maybe she's better off without me whatever the reason is that she's without me," Austin said.

"If you can't get it through your thick head that people make mistakes, and that's life, and we have to move on and learn when to take the good with the bad and when to let go, you're right," his mom said.

"She lied to me." Even as he said the words, they sounded stupid and hollow to him. Like a very weak excuse made by a man who would rather undergo a root canal than admit he'd been in the wrong.

"I don't want to hear that foolishness, boy." Leigh Anne said sternly. "Even if she did, and I'm not saying I believe she did, maybe she did it for you. For your own good."

"Hmph," Austin said.

"You're trying to pin this all on her, but the truth is, you're afraid, Austin."

"Afraid?" He snorted. "Of what?"

"Leaving Sweet Neck again."

"That's ridiculous. I go to Glennville all the time."

"You know what I mean." She tapped her foot impatiently and crossed her arms over her chest.

"No, I don't." He sank back into the couch.

Her expression softened. "I know you've been through a lot. I was there for a lot of it, remember? But you can't use that as an excuse to hide in Sweet Neck forever."

"And what am I hiding from?"

"You're hiding from what you really want and who you truly are. From the person who left here for New York at the ripe young age of eighteen. Now, sure, you went about it the wrong way back then, and you've paid the price and learned better how to handle things the next time around. And that next time has come around. You've grown up a lot. You dream big—or at least you used to—and that's not a bad thing at all. Don't be afraid of the life you really want to live."

"I'm living the life I want. The life I was meant to live."

"The life you think you were meant to live. Your father wanted to bring you back to your family, not trap you here forever. And he wanted to share something with you that meant a lot to him. Both of those things can be accomplished without you sacrificing your happiness, you know."

"But I am happy," he insisted.

"Sure, Austin. You go to that garage and you come back here just about every day. Most days, that's all you do besides work out, eat, and sleep. You're not even thirty quite yet. That's not a life for anyone—especially someone your age." She walked over to him. "But when Melody was here, you were a different man. A happier one."

He opened his mouth to protest, but she gave her head a firm shake, indicating she didn't want to hear it. He knew better than to argue with that particular headshake.

She patted his shoulder. "Just think about it. For once in your life, try not to be so impulsive and quick to jump to conclusions. And maybe, just maybe, if you're this miserable without her, you should at least give her a chance to explain. Right?" She walked out of the living room, leaving him alone with his dark thoughts to stare at the blank television screen.

When Donnie and Avery got home, he heard all three of them talking.

"He's just been laying there all day," Leigh Anne said. "I think he's taken up permanent residence on that couch."

"It's just as well," said Avery. "He was just about useless at the shop yesterday."

"Poor fool," Donnie said. "I don't think he even knows what he's doing to himself."

HIS MELODY

Dinner smelled heavenly as always—especially the gravy—but Austin couldn't be bothered to lift himself from the couch. He didn't think he'd be able to eat anyway. He rolled over and buried his face in the couch cushions.

It was Thursday. The showcase was two days away. She hadn't even tried to call him. Maybe she'd called Mom. Mom hadn't said anything if she had. Why would she try to call him? He guessed there was no reason to. He'd made it pretty clear he didn't want to talk to her ever again on Tuesday evening.

He flipped onto his back and stared at the ceiling. She was under his skin forever. There was no way of changing that. He should've never touched her, never kissed her, never held her. He couldn't quite say he regretted it though. Every moment with her had been worth it.

He glanced toward the kitchen. Were they right? Was he doing it to himself? No matter the reason she was gone, it was better to cut his losses. Whether or not she lied, whether she thought she cared about him or not, eventually it would've fallen apart. It was better to let go. He didn't know what he'd been thinking, getting involved with her.

And saying he'd go back to Atlanta—why had he done that? He acted like he'd gotten temporary amnesia or something. There was a reason he didn't get tangled up in relationships anymore. A very good reason. Really, more than one.

The phone rang. His mother picked it up.

"Oh, hi Melody darlin'! You're home?"

He clenched his teeth. Just knowing she was on the other end of Mom's phone conversation hurt. Austin flopped onto his stomach and buried his face in a throw pillow.

"Oh, I see," Mom said. "Well, I guess that's true. Yes, dear." She talked for a while longer before passing the phone around to Donnie and Avery.

Austin slunk up the stairs, passed the bathroom even though he sorely needed a shower, and went straight to his room. Shutting his eyes, he passed out.

He didn't know how long he slept, but he woke up to Regan's pounding at the door and loud voice.

"Come in," he called out hoarsely, sitting up.

She stood in the doorway and shook her head in disappointment. "You fool."

"Can't you let me wallow in my misery in peace?" he asked. "I've heard it all already."

"Not from me, you haven't." She took a few steps into the room.

"And what do you have to add?" To my self-loathing, he added silently.

"You love that woman. Anybody can see that. Heck, I bet even your thick-headed brother Donnie can see that."

"Please," Austin mumbled. "I barely even know her. She wasn't here for more than a couple weeks."

"What, there's a maturation date on love now?" she asked in a scornful tone. "Sure, love grows over the years, but it has to start somewhere, and it started between you two. That is, before you messed it up." Regan twisted her lips in a disapproving fashion. She stood there, legs akimbo, one black cowboy boot tapping on the floor, and glared down at him. She looked like she was accusing him of a crime and about to drag him off to jail.

"Even if that were true, I would've messed it up eventually anyway. Better sooner than later," he said, looking down at his black sheets. "I mean, look at what happened between you and me."

"If you don't stop holding that against yourself, I'm going to—I don't know—shake you until I shake some sense into you. I don't even hold that against you."

"I'm not the greatest guy."

"Well, knock me over with a feather. You're not perfect." She laughed a small humorless laugh. "You act like such a thing is possible. You screwed up, and you'll screw up again. That is, unless you sit here, wasting your life away, afraid to make any mistakes."

He laughed.

"What?"

"Nothing. You sound like Mom is all."

"Good. She's a smart woman, that mother of yours." Regan squatted down so that they were at eye level. "Just answer me one question. Don't you think she's worth it?"

"Maybe I'm not," Austin said, once again avoiding Regan's eyes.

"Maybe that's a decision you ought to leave up to her," Regan said. "After all, she knows about just about all your demons, and she's not the one who ran. No, you did worse than run. You pushed her away. You used some silly excuse to push her right on out of your life. Didn't you?"

Instead of answering, he lay back in the bed and stared at his desk across the room. He thought about the notebook he'd ripped to shreds last night and tossed in the trash.

"I think I've made my point," Regan said.

He didn't turn toward her, but he heard her leave the room.

CHAPTER THIRTY-SEVEN

Melody drove straight through, stopping only for restroom and coffee breaks. Driving was good because it kept her mind off things she had no business thinking about. She shut out thoughts of Austin kissing her, the way his skin looked and felt against hers, how good making love to him had been. No. She couldn't have those kinds of thoughts. If she did, she wouldn't be able to make it from one day to the next.

Once she made her way back o the interstate, she made excellent time. She got back to Midtown around one in the morning on Thursday.

Melody had rented an apartment in one of the new high rises in Midtown just a few months before Saeed had been hired and her job had become endangered. It was a nice place, and she'd been excited about the deal she got on it, but since she'd been fired, she wondered how she'd continue to afford it as her savings dwindled. Hopefully, she'd have a job soon. But all she had was a hope of a dream of a chance at the moment. No prospects. She had a lot of work ahead of her.

She dragged her suitcase and overnight bag into the apartment. She set her purse on the bar that separated the kitchen from the dining room and looked around the apartment. She had left a few things in the car that could wait until tomorrow. She'd left the suitcase Austin had bought her for their night together behind in Sweet Neck. She wasn't going to do that to herself. She'd learned the painful lesson in the past that it was best not to have things around that would only remind her of past heartbreaks she'd suffered.

Jen had been a good apartment sitter. She'd watered her plants and picked up the mail. There was a neat pile of it on the dining room table that could also wait until tomorrow. In fact, everything could wait until tomorrow—well, later that day anyway. She turned off the living room light after locking her front door. She kicked off her shoes on the way to the bedroom. She fell onto her bed, fully clothed, and crashed.

Melody awoke around ten Thursday morning, slowly blinking. Daylight streamed through the half open Venetian blinds. She smiled. That would be Jen's doing. Jen and her affinity for sunlight. Melody noted that all of her blackout curtains had been shoved aside.

Melody sat up slowly in bed and groped around for her phone. She was pretty sure she'd brought it to bed with her earlier that morning. Her fingers closed over it somewhere down by her ankle. She grabbed it and dialed first her mother's number and then Jen's.

"You're back you're back you're back!" Jen shouted into the phone. "Right?"

Melody laughed. "Yes. I'm here."

"So what are you doing today? Want to meet for lunch?" Jen asked.

"I have to deal with things over at New Face. I need to pick up my things, do some paperwork, all that fun stuff. And my last paycheck better be ready," Melody said with a grimace. "Wait a minute, we? Aren't you at work?"

"You need me," Jen said. "I'll take a half-day and meet you at your place at one, okay?"

Melody smiled. "Thanks."

"Of course."

After she got off the phone with Jen, Melody took a shower and dressed in a gray business suit and a light blue blouse. She paired the outfit with black heels. She didn't have to look like she'd let them win even if they had. Then she went through her mail, triaging the most important things, until Jen showed up.

Jen wore her dark chocolate brown hair up as she did most of the time for work. She wore a ruffle neck yellow blouse with a beige skirt and matching neutral heels and purse. Her oversized sunglasses rested on top of her head. She reached out for Melody with her short, thin porcelain-like arms, and Melody gratefully accepted the hug.

"Oh Mel," Jen said.

"It's such a long, crazy story."

"Tell me all about it," Jen said.

"Okay. On the way over to New Face." Melody grabbed her purse and keys and started telling Jen the story as they headed out of the door. She started with the night of the farewell dinner as that was where the updates Melody had been giving Jen over the phone had ended.

By the time they parked on the street in front of the building that housed New Face Records, Melody had told Jen the entire story.

"Mel, no," Jen said, her face showing her devastation. "I was so hoping things were going to work out for you two."

Melody smiled wryly. Jen, ever the optimist. "It's okay, Jen, really. It's not like I'm going to cry over it or anything." She refused to. "What's done is done. Time to move on." She sighed. "Speaking of which." She gestured up at the tall, downtown building. "Let's go."

They went in and were buzzed up to the floor where most of the New Face offices were. Everybody gave Melody sympathetic looks and goodbyes. Some added hugs.

"You will be missed. Sorely," said Melody's former assistant. She rolled her eyes at the door to Melody's old office. One of Melody's former colleagues, who'd always coveted the office, had taken it over according to the new name etched into the glass on the door.

"So will you," Melody said, giving the woman a hug.

"Call me if you strike out on your own," the woman whispered, shoving a business card into Melody's hand. Melody had mentioned doing so a couple times, but she might not ever have the money for such a thing even if it might otherwise have one day conceivably been a possibility.

"Sure will." Melody slipped the card into her purse. No point in crushing the woman's hopes.

When Melody got to Saeed's office, they signed all the appropriate paperwork, including that for the severance package that was Melody's right, whether she was fired or she quit, by contract.

"I'm sorry things couldn't be different," Saeed said.

"Me, too," Melody said, signing the last of the papers and pocketing her last paycheck, which was separate from the severance package.

"That demo you sent me really had promise." Saeed actually looked remorseful when he said that.

"I know." She tried to ignore the stab of pain she felt at the reminder of Austin.

"No hard feelings, just business," Saeed said, holding out his hand.

Melody shook his hand and nodded. "Where are my boxes?"

"Downstairs with security," Saeed said.

Melody walked to the door and was about to open it when Saeed called her name. She looked over her shoulder and said, "Yes?"

"There's no chance he'll be at the showcase Saturday, is there?" Saeed asked, a note of hopefulness in his voice.

"No," Melody said, forcing her voice not to waver. "I really don't think so."

Saeed nodded. Melody left the office and collected Jen from the waiting room. They went downstairs and retrieved

Melody's boxes from security. After the boxes were in the trunk, Melody said, "I want to go somewhere. Do something. I can't sit at home all day." Alone with my thoughts, she added silently.

"That's why I took the rest of the day off," Jen said.

"And why you're the best friend there is," Melody said.

Jen laughed. "Of course." She said, "Where do you want to go?"

"I don't know. Anywhere. I'm kind of hungry, though. So maybe we'll start with lunch?"

"Excellent idea." Jen rubbed her hand over her non-existent, concave stomach. "What do you want to eat?"

She almost said soul food, but then she thought of Rose's and Myrtle's. No. Nothing to remind her of any of that. "How about Caribbean? There's that new Haitian place that opened in the Highlands right before I left. I never got a chance to go. Hope it's still open." The spot the Haitian restaurant had taken over seemed to be cursed. No restaurant lasted there more than a few months.

"Yeah, it's still open." Jen said. "Let's go."

CHAPTER THIRTY-EIGHT

Melody started up the car and darted out into the flow of traffic. She was experiencing a temporary culture shock while she readjusted to life in Atlanta. Atlanta was a Southern city, and somewhat spread out and laidback as a result, but even so, everything was still so much bigger and faster paced than in Sweet Neck. She'd missed her home, sure, but she also missed Sweet Neck.

She missed walking to Main Street and waving to people sitting on their front porches on the way. Knowing everybody by name after just a few days of being there. The way Leigh Anne had stopped her truck in the middle of the road to have a conversation with a friend she hadn't seen in a while and nobody had seemed to mind. Regan's horse farm and how peaceful everything out there had been. She would love to go back one day if only it wasn't completely and utterly out of the question. She couldn't risk being that close to him ever again.

Jen patted her arm. "Mel, where you going? Slow down, you're going to miss the restaurant."

"Oh, right. Sorry," Melody said. She pulled into a metered spot that was a few blocks away from the restaurant. "All that Southern fried cooking back in Sweet Neck." She patted her hip. "I need to walk some of it off." That wasn't completely a lie. She needed to get back in the gym and soon.

"Oh, I'm thinking you worked all that off just fine," Jen said in a knowing tone.

Melody laughed. "Shut it," she said.

They walked to the restaurant.

Once they were seated, Jen asked, "What are you going to do about the showcase?"

"What do you mean?" Melody sipped her water. Kompa music played in the background, and brightly colored murals depicting scenes from the Port-au-Prince marketplace decorated the walls.

"Are you still going?"

"It's over, Jen. What would it matter?" Melody picked her menu up and flipped through it, letting her eyes skim over the words.

"You've always loved going to showcases. Even before you started working in A&R, you loved going to them. Plus, you have to start job searching at some point, and you know it's a good networking opportunity." Jen sat back in her chair and angled her head. "I'll come along for moral support."

"And to meet cute guys," Melody said.

They laughed.

"Of course. You always have to be on the lookout for those you know," Jen said.

Melody tapped her menu on the tabletop. Jen was right. She couldn't remain a hermit in her apartment for the rest of her life as much as she would've liked to. After all, she had to pay for that apartment somehow.

"Okay," Melody said slowly. "We'll go." Hopefully Saeed wouldn't be there. She couldn't bear the thought of looking at him again so soon. She counted on the fact that getting Saeed out to showcases was like pulling teeth. The only thing harder was getting him to listen to a demo. He'd listened to Austin's, though.

Austin.

Melody opened her menu again and tried to concentrate on the words that time. What did she want? So many choices. Maybe some griot. Or stewed goat. Whatever she got, she knew she was getting red beans and rice to go with it. And pumpkin soup.

She was back in the city where she belonged, having lunch with a friend at a new restaurant. This was her life. That other thing, whatever it had been, was just a detour. It would be best if she forgot all about anything having to do with that.

#

That evening, Melody made the call to Leigh Anne's house that she'd been putting off all day. She had to let everyone know she'd made it home safe, though. After she'd spoken to Donnie and Avery and Leigh Anne got back on the phone, Melody finally got the nerve up to ask.

"How's Austin?" She sat back on the couch and tucked her feet under her.

Leigh Anne didn't answer right away. Eventually, she said in a low voice that was almost a whisper, "He won't admit it, but I know he misses you."

Melody nodded even though Leigh Anne couldn't see her. "It's okay, Leigh Anne. You don't have to do that."

"Don't give up on my boy, please. He cares about you and he needs you, but he's difficult. Stubborn like his daddy."

Melody thought about what Blanche had said on the last day she'd seen the older woman in town. "I have to go. I just wanted to check in real quick, let you know I made it back okay and that I love and miss you all." Her breath caught in her throat. Taking a deep, calming breath, she said, "Tell Regan I made it back okay, and I said hello, okay?"

"Okay," Leigh Anne said.

Melody hated the sad note in Leigh Anne's voice, but there was nothing she could do about that.

"I'll talk to you soon," Melody said.

After a short pause, Leigh Anne said, "I sure hope so."

Melody put her phone on the coffee table and her head in her hands. So much had happened so quickly. She couldn't believe it was still Thursday.

She had a lot to do, and she didn't want to do any of it. First and most importantly, she had to update the resume. She hadn't touched that thing in so long, she didn't even want to think about how much of a pain that would be. Then she needed to get the dress that she wanted to wear to the showcase dry-cleaned. She would have to take it across town to the only next-day cleaners she trusted first thing tomorrow.

She also needed to make some calls and see who planned on being at the showcase and do her research on the industry people who'd be there as well as the acts who would be on stage. Now that she was jobless, every social event was also a business event. She had to network, get her name and face out there again. She had a ton of calls to make. She also needed to renew her subscriptions to a few industry journals and take care of some lapsed memberships as well. And she needed new business cards. All. Too. Much.

At least that should be enough to keep her from thinking about a certain someone. She knew that from experience. Just like after the divorce, she had to keep moving forward. Had losing her ex-husband hurt this much, though? With him, she mostly remembered feeling hurt pride that he would have the audacity to cheat on her. For better or worse, she loved Austin Holt with her whole heart. She was pretty sure she'd never felt anything this deeply for anyone. Ever. Not even her ex.

She forced herself up from the sofa because otherwise she would fall asleep on it. First things first. A hot shower and then bed. One step at a time.

CHAPTER THIRTY-NINE

When Austin opened his eyes Friday morning, his first thought was that the showcase was the next day. His second thought was that everything had been riding on that showcase for Melody. His third was that she'd been right and so had everybody else but him. His fourth was that he'd been a horse's ass.

He sat up on the side of the bed and rubbed a hand over his head. He'd done everything he'd done out of fear and a selfish sense of self-preservation. The garage was his father's dream, not his. He'd thought that could be enough for him; he wanted it to be because he felt like he owed that much to his dad. Maybe it would've been, too, if he'd never met Melody.

She'd changed him forever in a few short weeks. She woke him up and made him realize what was most important to him. He resented her for it, but he also loved her for it.

Loved?

Yes, he loved her. She needed to know that no matter what else happened. Even if she slammed the door in his face when he got there, he was determined to get those words out before she did so.

He went across the room, grabbed his duffel bag from the closet, and tossed it on the bed. He then began rifling through his closet for clothes to toss in the duffel.

There was a knock on his door. "You up yet?" his mom called.

"Yeah, come in," he said.

His mom opened the door. When her eyes landed on the duffel bag, she did her best to hide a smile. "Where you headed?"

He grinned. "I think you know." He walked to his dresser.

"You'll need her address," Mom said.

"Yeah, I guess so."

"I'll go get it," she said. She started out of the door, but then turned back and threw her arms around Austin. "You don't know how happy I am right now."

He patted her back. "Thank you."

Once he had Melody's address and was packed, he headed downstairs. Donnie clapped and cheered as he entered the kitchen.

"Shut your fool mouth." Austin laughed.

"You know, if you hadn't come to your senses, I was thinking I might have to find a way to kidnap you and take you to Atlanta myself," Avery said. "So, I guess it's a good thing you figured it out."

"Yeah, I guess so," Austin said.

"You'll need something on your stomach," Mom said.

He started to protest, but then he smiled at her. "I guess I could make an exception for breakfast just this once." He left his duffel bag by the doorway and went over to the table to pile a plate up with pancakes, eggs, and bacon.

"Tell Melody she better come back here and visit us soon," Avery said, taking a seat across from him.

Austin nodded, too busy stuffing his face to talk.

"Thank the Lord for that woman," Donnie said.

Donnie was right about that.

HIS MELODY

When Austin was done shoveling down his breakfast, he stood and grabbed his duffel from where he'd stashed it in earlier when he'd come into the kitchen to eat.

"I plan on asking her to marry me," he said. "I just thought you all should know that."

Avery nodded. His mother jumped up and made a hysterical sound. Running out of the room, she babbled something unintelligible. He thought he heard her call from somewhere down the hall, "Don't you leave yet!" but he couldn't be sure that was what he heard.

"Good." Donnie walked over and clapped Austin on the back. "Very good."

"Tell Mom I had to get going," Austin said, puzzled at where his mom had gone off to so quickly.

"Sure thing. Now go. Get her. You're wasting time." Avery shooed him out of the door.

"I'm going, I'm going." Austin laughed.

As Austin was about to climb into his truck, his mother came outside waving a small, black box. "Wait!" she cried. When she got closer, he saw that the box was velvet.

"What is it?" Austin asked, staring at the box. He was pretty sure he knew, though.

"It's your great-great-grandmother's engagement ring. She got it after the wedding, though."

"After the wedding?"

Mom laughed. "Do you know that when your great-great-grandfather asked your great-great-grandmother to marry him, he tied a piece of twine around her finger? He didn't have much more than his love for her and the clothes on his back at the time. But she loved him back just as much, and she believed in him. Together, they created a lot. This house, Bellevue, is their legacy." She glanced over her shoulder and smiled fondly at the house. Then she turned back to him. Her smile faded a little, but her eyes remained happy and bright. "She would've wanted you to give this to the woman you marry. They both would have. I think, son, you have found a love like theirs. And that's no easy task." She put the box in his hands and folded his fingers around it.

"Thank you," Austin said. He wanted her to know how much it meant to him to have that ring to give to Melody, but the words wouldn't come to him.

She threw her arms around him and squeezed tightly. "Just go get my future daughter-in-law, will you?"

Austin grinned. "Can and will do."

At least he hoped he could.

CHAPTER FORTY

Austin drove to Atlanta in record time and found the Midtown address that his mother had given him. He got there on Friday evening. Less than twenty-four hours to go until the showcase. He didn't have a plan. He didn't even know if they would let him perform. He knew only one thing at that moment. He had to see his Melody.

Walking up to her building, he took a deep breath. He stared at it for a moment, trying to think of what in the world he was going to say. What would it be like seeing her again? Especially after the way he'd stormed out like an idiot on Tuesday.

A voice interrupted his thoughts. "Coming in?" A slim, pretty blonde woman who appeared to be in her mid-twenties held the main entrance door to the building open for him. She gave him a warm, flirtatious smile.

"Yeah. Thanks." He smiled and walked through the door behind her. He wet his lips and headed through the lobby to the elevator bank. After pressing the up button, he paced back and forth for the few moments it took the elevator to get to him.

It took an eternity for the elevator to go up a few floors. As soon as the door opened, he strode down the hall to the door to apartment 436 and knocked. When Melody opened the door, the look of shock on her face was priceless. So was the look of the rest of her.

Only a tiny pair of shorts covered her long, silky legs. His gaze slowly moved up to the tight tank top that hugged her in all the right places. Especially since she wasn't wearing a bra.

His eyes met hers again, and he could tell she was pissed.

Before she could say a word, he pulled her to him and drove his lips against hers. They stumbled into the apartment together, and he shut the door behind them.

Backing her against a wall, he said, "I need you."

"You never gave me a chance to explain," she said between kisses. "You wouldn't listen to a word I had to say." She pulled her mouth away from his, but she seemed reluctant to do it.

"I know." He traced his fingers lightly over her throat.

"No." She put her hand over his and dragged it away from her neck. "You can be so pig-headed." She glared at him.

"I know that, too." He whispered the words against her skin.

"I said no. Do you have any idea how pissed I am right now?"

"I need you so much right now," he whispered before tugging at her earlobe with his teeth.

She moaned, pulling him in for another kiss before wrapping her legs around his hips. He unzipped his pants and pushed her shorts and panties aside. He filled her, and she gasped before resting her head on his shoulder. She dug her nails into his back, tightened her legs around him, and called out for him over and over again. He grunted into her hair. Being without her had been the hardest thing he'd ever done. He'd been crazy to think he could let her go. They fit together perfectly. This was where he belonged.

They pushed against each other harder and harder. He grabbed her hips, massaged his fingers into the flesh of her bottom. She came with shuddering gasps, which brought on his climax. Then she lay limp against him. He gently set her on the ground. She reached for his hand, and he gave it. She led him to her bedroom. She sat on the corner of the bed, and he stood in front of her. He brought both of her hands to his lips and kissed each of her fingers.

"You know, you can't just flit in and out of my life when you feel like it." She pulled her hands away from his. "And what we just did was nice—okay, really damned good—but a relationship is more than sex, Austin."

He nodded and grabbed her hands again. "I know that." He mumbled the words over her fingers. Then he said, "I don't have any plans to leave you ever again."

She raised her eyebrows. "Really? You seemed pretty dead set against every having anything to do with me when I left Wednesday."

He sat beside her on the bed. "When you left, I realized everybody had been right except me." He lay back on the bed and pulled her back with him. "I felt a hole in my heart as soon as I knew you were gone."

"What about your shop? And never leaving Sweet Neck?" She lay on her side and looked up at him. "My life is here in Atlanta."

He caressed her chin with his thumb. "Avery and Donnie can handle the shop. It was always more their dream than mine. In a way, Donnie was right when he said I stole it from him. That's probably part of the reason I was so mad about it." He pushed her tank top up to the undersides of her breasts and trailed his fingers over the skin of her abdomen. She shivered. He said, "I'm not giving up the shop completely, but I'll be more of a silent partner."

"I see," she said, shifting closer to him.

His fingers dipped down to play with the waistband of her shorts. "That C.D. that I snapped in half in your doorway right before I stomped out like a fool was an updated demo. It sounds more like the real me than the one you found."

"Yeah?" her voice was barely above a whisper.

"I brought a copy of it with me." He pushed her shorts and panties down her thighs, and she kicked them the rest of the way off.

"Are we done talking?" she asked.

He rolled on top of her, careful to settle most of his weight on his forearms. "Yeah," he said, looking into her eyes.

She spread her legs, letting them rest on either side of his hips. "Thank goodness."

He chuckled and kissed her lips before removing her tank top and turning his attention to her breasts.

CHAPTER FORTY-ONE

After they'd made love for the fourth time since Austin walked into her apartment a few hours earlier, Melody propped herself up on her elbow and looked down at him.

"What?" he asked. He slung his arm around her waist.

She smiled and spread her fingers out over his well-muscled chest. "Nothing."

"I doubt that," he said, pulling her fingers to his mouth. "Remember that night in my truck? Coming back from Myrtle's?"

She grinned. "Of course."

"You nearly killed me that night."

She laughed. "That was a good night."

"Sure was." He kissed her palm. "This showcase tomorrow night, there's not much of a chance they'd still let me perform, huh?"

She shook her head. "Nope."

He sighed against her hand. "I'm sorry."

She rubbed her hand over the bristles of his hair and slid down next to him in bed. "Jen and I are still going to go. It'll be a good networking opportunity if nothing else." She rested her head on his chest and looked up at him. "You want to come with us?"

"Of course I do," he said. "You, uh, you don't work at New Face anymore, do you?" He wouldn't look at her as he said that.

"No," she said.

"It's my fault. If I hadn't been a stubborn jackass—"

"Sh." She laid a finger over his lips. "It's a good thing. I was starting to hate it there, and Saeed was looking to push me out of the door anyway. This was just the nudge in the right direction I needed to move on to bigger and better things."

He gave her a wicked grin. "Am I a bigger and better thing?"

"Maybe," she said.

"Oh?"

"We'll have to see." She laughed as he grabbed her and pulled her to a sitting position on his stomach.

"Okay, well, let me show you," he said. He traced circles against her inner thigh before pulling her close enough to kiss it. They were going for number five.

#

Saturday night, Austin and Melody met Jen and her co-worker, Chad, at The Spot. Jen wore a trendy, bright green knee-length dress with silver jewelry. She wore her brown, silky hair down over her shoulders. Chad was definitely Jen's type—tall, dark, and handsome. He had short, dark brown hair and was olive-skinned. He wore dark jeans with a blazer and a crisp, white shirt.

Jen and Melody made the introductions. However, Melody already knew a lot more about Chad than he probably knew about her. Jen talked about him a lot. Chad's parents were Italian immigrants, but Chad had been born in New York. He had moved to Atlanta for college and decided to stay after he graduated. Jen had had her eye on him for a while, but they had never been out together socially, not even as friends or co-workers, before that night.

Austin and Chad started up a conversation, and Melody pulled Jen aside.

"I see what you meant about Chad," Melody said. "He's gorgeous."

Jen seemed to be restraining herself from dancing with joy. "I have good taste, right? As do you." Jen smiled. "I see Grayson's back."

Melody's cheeks grew warm, and she nodded. "He showed up at my place last night." She didn't know where things were going to end up with Austin, but she was glad he was back. The fact that it didn't take much to make him run wasn't making her eager about talking about whether they had a future together. She'd had her fill of fickle men. Love wasn't worth the pain them leaving caused. She was already in deep enough. If she fell any more for him, he'd destroy her if—or should she say when?—he left again.

"Oh. We have a lot to talk about. You look great, by the way," Jen said.

"Thanks," she said. Melody wore a slinky, low-cut burgundy dress and the brand-new Jimmy Choos she'd bought herself as retail therapy yesterday before Austin showed up at her door. "You look great, too."

Jen twirled and struck a pose. They laughed.

They wandered back over to Austin and Chad. The four of them sat at the reserved table that the owner of the club, whom Melody knew, had set up for them in the area where industry folks sat. Austin was getting a lot of looks. Melody wondered if people were trying to figure out whether he was Grayson the way she had at first, or if they were staring because he was friggin' stunning, or both.

He wore dark slacks and a collared shirt that hinted at the incredible body it hid. She wanted to rip both off him at every moment. She settled for holding his hand. She thought back to the demo C.D. he'd played for her last night before they'd finally gone to sleep. It was different from the first demo she'd heard, but in a good way. It was more mature, and he was right about it sounding more like him. He definitely had his own unique sound.

Halfway through the acts, at intermission, Melody introduced Austin to some of the people she knew—execs at other labels, agents, and the managers for a couple of acts she'd courted while at New Face. Acts that her bosses had vetoed and who'd then gone on to be successful with other labels. They were walking through the club, making their way back to their table, when Melody spotted the woman who was undoubtedly the most important person in the room that night.

"That's Ebony Brown," Melody said to Austin, nodding to a tall woman whose considerable height was exaggerated by three-inch heels. She'd paired a black power suit with a gray blouse, and her smile was like everything else about her—tight, controlled, and a little frosty. "She works for a division of Global Records."

"Global," Austin said. "Isn't that the huge conglomerate that just swallowed up a bunch of smaller independent record companies throughout the South? They're the next big thing, right?"

"Yeah," Melody said. She'd heard that they'd most recently gobbled up her ex-husband's label out in California as well, but she didn't want to bring him up in even that small way that night. A small frown of confusion tugged at the corners of her lips. "It looks like she's coming over here."

"Yeah. Looks like," Austin said.

"Why?"

"I'm guessing she wants to talk to you."

"Why would she want to do that?" Melody muttered.

Before Austin could respond, Ebony reached them and said, "Ebony Brown." She offered her hand. "Melody James, right?"

Dazed, Melody nodded and shook the woman's hand. "Yes."

"You were with New Face, correct?"

Were. News certainly traveled fast. Melody said, "Yes, I was until earlier this week."

"Perfect." Ebony nodded. "I thought I'd seen you around. I believe we were at some of the same private parties at the Essence Music Festival last summer. I've seen you at events here in Atlanta, too," Ebony said in her brusque, business-like tone.

"Okay." Melody still wasn't sure where this conversation was going. Surely, Ebony had more important people to talk to than a former A&R exec who'd been fired from a failing record company.

"I was really surprised to hear that Saeed let you go," Ebony said. "Between you and me, it seems like you were the only thing keeping that company afloat."

"Really?" Taken off guard, Melody wasn't able to hide her true reaction—which was shock—to that statement.

"Everybody thinks so," Ebony said. She spoke as if what she'd said was indeed common knowledge. "Do you have your next move planned yet?"

"I have a few things in the works," Melody said. She glanced at Austin who gave her a reassuring smile.

"Don't make any final decisions without calling me first." Ebony whipped a business card out of her black satin clutch and handed it to Melody. "Global could use talent like yours. Have my assistant set up a lunch for us next week."

Melody took the card. "I will." She tried to keep her hand from shaking as she tucked the card into her own clutch. "Thanks."

"I have to go. I have a couple other engagements tonight. I wanted to make sure I talked with you before I left, though," Ebony said.

"Well, it was good talking to you," Melody said.

"You, too." She was gone as quickly as she'd come.

"Looks like big things are headed your way," Austin said.

"Our way." Melody wrapped her hand around his. He held her close.

When they made their way back to the table, Jen jumped up and leaned across it.

"Saeed is here," she said. "And he's pissed. He saw you talking to Ebony. He also wants to know why Austin's here and why you lied to him."

"Where is he?" Melody asked, looking behind her at the tables that filled the dimly lit room. She also scanned the stools that surrounded the bar. She didn't see him anywhere.

Jen shrugged. "I don't know where he is right now, but he'll be back. He said he'd catch up with you before the night was over. Not to worry about that."

True to his word, Saeed came up to the table, huffing and puffing, in the middle of a set.

"Can I speak to you outside?" he hissed.

"Why?" she asked.

"Now," he growled. He reached out to grab her arm, but Austin stopped him. The way he gripped Saeed's upper arm seemed painful, and the grimace on Saeed's face also indicated that was the case.

Austin spoke without relaxing his grip. "I think Melody asked you a question, and you'd better answer it if you want her to go anywhere with you."

"Okay, okay," he said. "Leggo my arm," he snarled at Austin. Austin let go. Saeed glared at him before turning his hateful eyes to Melody. "You lied to me."

"No, I didn't," Melody said.

"Yes, you did!" He insisted. They got a few dirty looks from nearby tables and some people shushed them.

"We'll be right back," Melody said to Jen and Chad. They nodded. She stood and gathered her clutch. She, Saeed, and Austin went outside.

"If you didn't lie to me, what is he doing here?" Saeed jerked a thumb in Austin's direction while looking at Melody. "You're cutting deals behind my back with that sea witch, Ebony, and don't you try to deny it."

Austin spoke up. "The reason I'm here has nothing to do with you, but I will tell you this much. She didn't lie to you. As far as she knew, I wasn't coming tonight. You didn't see me perform, did you?"

Saeed turned to Austin. If he were a cartoon character, there would've been dollar signs in his eyes. Saeed said, "But you could perform tonight. We could arrange it." His eyes pinged back and forth between the two of them. "Exceptions can and will be made tonight. Just say the word. Say you'll get on stage tonight."

"No," Melody said. "He doesn't want anything to do with New Face."

"I'm not talking to you," Saeed said roughly to Melody.

"She's right," Austin said, stepping between Saeed and Melody. "After what I've seen, after the way you've treated Melody, there's no way I would work with your company."

"But you haven't given me any chance to explain."

"Don't need to," Austin said. His eyes were hard and cold as he focused them on Saeed.

"She can have her job back. Just please, come by the office tomorrow. Both of you. Let's talk." He looked frantically between the two of them.

"There's nothing for us to talk about," Austin said. He turned to Melody. "Ready to go back in?" He held out his arm.

She smiled. "Yeah." She linked her arm through his, and they walked back inside together, leaving Saeed behind them and speechless for once.

CHAPTER FORTY-TWO

Melody met with Ebony for lunch a few days after the showcase. They had lunch at a popular restaurant downtown that Melody's meager New Face expense account had never led her to.

"You know I'm not the type to mince words or play games," Ebony said.

Melody nodded and sipped her water. Ebony's reputation preceded her. "I've heard that," Melody said.

"I know what I want, and I know talent when I see it. You could flourish if given the chance, and at Global, we want to give you that chance. We're starting up a new sublabel, and we want to focus on the sort of repertoire it seems you were trying to build at New Face. A jazz fusion sound. A little something like Q-Tip meets A Tribe Called Quest. And maybe a little P.M. Dawn. That's just a basic idea. You'd have complete control over developing artists for the label."

Melody's heart beat faster. This seemed too good to be true. She took a deep breath and tried to keep her cool. "Okay," she said, taking what was carefully contrived to look like a casual glance at her menu before tossing it aside.

"As I've already hinted at, we're looking for someone to head up A&R for this new label, and we want you."

Speechless, Melody could only nod.

"Do you have any artists in mind?" Ebony asked.

"Actually, I do. Do you remember the man who was with me at the showcase?" Melody asked.

Ebony nodded. "Yes. The blond, right?"

"That's him." Melody went on to tell her about Austin while trying not to seem too eager. When she was finished, Ebony said, "Sounds promising. I'll tell you what. You bring his demo to the Global offices downtown with you tomorrow. That is, if you think you're interested in talking about a deal. I can let you have a little time to think this over if you need to, but we need to move quickly on this."

"Yes. I'll be there tomorrow. Yes," Melody said. She wanted to scream it from the rooftops, but instead she inquired about exactly what Ebony had in mind as far as Melody's rights and responsibilities, especially when it came to her freedom in acquiring and developing talent.

#

When Melody got home, she told Austin through kisses how well her meeting had gone with Ebony. Everything had been happening so quickly since the night of the showcase. Life was blowing by at the speed of light.

"Are you even listening to me?" she asked, laughing as he teased her skin with his teeth.

"Of course I am," he said as he helped her out of her blouse.

"What'd I say then?" she asked.

He pulled off his shirt and tossed it onto the couch. "You said you're going to make all our dreams come true, and I never doubted you would." He pulled her to him and lifted her from the ground. "You already did that for me Friday when you opened that door and didn't slam it back in my face."

"I thought about slamming it," she said. She really had. He'd come a little too close to proving to her that she couldn't rely on anybody but herself.

He grinned briefly. "Yeah, but you didn't." He hugged her close. "I'm glad you let me in."

She pressed her cheek to his chest. "I'm glad I did, too." She pulled back and looked up at him. "We do need to talk, though." She grabbed her blouse from the couch and held it to her chest.

"Okay." His dark green eyes searched her face.

"We haven't really talked about what we're doing here. You and me," Melody said.

"What do you mean by that?"

"You showed up, and we've been having amazing sex. And I'm happy that we're getting your career going and that you figured out what you really want to do. What makes you happy."

"You make me happy."

She smiled. "I just think we need to take it a little slower. I'm not sure you know what you really want. In any case, I can't trust that I'm nit. Not after the way you could just throw me away like you did."

"But I couldn't. I was miserable the moment you left." Pain flickered through his green eyes. "I couldn't see any peace until I followed you here."

"How can I trust you won't run off like that again? Especially when you'll soon be surrounded by gorgeous women who will want nothing more than to sleep with you," she said. She'd seen plenty of musicians in action. Not to mention her own greedy ex-husband. What had she ever seen in that man?

"You have nothing to worry about," Austin said. "The only gorgeous woman I want is right here in front of me. Besides, you can't be jealous of imaginary groupies when I haven't even met with these Global people yet."

"No. I mean...I don't know what I mean." She sighed and pressed her head to his shoulder. "I think you should take the spare bedroom for a little while. I need to think about this. We both do. To make sure we're making the right decision." She looked up at him. "Is that okay with you?"

He nodded. "If it's what you need, sure."

\#

At least she didn't kick me out, Austin thought. He kissed Melody's bare shoulder. He ran his thumb back and forth over the skin between her shoulder blades. It was good news about Global, sure, but nothing could compare to having his Melody back. He'd been so stupid to risk losing her forever while nursing his hurt pride. He wasn't going to mess it all up again. He would give her space and anything else she asked for, but he planned on ending up with her when all was said and done.

She looked up at him. "You're so quiet all of a sudden."

He responded to that by kissing her, letting his lips linger over the soft, full mouth he'd missed so much in just the few days they'd been separated. "I was just wondering if I can take you out to dinner tonight."

"Of course you can." She grinned. "I'd like that."

"Okay. Let me move my things into the guest room and grab a shower. And we'll go," he said.

"Sure," she said. "I'll go get ready, too."

He walked to her room and grabbed his things. He checked inside his shaving kit to make sure the black velvet box was safely inside before tucking it under his arm.

He knew he wanted to marry her. He already had the ring—the family heirloom his mother had given him was tucked away in his shaving kit. He just didn't know when to ask. After the way he'd acted, he wasn't sure she would take him seriously. She might not believe that he wanted to spend the rest of his life with her even though it was the thing he wanted most in the world.

CHAPTER FORTY-THREE

Austin and Melody went to a restaurant downtown known for its Southern comfort food—especially the fried chicken. They ordered and sat back sipping their drinks and talking about the meeting coming up with Global. The food she saw going past her on servers' trays looked good, but the place made her miss Rose's diner. Once again, she was sad about leaving Sweet Neck behind. At least she had an important part of it back with her.

She smiled and reached across the table for Austin's hand. He gave it and rubbed his thumb over her knuckles.

"What?" he asked softly.

"Just thinking of how happy I am right now. That you're here." Her biggest fear was that it wouldn't be permanent. He'd been so quick to believe she would betray him without giving her a chance to explain. And then there was the fact that she had no idea what would happen when he got his contract with Global. There was no question in her mind that it was when and not if. Would the celebrity life take him away from her? Maybe it wouldn't be smart to take anything Austin said seriously. Falling in love with a musician hadn't gotten her mother far. Not far at all. And falling for a music exec had gotten Melody less far than her mother had gotten.

"It seems like there's some much more intense thinking than that going on over there." Austin reached for her other hand, and she laid it against his palm. His big fingers closed over it, engulfing her small hand in his much larger one.

"I think you have some admirers over there," Melody said both to change the subject and because it was true.

"Who?" Austin raised an eyebrow.

"Those two women sitting to the right of us." Melody nodded her head subtly in the direction of the women's table. "They keep looking over here and then giggling and saying something to each other and making these wild hand gestures." She grinned. "And I don't think it's because of me."

Their food came. After they thanked the server, they started eating. Austin didn't say anything else about the women. She couldn't tell if it was because he was much more interested in the food or if the idea of having admirers bothered him. If the latter was the case, he was going to have to get used to it. For a musician, admirers paid the bills.

Later, as the two women were leaving the restaurant, they stopped at Melody and Austin's table. One was Korean-American and her friend was a redhead. They both seemed a little tipsy.

"Hi. We don't mean to interrupt your dinner, but we have to ask you something," the redhead said. She spoke with a faint Jamaican accent. She pushed her red braids back over her shoulders and looked at her friend.

Her friend nodded. "We just had to know—are you Grayson Meadows?"

Austin's eyes hardened for a moment, and Melody thought he was going to deny it or do something worse like ignore the women or snap at them. Then he composed himself, pasted on a smile, and looked up at them. "Yeah," he said. "I go by Austin now, though."

They squealed and turned to each other. "I told you so!" the redhead said to her friend. She turned back to Austin. "I just loved your show. We both did."

Her friend eagerly agreed.

"We were just wondering..." the friend started to say.

"Could we have a picture with you?" the redhead finished. She whipped out a smart phone. She looked across the table and smiled at Melody.

"Sure," Austin said. It was clear he'd made their night by their reactions.

"Could you...would you mind taking the picture?" She held out the phone to Melody.

"No problem." Melody took the phone. The women pressed in on either side of Austin—much closer than was necessary—and Melody took the picture. They then chattered on for a while, eventually asking Austin to sign whatever they could find. He signed a napkin for the redhead and a compact case for her friend. After a little more gushing, they finally said goodbye.

After the women walked away, he put a hand over the lower half of his face and closed his eyes. Melody pulled his hand away from his face and folded hers inside of it. He opened his eyes, and she smiled at him.

"It's no use." He heaved a huge sigh. "No matter what I do, I'll always be Grayson Meadows. I'll never be able to get rid of him." He looked up at her with doleful eyes. "Will I?"

"He'll always be a part of you, yes," she said. "But just a part. There's so much to you, Austin. You're funny, smart, ornery—all sorts of things. And Grayson's just a part of that. A part you learned from and that makes you the wonderful man I. Well. The wonderful man sitting in front of me."

"What were you going to say?" He brought the heel of her palm to his lips and kissed it moistly. "The wonderful man you what?"

"There's no point in denying it, I guess." Rational thought was hard with his lips pressed against her skin. "I love you, Austin."

"I love you, too, Melody." The look he gave her melted her. She almost told him she wanted him to move back into her room.

"But we have to be sure that a relationship is what we both want." That you won't get swept away by your new career and the groupies that come with it, or fly off at the handle for something you won't let me explain and leave me behind. For good this time, she added silently.

"I'm sure it's what I want," he said. "I'm just waiting on you." He kissed the inside of her wrist. "In the meantime, I plan on doing everything in my power to convince you of just how serious I am."

She could see some serious benefits coming out of that plan.

#

Thursday night, after their meeting with Global, Melody and Austin sprawled out on the floor with takeout from a great Korean place in Duluth. They'd picked up soup, some noodles, and kimbap. Austin sat with his back against the couch, watching Melody who sat across from him. She'd been pretty quiet since the meeting. She'd seemed so far away from him. The one thing she kept stressing was how fast all of this was happening. He'd definitely noticed. He wasn't sure how he felt about that, but he could safely say he wasn't thrilled.

"So what's our next move, manager?" Austin asked. He popped a kimbap into his mouth. Flavor exploded on his tongue.

"I can't be your manager. I'm thinking that's a serious conflict of interest," she said. "I don't know what we're going to do for a manager."

"That's what you really want, though, right?" he asked. "You push me to follow my dreams, but you're going to work under someone else again instead of being your own boss."

She stared into the bowl of noodles that rested on her lap. "I'm not ready yet. I don't have enough money saved."

"There'll always be an excuse. Trust me. That's one thing I definitely do know. I'm the king of excuses as you well know. You called me on my denial. Now I'm calling you on yours."

She took a bite of her noodles and took her time chewing. When she was done, she said, "Right now, we need to focus on you. We have to find you a lawyer. The next meeting with Global is coming up quickly. Have you looked through that list of contacts I gave you?"

He stared at the paper that laid on the coffee table where he'd left it right after she gave it to him. "I've been trying to find somebody. It's hard for me to put that much trust in a stranger, though." The truth was he wasn't in any particular hurry. The longer he put it off, the longer he didn't have to think about the fact that everything in his life was about to change again. The last time he'd gone this route, it hadn't gone well at all. Sure, the circumstances were different this time, but he couldn't help but think about how big he'd crashed and burned the last time.

"The list of lawyers I gave you are business contacts of mine. These are people I know, Austin. Don't you trust me?"

"That's the same question I find myself asking about you," Austin said. "Do you trust me, Melody?"

Instead of answering him, she looked down at the notes she'd made in the Global meeting. She could be downright infuriating when she wanted to be.

He reached over and put his fingers under her chin. Tilting her head up gently, he forced her to meet his gaze. "We haven't talked about what's going to happen between us since that night you asked me to move out of your bedroom. I respect that you're not willing to jump back into my arms, and that I'll have to work for it, but I would like to know where I stand with you. Give me some idea of how to go about fighting for you. Which I fully intend to do."

He kissed the corner of her mouth, and she sighed. It was clear she wanted more. At least he knew she was missing his touch as much as he missed hers. "You're distracting us from the most important thing right now. We need to find you a lawyer."

"No, I'm not," he said simply. "You're the most important thing." He ran his fingers up and down her arms, and he felt goose bumps raise under his fingertips. They hadn't made love since the night she'd kicked him out of her room. Every inch of his body missed her body. He was trying to be patient, but he felt like he was going to explode every time he was near her. He kept thinking of the silky skin of her thighs, cupping her perfectly round breasts in his hands, and other things that heated his blood. All he could think about was being inside her again.

"I was thinking we could go to the beach this weekend. Clear our heads. Get ready for our next meeting with Global," she said. "Maybe we could talk about it then."

"Okay," he said. "I just want you to know that I mean every single thing I've said. I can't remember ever wanting anything more than I want to be with you. You changed the way I think about everything. I hope you're not asking me to give that up now." His breath was warm against her throat.

"You're making it impossible for me to think right now," she whispered.

"Maybe you do too much thinking."

CHAPTER FORTY-FOUR

The weekend after Austin and Melody's meeting with Global, Melody decided they needed a beach weekend. They drove out to Tybee Island, which was near Savanna. It was a bit of a drive, but Melody knew it was worth it the moment she saw the sparkling blue-green ocean.

She and Austin spread an old blanket out over the sand and collapsed onto it. After the whirlwind of the past few days—getting fired, having unbelievable luck by getting hired by a fast-growing label that was sure to be a major label soon, losing Austin, getting Austin back and getting him on the road to a record deal—some downtime was essential.

Melody adjusted her black bikini halter-top before flopping onto the blanket and nestling her cheek against it. Austin sat next to her in only a pair of gray swim trunks. She lifted her head a little to appreciate the view of his perfect golden body. He stretched, and his back muscles rippled in a delicious way. Staring at a half-naked Austin wasn't a bad way at all to spend a day.

He grinned down at her. "Am I being objectified?"

She slid her sunglasses down her nose. "You'd better enjoy it while you're young and gorgeous. You'll be flabby and gray one day, you know."

"Growing old won't be so bad so long as I get to do it with you." He lay down on his side and propped his upper body up with his elbow.

Her heart beat a little faster. It always did when he mentioned anything about them having a future together. "I don't plan on letting you go anywhere," she said. Then she smiled playfully. "You're my meal ticket."

"Hey. I haven't signed the contract yet," he said. He had a draft of the Global contract. He just had to get a lawyer to look over it before he signed it. Melody had a few friends in entertainment law that he was supposed to meet with after they got back to Atlanta at the end of the weekend. She'd finally made him pick out a few to meet with, insisting he have a lawyer before he met with Global again.

"You know I'm kidding," she said.

He twined their fingers together. "Of course I do."

She squeezed his hand. "I'm so happy right now."

He kissed her fingers. "Me, too."

"I know I keep saying this, but I can't believe how fast it all happened." She didn't want him to take that the wrong way. She wasn't saying she was ready to take the next step with him romantically. "You could be signing a contract next week."

"Hm." Austin moved closer and grabbed a bottle of suntan lotion from her bag. He poured some into his hands and began rubbing it into her shoulders.

"That feels nice," she said.

"Yeah," he said in a distant tone.

"What are you thinking about?"

"Huh?" his firm, capable hands moved between her shoulder blades.

"You seem distracted." She melted under his kneading fingers. "What's distracting you?"

"Besides the obvious?" His hand slipped under her top and caressed the side of her breast. A spark of warmth spread through her.

She grinned. "Besides the obvious."

"I'm thinking of how incredibly lucky I have been to have you in my life from the moment you stepped out of Regan's truck and I first saw you." His hands made their way to her lower back.

She closed her eyes, enjoying the sun beating down on her back and the feel of Austin's strong hands probing deeper. He worked lotion into the backs and sides of her thighs. "That stupid car breaking down is the best thing that ever happened to me."

"It's the best thing that ever happened to me, too." His hand dipped between her thighs and gave the sensitive skin there a quick rub. He slipped his fingers into the bottom of her bikini for a moment, stroking her skin quickly but in a way that made her gasp and writhe under his fingers. He leaned over and kissed the top of her ear. "You booked one room. With one king bed."

She grinned, her eyes closed. "I had my reasons."

"Good." He moved his lips to her neck.

"This better be a preview of what I'm getting tonight." The thought of going back to the hotel with him that night warmed her all over. They hadn't made love since the night she told him she needed a little time to think. Nearly a week had passed since then, but it felt like years had passed. She couldn't fight the temptation any longer.

"We'll see." He closed the top on the suntan lotion bottle.

"Tease." She grinned up at him.

He scooted down next to her and kissed her full on the lips. "We'll see about that."

"Why'd you stop?" She pouted and nodded her head in the direction of the suntan lotion bottle.

"Because I was getting the kind of ideas that could get us arrested out here." He stretched before giving her bottom a light tap. "Speaking of which, I think I need to go for a swim. Get my mind on other things."

She sat up. "I'll come with you."

HIS MELODY

They went down to the water. She shrieked the moment it touched her. The cold water was a shock against her hot skin.

"Jump in. Get it over with," Austin said before running in deeper and diving in. She followed his lead. She swam next to him for a while before leaning back and treading water. She watched him swim, admiring his powerful shoulders and back as he cut through the undulating water.

After their swim, they went back to their blanket. Melody passed out and took a much needed, very long nap. When she woke up, the late afternoon sun had dipped lower in the sky. She looked around for Austin and found him down the beach a little playing a pickup game of touch football with some new friends he must have made while she was asleep. She sat up and watched him, satisfied with the knowledge that he was hers. All hers.

#

When they got back to the hotel room that night, he grabbed her as soon as the door shut. Pulling her to him, he kissed her softly yet deeply in that way that always made her knees buckle.

"Hold it," she murmured reluctantly between kisses.

"Why?" he asked. Very good question. She almost forgot the answer as he nibbled away at that sensitive spot he'd found behind her ear a while ago. He wasn't playing fair; he knew how crazy that drove her.

"I need a shower. I have sand in places I don't even want to think about."

"I wish I was that sand," he said. "Here. Let me help." He had her cover-up and swimsuit off in no time. She stood before him wearing nothing but her sandals. He bit his lower lip and caressed the sides of her breasts with his thumbs.

"I'll be right back," she said even though she was rooted to the spot. She couldn't make herself move away from his touches.

"I'll come with you." He followed her into the bathroom. He stood behind her as they faced the bathroom mirror. She felt the rough fabric of his shorts against the backs of her thighs, her butt. He pressed closer, and she felt the hard ridge of his erection against her back. His hands moved over her breasts, down her sides, rested at her hips. She tracked his movements in the mirror with her eyes.

"Shower," she whispered.

He walked her over to the shower. She turned on the water and adjusted the temperature while he stripped. Together, they stepped under the spray of the showerhead. She was able to rinse off the sand before he grabbed her and pushed her against the wall. After pressing her thighs open with his, he stepped between them.

"You have no idea what you did to me on that beach today," he whispered before biting gently at her ear.

"Same things you did to me?" she said, her tone teasing.

He grunted and lifted her onto his hips. "I need this."

"Me, too." She gasped as he entered her with little warning. She was more than ready for it, though. He pumped his hips against hers a few times. He didn't last long, but neither did she. After they came together, he pressed his forehead to hers and let her down from his hips. She kissed his lower lip. He pulled her back under the water spray.

He grabbed a bar of soap from the tray of soaps that had been left out for them. He lathered her arms, kissed the space between her breasts before lathering that as well. Holding her close, he soaped her butt. She moaned, pressing her body to his.

After spending over an hour in the shower, they finally managed to get clean and get out. Wrapping themselves in towels, they made their way to the bed. Austin whipped away the towel he'd put around her just a few moments ago. Stroking her inner thigh, he gazed down at her. His eyes roamed over her body before finally meeting hers.

"You're so beautiful," he murmured. "Do you know how beautiful you are?" He dipped his head and kissed her behind her knee and made his way up until his kisses were crossing her abdomen. She shivered with anticipation and writhed with desire.

He kissed his way up to her lips. Still kissing her, he slipped inside her again for the first time outside of the shower that night.

Later that night, after making love several times, they lay in the king-sized bed. She was wrapped in his arms. She snuggled against him, resting the her head against his chest.

"This has been the most perfect day," she said with a sigh.

He brushed her hair away from her temple and kissed it softly. "Yeah."

"I want every day to be like this."

"Does this mean I can move back into your room?"

She laughed. "Yes. I give up." Squeezing the arm he had around her waist, she said, "As soon as we get home."

"Good."

Whatever her fears and other reservations, any time spent pushing Austin away was wasted time. She wanted as much of him as she could have as often as she could have it.

CHAPTER FORTY-FIVE

Austin settled on a lawyer by Tuesday night. Her name was Zaria, and she and Melody had a mutual friend. He and Melody met Zaria later that week to go over the contract. Zaria made a few suggestions and worked on a negotiation strategy with them. They set up a meeting with Global for the following Wednesday.

The three of them walked into the Global offices together on Wednesday. Austin wore a black collared shirt with black slacks. Melody wore a beige business suit. Austin's eyes kept drifting down to her high heels and perfect legs.

Zaria wore a sleek charcoal gray pants suit and looked ready for business. Zaria was a tall woman, and with the black heels she wore, she towered over them and most of the people they passed on their way to the elevator bay in the center of the lobby.

Global was headquartered in Atlanta, and they rented a few floors of a large downtown building to house their Atlanta offices. The building was one of the high rises on Peachtree Street. Austin hadn't been in a building that size since he left New York.

Thinking about New York made him a little uneasy. He looked over at Melody as they rode up in the elevator, and she gave him a reassuring smile. She was right. It would be different this time. He could trust her. He knew that now.

They got off the elevator on the floor of the Global offices where Ebony's office was located. Ebony's assistant led them to a conference room and held the door open for them.

Ebony welcomed them and made introductions between her team from Global and Melody, Austin, and Zaria.

"Melody is the A&R genius I was telling you about," Ebony said to a tall, broad-shouldered man with graying hair. He wore a finely cut black suit and his graying hair was also thinning. He stood next to the leather chair at the head of the table and was clearly running the show. Ebony had introduced the man as Max.

Max nodded. "If she discovered Austin, then I have to agree with you." After shaking hands with them, he gestured to three empty seats at the table. "Please, have a seat. Let's get started, shall we?"

They sat.

Zaria pulled a legal pad and a copy of the contract from her briefcase. Then she whipped out a black fountain pen. Her black-framed reading glasses were perched smartly near the end of her nose. She exuded power and confidence. Austin could have seen himself making a move if he didn't already have the only woman in the world for him right next to him.

Stupidity wouldn't make him risk losing Melody ever again. He'd come dangerously close to pushing her away, and he wasn't going anywhere near that road again. He grabbed Melody's hand under the table. She squeezed his fingers.

Zaria started in on business right away. "We've looked over the contract, and it there is a lot here that works for us, but if you want Austin to agree to a 360 deal, there are a few points we need to discuss."

"What do you have in mind?" Max folded his hands together on the table.

Zaria gave a wolfish smile and began laying out her terms.

As it had been explained to him by Melody and Zaria, 360 deals—or multiple rights deals—were the way most of the major record labels were going those days. In essence, Austin would allow the label to share in profits that the artist usually kept exclusive of the record company such as concert revenues, "merch"—or merchandise sales—and ringtones. In exchange, the label would spend more time and money on promoting him than they otherwise would, they would try and develop new opportunities for him, and they would focus more on his entire career than just his record sales.

He would also get the reputation of the Global name behind him, and Global had signed some of the biggest name acts in the South over the past few years. They had also acquired other big name artists by buying up a lot of smaller independent labels. Hopefully, he'd get a bigger advance, too. That was one of Zaria's talking points. The main thing he had to make sure of was that he wasn't going to lose too much control. If it started to look like he was, he would get up and walk right out of that boardroom. He didn't care who didn't like it.

When Max started to waffle and hesitate, Zaria's face and stiff posture gave away no clues as to what she was thinking. She must have been an excellent poker player.

Max straightened a stack of papers. "You're asking an awful lot for a new act who has no following. We have no proof of what he can do." Max ticked off a finger for each of his next points. "He doesn't have any mixtapes out, does he?"

"No." Zaria settled her long, black hair back over her shoulders.

"He's not known in the underground hip-hop world at all."

"Correct." Zaria studied Max with her serious dark brown eyes.

"And we've done our research. He has quite a past." Max tapped a manila folder that lay in front of him. "Grayson Meadows."

"The right P.R. person can spin that past to your advantage," Zaria said smoothly, not missing a beat. "You're really getting him for a bargain. If you get him at all, that is. If you miss your chance of signing him, well, that'd really be too bad." She went on to talk about several Global artists Austin would collaborate well with and then talked about other labels she was shopping his demo to. She bluffed a little by saying they'd already set up meetings with Universal's Def Jam and someone at one of Sony's sub-labels.

Max looked down at the CD in front of him, and then he glanced at the manila folder that seemed filled with info about Austin, or Grayson, or both from the way Max had referred to it. He then looked over at Ebony. Ebony gave him a slight, almost imperceptible nod.

"If you'll excuse us, I need to meet with my team outside for a moment," Max said.

Zaria nodded. "Of course."

When Max, Ebony, and the other Global executives went into the hall, Zaria cracked her first smile of the morning. "I think they're about to cave," she said.

He returned the grin although he still felt a little uneasy. He put his arm around Melody. He'd put his trust in her, and he didn't regret that. "Me, too." He kissed Melody's cheek. "Thank you so much."

She hugged him.

When Max and the others came back in, they looked solemn. Max raked his hands through his thinning hair and said to Zaria, "You drive a hard bargain, Ms. Washington."

"Thank you," Zaria said with an unreadable expression.

Max ran a hand over his face. The percentages you want are yours with the exception of royalties. We'll meet you in the middle on the royalty rate."

"For C.D.'s or mp3's?"

"Both," Max said.

"We can live with that." Zaria made a note on her legal pad.

"We will introduce Austin to producers, and he gets input, but we have the final say."

Zaria looked at Austin.

Austin shook his head. "Won't work. I choose my producer." He wasn't going to start out the wrong way and let them take control over his career from him in any way. That was how things started to go bad last time.

A man to Max's left wrote something on a piece of paper, underlined it twice, and passed it to him. Max had introduced the man as the head of his legal team earlier. Ebony turned her head so that her face wasn't visible to Austin and mouthed something to Max.

Max said uneasily, "It's customary for us to choose the producer. We're investing a lot here, and we have a vested interest in making sure that investment pays off."

"I don't care. This is my future we're talking about here." Austin sat forward in his chair. "I choose the producer, or there's no deal." He spoke each word slowly. He was ready to walk out if Max gave the wrong answer.

Max heaved a sigh and nodded, looking at the paper the man had passed him earlier. "How about this. The label will suggest producers to Austin, but he gets final say on the producer chosen. He can only be overridden by a unanimous vote of the entire executive board." Max looked directly at Austin. "That's a deal no one, and I mean no one else we've signed has." He grimaced like the deal was giving him heartburn.

"Works for me." Austin settled back in his chair. He had no plans of giving up as much power over his life as he had last time. No career was worth giving away his soul.

Zaria scribbled more notes on her legal pad.

"You go into the studio right away," Max said. "As soon as you find a producer."

"Fine with me." He had a lot of material he was ready to try out. He'd been waiting a long time for this moment. Longer than he'd even realized. How could it be possible that after such a short time, Melody had come to know him better than he knew himself?

"We'll have you meet with some producers next week. Starting Monday if possible," Max said.

"Just let me know what time."

"That's what I like to hear," Max said firmly. He gestured to a dark-skinned woman with dreadlocks who sat near the end of the table. "Fatimah, get a list together. Producers you think would work well with Austin."

"On it," Fatimah said. She tapped the screen of her tablet computer. Then she slid her fingers around on the screen a few times before she began typing furiously on it.

"We'll have to run all of this by our president, of course," Max said. "We've made a fair number of changes to the contract, but I'm not anticipating any major problems with her." Max looked at each of them in turn.

"Okay," Zaria said while still scribbling notes.

"I'll have a final draft emailed out to you in a few days, Ms. Washington," Max said to Zaria. He glanced at the Global lawyer on his left as if to confirm this. The man nodded.

"I'll let you know when I've received it and we've had a chance to look over it," Zaria said.

"Good," Max said. "We want your first album out as soon as possible."

"Me, too," Austin said. He'd waited long enough for this.

When Ebony walked them out of the meeting, she said, "Welcome to the Global family, Austin."

"The contract's not signed yet," Zaria said with a smile in a light tone that carried an undertone of seriousness. "And we'll need to hammer out something for the music publishing side of things." Global had their own music publisher, and Austin planned on writing his own material to publish with them. The real money was in writing the songs.

"I'm sure Austin has seen the light," Ebony said in a matching tone.

After saying goodbye to the three of them at the elevator, Ebony walked in the direction of the conference room.

They parted ways with Zaria in the parking lot and walked over to the car that had brought them together—Melody's old red beater. It ran better than ever now, and Austin couldn't help but pat himself on the back a little for that.

"So what do we do now?" she asked, leaning against the trunk.

He wrapped his arms around her and mumbled against her ear. "We celebrate."

CHAPTER FORTY-SIX

As soon as Austin signed the contract, a date was set for an unofficial welcome party to introduce Austin to the Global execs and to celebrate Melody's position as head of A&R for the new sub-label. They'd made up some fancy title for her that was something like Vice President of Talent Acquisitions. She wasn't too worried about the title. What thrilled her was knowing she had control over which artists the label would sign. Of course, if her artists didn't make money for Global, she would be asked to step down or leave, but that was the least of her worries at the moment. She was solely focused on finally being given the chance to shine.

The party was to be held at a penthouse apartment that Global rented out for business purposes downtown, not far from their Peachtree Street office. Melody and Austin made sure that all the important names were on the guest list. Melody's mom, Jen, Chad, Leigh Anne, Avery, Donnie, and Regan had all been invited.

"I hope everyone shows up tonight," Melody said, biting her bottom lip. She studied her worried expression in the mirror as she rolled a tube of lip gloss back and forth on her vanity.

She watched Austin walk up behind her in the mirror and put his hands on her shoulders. She wore only a cream colored slip—she hadn't put her dress on yet because she was terrified of getting a stain on the nude silk dress she planned on wearing to the party and ruining it before she even left the apartment.

He toyed with the straps of her slip. "They'll be here," he said. "They're on their way now."

She looked up at him. "You sure?"

He kissed the tip of her nose. "Positive. Mom called to say they passed through Peachtree City not too long ago. Don't worry. They wouldn't miss this for anything." His hands slipped over her shoulders. "They'll meet us over there."

"I hope things won't get too wild for them tonight."

"This is the fancy suit party, remember? To impress the execs and make sure they know they're getting their money's worth." He squeezed her shoulder. "I don't think you have anything to worry about."

"Yeah. Zaria made sure to drill that part home, huh?"

"Don't worry. I'll behave." He gave her a suggestive smile. "There'll be plenty of time to get wild later."

"I'll bet," she said. "You have any idea of what you're performing tonight?" A few other Global acts were the entertainment that night, but Austin was supposed to do one song as well.

He grinned. "Not one clue."

"Austin…"

"Don't worry. It'll come to me."

"It better."

"It will."

After she finished with her makeup, she slipped on the dress and paired it with gold jewelry and strappy gold sandals. She looked up to find Austin staring at her. "What?" she asked, unable to fight a smile.

"I am so glad that dress is sleeveless." He ran his hands up her arms. "I do love these shoulders." He gave each shoulder a slow, lingering kiss.

"Hm," she murmured. "You look good. Smell good, too."

"Glad you think so," he said. His gray shirt hinted at the ripped body beneath it. He'd paired it with a black blazer and dark designer jeans.

"I guess we'd better get going," she said.

"Yeah. Otherwise, we're going to be really late." He gave her a wicked grin.

#

From the moment they walked into the darkened penthouse, they were bombarded with people. Sometimes they were pulled in the same direction, and sometimes they were pulled in separate ones to shake hands and meet all the important people. It was impossible to keep faces with names. Ebony and Fatimah moved them around the room so quickly that Austin couldn't concentrate on any one person long enough to learn anything of substance about them.

The music was good. Several acts took the stage that had been set up in the middle of the living room that night. Some Austin had heard of, and others he hadn't. In any case, no one who performed lacked talent.

Every time he thought he was going to steal a moment alone with Melody, Ebony and Fatimah took them off to meet more industry folks. They got a few minutes to talk to Zaria, the lawyer who'd made all this possible, when she showed up. That didn't last long, though. Soon after she arrived, Austin lost track of her. He made a mental note to find her later and ask her how the contract was coming along. And to thank her again, too. He couldn't thank her enough.

Finally, when Austin's family arrived, he was able to break away from the crowd. Melody walked up to them. She had several people with her—Jen and her date, as well as an attractive older woman who must have been Melody's mother. She must have found them while the two of them were separated.

Introductions were made all around.

"So. You're Austin," Melody's mother, who'd been introduced as Yvette, said.

"Yes. It's so nice to meet you," Austin said, extending his hand.

Melody's mother raised her eyebrows. "I'm not as easily charmed as my daughter. Keep that in mind." She reached out to shake his extended hand, and he brought her hand to his lips for a light kiss.

"Yes, ma'am."

A smile broke out over Yvette's face. "He doesn't even have to try, does he?" Yvette asked Melody.

Melody laughed. "Not really." She linked her fingers through Austin's. He squeezed them.

They all stood around getting to know each other until Austin was whisked away from the group by Fatimah. He'd gleaned that night that Fatimah was going to be his handler at Global. Fatimah took him to a room in the back of the penthouse and ran over his performance with him. He was only doing one song. She asked if he knew which one. He told her he was doing the first song he'd written for Melody, So Beautiful. He had turned the poem he'd written for the open mic night at Myrtle's into a song.

Fatimah nodded while typing something onto the screen of her phone. "Good." She looked up at him. "It's time for you to get out there."

"Okay." He was anxious to do something besides stand there waiting around.

His song was a hit with the crowd. He had a bias toward anything to do with Melody, so he had to agree with them. Fatimah and Ebony seemed pleased as well. They walked him back over to Melody, his family, and the others, talking about how they couldn't wait to get him in the studio on

Monday. Zaria kept reminding everyone that all of this was unofficial because no contract had been signed yet.

"I think you're going to like Robert," Fatimah said. Robert was apparently the producer they were having him meet on Monday. "You two would work well together."

"We'll find out in a couple days," Austin said.

Melody threw her arms around him. "You were so good."

Ebony gave Melody a sincere smile. "Good work, Melody. You've done great things for Global. We'll return the favor."

"I believe it after everything I've seen so far," Melody said to Ebony while still looking at Austin.

Ebony nodded. Melody and Austin introduced Fatimah and Ebony to their friends and families. Everyone raved over Austin's performance until Fatimah and Ebony had to return to the bedroom that was serving as a backstage area.

Austin stood with his arm around Melody's waist. That night felt like the true beginning to a new life. He finally felt like he was on the path he'd been meant to walk. And he was glad Melody was walking it with him.

CHAPTER FORTY-SEVEN

Near the end of the night, Austin finally got Melody alone. They went out to the balcony, which overlooked the twinkling city lights. A gentle breeze stirred the air.

Melody brushed her hair away from her face. "It's beautiful out here."

"Yeah."

She leaned against the railing and looked over at him. "What do you think of tonight?"

"Think it went pretty well."

"Pretty well? Give yourself more credit than that. It was perfect. Especially your performance."

"Not perfect quite yet." He put his hand on her shoulder and turned her to face him.

"What do you mean?" She gave him a quizzical look.

"I never felt as low as I did after I sent you away. I don't want to feel that way ever again." He brushed the backs of his fingers against her cheek. "I know I'll make plenty of mistakes in the future, but I don't want one of them to be letting you get away ever again."

He dropped to one knee before her. She stared at the black box he held in his hands.

"I want you to share every aspect of my life," he said. "I want you as a business partner, yes, but I also want you to be my partner in life." He opened the box, and a huge diamond sparkled against the black velvet and ivory satin background. "Be my wife."

"Austin," she whispered.

"Is that a yes or no?" he asked.

She grinned. "Technically, you didn't ask a question."

He laughed. "Well, then. Will you be my wife, Melody James?"

"Yes, yes, yes." She slid into his arms, kissing him. They stayed locked together until the balcony glass door slid open, alerting them that they were no longer alone.

He looked over and saw Jen standing in the doorway.

"What are you two doing out here besides making out like the world is about to end?" she asked.

Melody turned to her. "We're getting married!" She held up her left hand and wriggled her fingers.

Jen screamed, grabbed Melody's hand, and pulled her back into the penthouse, shouting the news. Austin followed.

Leigh Anne walked up and hugged them both. Melody turned to Yvette, and Leigh Anne reached up to put a hand on Austin's shoulder.

"Congratulations, son."

He bent down, and she hugged him. "It wouldn't have happened without you bringing me to my senses," he said.

"That's what I'm here for. To keep you from messing up as much as I can."

They laughed.

Once the excitement died down, Austin pulled Melody aside. He held her close. "I can't believe how lucky I am." He kissed her softly. "Thank you."

She grinned. "Thank my stupid car."

"Are you kidding me? I love that car. If it weren't for that car, I would've never met you. I don't even want to think about a thing as horrible as never meeting you."

"Considering how well this all worked out, I might have to agree with you." She rested her head against his shoulder.

"You just might," he said. He wrapped his arms around her waist. He had no plans to ever let go of his Melody.

THE END

ABOUT THE AUTHOR

Nicole Green is the author of three romance novels and one novella. In chronological order, they are: Love Out of Order (Genesis Press, February 2010), The Davis Years (Genesis Press, February 2011), Holding Her Breath (Genesis Press, July 2011), and Pink Champagne (February 2012). She is always at work on her next novel and constantly seeking out people who love to read her novels as much as she loves to write them. She believes love comes in all colors, shapes and sizes. And yes, that love comes even to the imperfect. She hopes that her novels reflect those beliefs. You can learn more about Nicole at http://www.nicolegreen.webs.com.

You can also get in touch with her through email at niki.g82@gmail.com. She would love to hear from you. She sincerely hopes you enjoyed reading this novel as much as she enjoyed writing it.

Made in the USA
Lexington, KY
14 August 2012